Cartoon Heroes

Anthony Harwood

Published by Anthony Harwood

ISBN: 978-0-9567479-2-1

Here we go....

The explosion rocked not only the foundations, but shook up the lives of hundreds of people around the city. In a world where the most isolated township was also the largest, normalcy had been shaken to the very core, even torn asunder, thrown to the winds. But in a world where there was strangeness, it was about to be introduced to the true meaning of weird.

CHAPTER ONE

Five minutes before the explosion, a plain white van had entered the car park. Stopping and starting behind the other couple of cars making their way inside before heading slowly to the third floor of the seven storey structure. It was Sunday, ten past six when it pulled into a bay not far from the elevators and stairs. The doors to both were closed.

One man in a dark jumpsuit hopped from the passenger side door, the left in this case, and pulled open the side slider. Inside was dark, even the dim lights from the building did little to light the interior. The man vanished inside. The driver, his window wound down, tapped anxiously on the outside of the door to an unsteady and erratic beat.

$$* \quad * \quad *$$

Two minutes before the explosion, a plain, pale faced young man dressed in formal shirt, tie and trousers, made his way across the busy street below the car park and entered the building by way of a glass door that led to the stairwell. Inside, he took the first few steps slowly. Judging each one for their merit of existence. Why were they there instead of a giant black hole that would swallow him whole? Why couldn't he plummet into a void of nothingness? Typical angst ridden thoughts. Hesitating, he reached into his shirt breast pocket and pulled forth a name badge that read Russell, above that, in big black letters, the name of one of the largest department store chains in the country, irrelevant to him; although he enjoyed working there. It was the presence of his badge he was concerned about. Reassured, he replaced the badge and began to take the stairs two at a time, before slowing on the landing of the second floor. He reached into his trouser pocket and took out his keys as he stepped into the main building.

His eyes darted around at the lines of cars in front of him, at the grey wall that partitioned the centre off from the rest of the car park. This was the second floor. The exit floor. Behind the grey partition were two ramps leading down to the pay offices which in turn led onto the street. A third ramp came up from a secondary entrance, less used, less known about.

He clicked his tongue and spun back into the stairwell. This was not his floor.

His thumb played absent mindedly with a small black button on his key ring. It was located on a rectangular object, the fulcrum of the chain itself. A red light blinked on and off, indicating the object was working. A simple piece of electronics, useless now the motion detector, used as a security precaution at his parent's office, had run out of batteries, now sitting dormant, but ever vigilant in the centre of the ceiling.

The keys rattled as he made his way up to the next landing, his thumb still active as he opened the door.

The next and last time he pushed the black button, he was able to catch a glimpse of the white van, the intricately detailed electronics within and the orange boot of his own car jutting out just behind the larger vehicle. He was then thrown backward against and through the wall of the stairwell, over the street he had just crossed and through the window of a vacant office on the other side. He was, however, only aware of what was happening around him up until the blast of orange light he thought came from his car hit him square in the face.

*   *   *

Several seconds before the explosion, the man within the van's dark interior exited the vehicle once more, the driver following suit.

"Right?"

The passenger mumbled a reply before running back down the sloping roadway they had just driven up. Another car would be parked, waiting for them. They had time, as long as nothing went wrong. Nothing would, though. A foolproof plan. It would work perfectly.

They didn't, however, count on the motion detector sitting battery-dead in the centre of a ceiling at least twenty kilometres away, nor its counterpart that was merely metres away, nor the effect of the signal frequency the all but redundant key ring gave off when it was activated.

They did feel the blast wave as their van exploded barely a floor above them, orange flame consuming that whole floor and rapidly spilling both up and down the building's interior and exterior.

*   *   *

At the time of the explosion, several dozen people around the building screamed and bolted for cover while others turned in awe of the belching car park that billowed plumes of orange fire and smoke. The blast wave erupted from the windowless sides of the structure, reaching far across the sky, barely metres from the ground, and sweeping past but barely affecting the buildings around it.

Shards and whole portions of cars were swept along with it. In one case, some observers claimed later, it appeared someone had been ejected through a wall, though some put it down to imagination or claims it was simply a piece of vehicle being expelled by the force of the explosion. As yet, there are no known fatalities or injuries.

The flames then travelled upward and down the side of the building, crawling, even dripping over the concrete walls, consuming the structure in a heatless fire that, as soon as it began, was starting to evaporate into thin air.

"An extraordinary sight one rarely sees effectively displayed in a science fiction movie these days," one bystander was quoted as saying.

The smoke lingered above the city before dissipating into the atmosphere, leaving little trace that anything had occurred at all, excepting the emergency vehicles, the gathering crowds and the lingering thought in some onlookers' heads that someone may be lying injured somewhere.

*   *   *

An hour after the explosion, in the back of a darkened room, the only light was shining through the broken window, once covered in black paint, now open to the weather and city beyond. Around him, wooden crates and cardboard boxes were amassed. Some stacked, others fallen, or threatening to topple after his impact with them. Effectively, he was hidden from the world in general by towering and foreboding square objects of which he had no idea how they got there, nor where 'There' was. He pushed himself up on his elbow, letting it dig into the packaging materials that had exploded from one of the said crates that he had landed on, smashing into useless shards and planks. He winced as he looked at his other arm.

A nail from a crate had found its way into his right forearm. But he merely winced. It was a deep wound. Should have been quite painful. But he found himself shudder more at the appearance of the wound than the pain. It was probably just numb for being slept on.

His body shuddered, a shiver passing down his spine as if, as the old wife's tale went, someone had walked over his grave. He had once thought, as he recalled even now, how he found it rather distasteful in any future society that someone would have the gall to actually attempt such an activity. That was if the theory pertained to someone in the future walking over your grave. In the other theory that it was the site of your grave that was being walked over, one got to thinking, where that site actually was and was it already part of a cemetery or a planned expansion of one. The thought of the growing sizes of cemeteries around the world was disheartening to say the least. One day they would break into the expensive land development sites for the main reason that the development of cemeteries didn't entail building an extra level on top. There was no vertical expansion, only horizontal. The whole idea of growing cemeteries led to problems in urban planning, in land management, unless of course the idea of mass morgues instead of ground planting burials was initiated. One day people would be laid to rest in large buildings with many body sized compartments allotted for each member of the community not wishing to be cremated or put to sea, if such an option was viable, let alone legal or environmentally friendly. It would be like a giant body bank, except there would be very few, if any, withdrawals. And they would be freeze dried to aid in autopsies or exhuming the body for investigative reasons. That way there would be no decomposition, thus no natural gag reaction to the putrefying smell of fetid flesh.

As to why people gag on the smell of rotten things, the strength of such smells being a major influence, and yet enjoying the excessive, yet sickly sweet smell of a room full of flowers, air fresheners and the like, being just as strong, is rather amazing.

Russell tried to clear his mind and his vision as unconsciousness tried to drag him back toward a sleep of indifference.

A doctor, was his first clear thought, I need a doctor.

He scuffled his way through the debris, managing to get awkwardly to his feet that felt almost as if they weren't really there. Now he could see. The light spilling in from outside washed the room with a fading yellow glow. The sun seemed to be setting.

It was an empty room, apart from all the boxes and crates and a desk or three, dust covered and drawless. The floor was of wooden boards, some cracked, and others covered in dead wiring, broken bits of crate, furniture or glass.

He pushed his way with his uninjured arm into the open part of the room, standing in the light, feeling its fading warmth caress his dust covered and muscle weary body. He closed his eyes for a moment, a reaction from the drawing of sleep, the comfort of the light, the light-headedness he was feeling and found himself falling. Falling, but never hitting the ground. Drifting into the darkness of unconsciousness.

CHAPTER TWO

It was funny how time didn't register in unconsciousness, where as in dreams, there was always that passage. Yet, in unconsciousness, there was nothing, no subconscious images making stories for your sleeping mind to toy with, to torment you with. Perhaps this was what sleep should be like, no nightmares. But no pleasures either. No dreams of happy times, no memories relived. No fantastical stories of magical rides, or even flying. But in this unconsciousness, even without the dreams, Russell still felt he was flying. He recalled the feeling as he began to regain his senses – Sight, hearing, taste, smell and touch. He could see the shadows that had reclaimed the room, the sun having set. He could hear the distant cars, few and far between, but still passing below the window. He could taste the dryness in his mouth; the almost sick taste as if he had thrown up recently, though he hadn't. He could smell the dust, the must that infested the office and could feel the dull throb in his arm from the nail. The rubbing of his clothes on his skin. The gentle breeze that seemed to encircle him in a cocoon of air. He lounged in the sensation as the current circled his body, above him, below him, all around him, a gentle breeze, cool on his skin, a nice contrast to the warm summer air outside.

And then he blinked.

Above him. Below him. All around him. Air.

Blinking again, he looked down at the floor below him. At least half a metre below him. He didn't blink again, not for a while. Not until he hit the floor moments later did the shock hit him. Not only the fact he was lying on nothing but air, but the whole explosion, the orange flames, everything. His mind was consumed by wild thoughts of everything that had occurred and of nothing important. Nothing coherent anyway.

Distracted, he was jarred to sensibility as his backside made contact with the wooden boards below.

He didn't bother calling out in pain. No one would hear. It was only a childish response adults carried on. Even if it didn't really hurt, there was always that need to say "Ouch" or "Ow" if someone was around. Sympathy gets you attention. None to be gained from this crowd, Russell figured before jumping to his feet, still surprised his wound was only mildly throbbing.

Right now, though, all he could really think about was bed. He was tired, heavy, even nauseous. But first, he would see a doctor.

All he'd have to do is drive up the road to the hospital, then back to the other side of the city to his apartment.

His car! The last he had seen of it was the boot before the explosion. The explosion! What had happened! Was the building still standing! His car?

Though he had no real hope for his car, he heaved his heavy, now throbbing body to the window and once again felt the breeze from

9

outside. He checked to make sure his feet were firmly planted on the wooden floorboards before looking out at the building opposite. Even in the limited starlight and the faint glow from the street lamps and the other city lights, he could tell it was reasonably unharmed on the exterior. A few added police lines, security guards, bits of shrapnel made it stand out a little more, and then there were the torches. On the floor directly opposite, he could see a series of torches playing off the remains of vehicles and walls. When referring to remains, in this sense, one referred mainly to the husks and scraps left over from the blast. It was only a few metres away, the walls were only slightly higher than waist high around the side of each level, he could see pretty clearly the devastation inside and that there were at least five people with torches moving around. Two of the spotlights danced together, playing a game of chasey over what looked to be the remnants of a white van.

Straining his ears, Russell tried to hear what they were saying.

*   *   *

"They say it started here."

"Figures," the detective let his own torch examine what remained of a white Mazda van. It had been ripped open from the inside out, like some giant monster trying to escape figured that spontaneous combustion was the most viable option. In such a case, as Detective Warwick Jones was thinking, he believed the monster should only have tried the lock. Then it would have saved himself and the whole downtown police squad the major headache of Catastrophe Control.

Thankfully it hadn't been bad. The three security guards in the building had been unharmed, complaining of fume affection, dizziness and the like. There had been seven other people in the building at various points; two had been unaware of any of the events, having been making out in one of the four stairwells on the top floor. The other five, an elderly couple on the first, a teenage girl on the fourth and two men on the second had all been offered counselling. Only the teenager accepted.

"Figures," Jones repeated to the notion of the young girl being the only taker. He believed, as many others did, that crisis counselling might be beneficial in such cases as plane crashes, near death experiences. But for the more trivial occasions, when there was maybe only a slight chance you may trip over your own feet due to mild anxiety, Jones thought it to be a waste of time, money and, well, made people too emotionally dependant on other people's support. He was from the old school – survival of the fittest.

It was plain to see on this level, though, that the winner of that competition was the Volvo parked two cars away from the van. Anyone inside probably would have noticed the tremor, maybe even the flash of light through their tinted windows, but that would have been all. Good car, Jones thought. His wife's car was a Volvo. Sturdy, safe. Heck, she'd survived at least six head on collisions already, each time the light post, the tree, the cyclist and the other cars had come off far worse.

The lieutenant nodded humbly to the detective's statement. As to why it figures as such, that wasn't for him to question.

There was a loud clatter from one end of the floor followed by a "Sorry!" as one of the policemen went to work on some old car, or cars as the case may be.

"Sir!"

"Hmm?" Jones looked up at the caller. Another officer, he assumed in the darkness. The young git's flashlight was shining in his face. He raised his hand against the glaring beam.

"I think I found something."

The detective turned and moved to where the torch was seemingly suspended in mid air, squinting through the glare, trying to make out the man's face. All the way, the light remained. Jones grabbed the young officer's hand and twisted both it and the light out of his face. There was a cry in the darkness before the light clattered to the floor, "Next time it won't be your torch you'll be losing, son. Now what are you on about?"

Jones was far from respected by the team. He was rude, rough and down right dirty, in almost every sense of the word.

The officer scrambled for his still lit torch, whimpering under the harsh onslaught of Jones' torch, which the detective had aimed at the young lad's face, effectively blinding him.

Two wrongs and all that was not part of Jones' philosophy to life. Eye for an Eye was one of his, though.

Once the officer, Parks by his name badge, had retrieved his torch, he hurried to a large black door. It had once been a creamy colour but had been seared by the exploding cars.

"So?"

The officer pulled the door open, holding it open for his colleagues to look inside.

Beyond, in an otherwise unscarred stairwell, a large gaping hole was located just opposite the door. Bricks, strips of paint all hung down and around the edges of the exploded orifice.

"So? Couldn't a piece of one of these cars done that?"

"Umm, sir, the door opens inward. Or outward if you're in the stairwell."

"And?"

The Lieutenant who had been with him all along dawned on the idea, "Sir. If a car had caused this, for it to have made this hole and yet left the door intact, one would assume it had opened the door first."

"What exactly are you saying?"

Parks cleared his throat nervously; "This hole couldn't have been made unless the door was open. But that isn't possible, watch," with that, he let

11

go of the door and the three men watched as it swung shut as an automatic response, "There is no way, unless someone had opened it. That hole wasn't caused by a car, or any part of one. That was made by a human being."

They remained in silence before Jones stepped forward to examine the hole more closely. No blood. He peered over the edge, letting his torch dance on the pavement below. No body. Then he looked up, the torch going with his line of sight until it shone on a window directly opposite the hole. In it, a man, or a youth of about eighteen years stood gaping stupidly at them like a kangaroo caught in headlights.

"Get him. I want him for questioning."

The two didn't move, neither sure whether they were looking at the person who had gone through the wall or just an unlucky individual who crossed Jones' path. Either way, with the dorky expression on his face, they weren't too sure if he were alive or not.

"Now!"

The detective's voice echoed through the heart of the building and spewed forth, much as the fire did, into the street below.

*   *   *

The world was a rush.

From the moment the light captivated him from across the street, to when the door burst in as several armed policemen made their way forcibly into the room. He wasn't arrested, according to the detective in charge; protective custody was what he called it.

Reporters, who were already on the scene, trying to pick what was left out of what seemed to be an already dead story, ambushed him the moment Russell and the police emerged from the building. The officers did their best to shield him from the prying cameras, flashing like a miniature lightening storm, but every now and then he would have to flinch, even recoil as both the harsh assault of light and lollypop looking microphones were thrust at him. He remained silent the whole way to one of the cars. He couldn't make out the questions in all the din, let alone know what he would say anyway. From the time he opened the third storey door to when he finally spotted the car he was being led to, the world seemed a confusing ball of nonsense. So much for his early woes and betides he had squirming inside of his head as he entered the building itself. They were nowhere to be seen for the present.

He spotted the patrol car ahead of the group. A white vehicle with a blue checked line around the side. The lights were flashing red and blue, but there was no siren.

Of this, Russell wasn't entirely sure, though. How could you tell with at least thirty reporters yelling questions, eight police yelling warnings and the general rush of the gathered populous at the scene?

It was starting to consume him.

From his left, someone shoved through the police barricade of bodies, knocking him sideways into someone else, effectively destroying his safety bubble. A wave of microphones darted through the hole, some hitting him in the head, bouncing off, but annoying him no end.

What kind of people were these?

He had studied journalism at university. He knew some of the methods of obtaining information were uncouth, but this was ridiculous. He'd never been on the targeted side before. But this wasn't about getting the story. This was about getting the story first.

They didn't care if he was hurt, if he knew what had happened or how. They didn't even care if he had caused the explosion in the first place. They only cared about beating their 'colleagues' to the deadline.

Claustrophobia has been one of Russell's little problems throughout the years. Nothing major. Just the inability to go into caves, tight tunnels, anywhere he couldn't move freely or have a way out. Trapped in other words.

He was starting to feel this now.

All around him people had begun pushing and shoving, the police were unable to do anything about the forceful attacks of these sturdy journalist monsters craving recognition that, frankly, they didn't deserve. Then there was the sound. Screaming, yelling, and yes, the sirens were going, he could tell now as he moved, or was pushed, closer to the car.

An ongoing onslaught on his ears and subsequently his brain, thumping him from the inside out, racking his body with waves of nausea, confusion, anger. He could feel it welling up inside of him. The crowd around him became a mass of faces, no longer individuals. The fearful look on the policeman's face beside him seemed to super impose on the maniacally hungry snout of the journalist pig beside him. They were everywhere, monsters that had once been people. Pushing, shoving, yelling, screaming!

All he wanted was for them all to shut up and stop pushing.

Someone belted him in the back with their knee and he lurched forward, collapsing onto the pavement.

Then they were on top of him. Not on purpose. They were being pushed from all sides, there was now a gap to fill and the closest bodies to him filled it, squashing him onto the ground, creating a tiny cocoon around him.

He could see lights between the legs around him. Legs that flailed and kicked and stepped and trod everywhere and yet going nowhere.

And he could feel the breeze. A cool breeze, winding its way through the masses, curling, licking at the bodies. In his daze, he could almost imagine that he saw it. A beautiful swirl of clouded, yet strangely transparent air. Like it was physically there, but still invisible.

But it didn't matter. He wanted out. He wanted to get these people off. He curled into a tiny ball on the concrete; letting the air wash over him, comfort him.

The screams were slightly muffled from above, but still managed to grow in intensity. He wanted it to stop. They had to go away. But they weren't. Shut up, it ran through his mind. Enough. He thought his blood was boiling, the anger, frustration and confusion congealed into a white-hot ball of emotion within his brain wanting to escape. Enough! They kept kicking and pushing above him, a riot of movement and sound, trapping him like some wild creature, no longer interested in him, but what he has to say. Maybe now not even that, but their own fight for survival in such an anarchistic mob.

"Enough!"

The Air rushed in from between the legs, a force in itself to be reckoned with as it knocked some people off their feet. He could feel it coming for him; he opened his eyes, watching the silvery clouds come like a heavenly wave sent from God.

He could hear it calling out to him. Maybe he was dying. Maybe he was losing his mind. He didn't know. He was lost in the middle of confusion, not only around him, but in his own mind. He wanted them to leave him alone!

The wave of Air finally reached him, somehow managing to ease over his prone body before –

"ENOUGH!" He yelled, not only to the people around him, but to his own frantic thoughts.

The silver waves crashed together above him, their ethereal breaking created the loudest thunderclap he'd ever heard. Though not technically or scientifically such, it was as loud and shook the very ground he was lying on, not to mention his bones and nerves.

The resulting explosion of the silver air pushed upward and outward like a volcano through the people piled above him, pushing them backward like a set of dominos, air rushing underneath them, through their legs, only to explode forth back at them, blasting them backward, freeing Russell from his cocoon.

There was silence.

Even the sirens had ceased to work. People lay prone, unhurt, but dazed in a circle around Russell who was slowly getting to his feet. They stared in wonder at each other, at Russell; unsure of what had happened, too scared to ask.

As he looked around, it was like an explosion had gone off in the middle of a forest of people, a blast wave knocking them all back in a circular pattern.

It looked amazing, something he wished he could capture on camera. Maybe one of the journalists would get it. The thought angered him once more, but nowhere near the level of frustration he had felt while consumed and concealed beneath the mound of bodies.

He was ready to leave now. He stepped over the people who watched him in what may have been awe or just downright dumbstruck confusion.

The car was only a couple of metres away. He opened the rear driver's side door and got in, slamming it shut behind him.

*   *   *

The hospital had been alerted to his arrival. They had made sure his entrance would be unattended by journalists. They were ready to cart him inside and treat his wounds, whatever they may be.

It was only two minutes drive from the car park, but as Russell pondered the events of the evening, it felt like an eternity. But his mind drifted elsewhere once he arrived.

The doctors fussed over how healthy he was, having been blown through a wall and across the street with such force only to receive a couple of scrapes on his back, not to mention the nail in his arm.

They talked excitedly about the remarkable feat of survival, the strength of the human body and set about treating his wounds, but Russell didn't listen. Their lively conversation seemed more like the droning of a fly stuck in one's bedroom, unable to escape, who finds it necessary to occupy the airspace around your ear as you try to fall asleep.

He didn't care what they had to say. He had worries of his own to tend to.

Like Kristen. Odd that even at this point in time she would arise in his thoughts.

Infatuation was perhaps the most appropriate term, maybe even lust. But it wasn't physical. Not yet anyway. She worked with him. A sales assistant; only metres from his own counter. She was tall, attractive with even features on a long heart shaped face. Her hair was short, boyish even, but growing out. And her eyes were a piercing blue, not just in the colour but in the manner she looked at you. From the second moment he laid eyes on her, Russell was lost. It wasn't love at first sight. Maybe second, but it wasn't just her appearance that captivated him. She had a brain inside that beautiful body. She was kind, knowledgeable, trendy, even compassionate when she needed to be. She seemed to fit in wherever she was, even if she remained on the outskirts of the activity. No one would question her presence, merely smile, acknowledge her, and maybe even joke with her.

She sold computers. And as far as Russell could tell, she did it well. She was a competent worker, she was a spirited personality, she was, for all Russell could see, perfect.

She was also very much in control of his heart without even knowing it.

15

He let out a sigh at the mere thought of his own unrequited love, as he liked to refer to it.

Oh they flirted. Little jibes, quips, even polite conversation. But what did that mean? Was she interested or merely being friendly? Russell didn't know and it had gotten to him.

Light flared in his eyes, bringing him back from his reverie.

"Mister Paige, how did you escape from the blast?"

"Is it true you were thrown through a foot of concrete and across the very street?"

"Mister Paige, our viewers would appreciate a true account of your remarkable survival."

Reporters! Again!

He squinted against the video cameras and the odd flash bulb, raising his arms against them.

He realised he was no longer lying down, but had been transferred to a wheel chair which was now being pushed through the mob that had gathered within the hospital.

Then the police were there, once more holding them back. It was becoming farcical. That wasn't to say Russell was amused by his becoming a media spectacle. Just the opposite. He quickly tired of it and was now getting annoyed once more.

Then a door opened ahead of him and he was wheeled into a private room.

Even after the door had shut behind him, he could still hear the crowd beyond. It was already a long night, how much longer would it last?

The intern wheeled him around and reversed him into a position beside a bed.

"What are you doing?"

"Moving you onto the bed."

What? Russell finally regained his senses; "I'm not staying here."

"But, sir..."

He pushed up from the chair, using both arms as leverage, the dull throb from his injured one barely noticeable. He swung around to face the lady who had steered him through the fracas. She was in her thirties and ovular in face and body. She would have seemed motherly if her face wasn't so young.

"No, seriously, I'm fine. I can barely feel it," to emphasise this he shook his arm around in the air, "I mean, is there any medical reasoning behind my staying the night?"

The stunned intern shook her head.

"Well, I don't want to be paying huge medical bills that I can't afford. So I'll be on my way."

He knew he was being rude, but it seemed right. Not that this innocent woman deserved it all, but all those reporters behind the door were behaving worse than he was; besides, he was only being honest.

"Yes, sir. But first, there will be a few bits of paper work to sign you out. I'll be right back."

She disappeared out the door; the volume level of the crowd beyond having slightly decreased rose to an ear splitting pitch once more before the door closed.

Russell shook his head and moved to the window. He was three stories up on one side of the building facing away from the street. In fact it looked onto the church grounds next door. A large cathedral lit by strategically placed spots to look even more archaic and mysterious. A beautiful building with a history Russell couldn't even begin to imagine. But it was nice to look at. So he did until the intern returned.

The crowd outside the door had thinned out; the police having forced them to leave under the pretence Russell needed rest. How were they to know differently?

It didn't take long for him to fill the necessary forms before being sat back in the wheelchair and wheeled toward one of the smaller exits.

As he moved, he was joined by a man in a dark suit. An elderly gentleman with a friendly face.

"Mister Paige?"

"Yes?"

"Detective Corrigan, how are you feeling?"

"Fine thanks and you?"

The detective smiled at his polite response, slightly unsure as to whether it was a joke or not, "As well as can be expected after the events of this evening."

Russell smiled, "I know what you mean. How can I help you?"

"I just wanted to inform you that we will need to gather a statement from you and ask a few questions."

"Fine with me."

"Great, I'll have someone get in contact with you in a day or two."

The detective didn't walk with him the rest of the way.

Once outside the building, Russell stood and stretched his legs.

"Oh, excuse me," He turned after the intern who was quickly disappearing inside.

She faltered before turning, "Yes, sir?"

"I'm sorry about being so rude back there."

She smiled sweetly before resuming her exit, "All in a days work."

Work! Bugger! Russell remembered he had a full day of work the next morning.

Oh well.

He put his hands in his pockets, finding his keys had somehow made their way back there, and set out for home. Along the way his mind flashed through the events of the night, never anchoring on one thought for long before flitting away to a completely new train of thought. He was too tired and confused to think straight, but too weary to turn his mind off.

CHAPTER THREE

An hour later and he had made it. It was only a small apartment located above a pastry and pie place on the outer rim of the central business district. He was lucky to have found the joint, let alone score it. The small façade of the pastry place was quaint, with a central door set back from the main path. Two display windows then jutted forward and ran for a couple of metres on either side along the concrete walkway. The frames were made of polished wood creating the aged appearance of an old candy store you could imagine back in the turn of the last century. Already the smells of fresh bread and other delicacies were wafting through the air as the young couple who owned the shop set about cooking their supplies for the following day.

The warm smell drew Russell's thoughts away from the events of the day, replacing his worries with an almost peaceful longing to be safe and sound in his own bed. Not long now.

Beside the shop was a small doorway. Russell unlocked the deadbolt and the handle lock and went inside. A sensor light flashed on in reaction to the door's movement, allowing enough light for Russell to re-lock the door and make his way up a narrow flight of stairs to his apartment.

Once inside he threw his keys, badge and wallet on the kitchen counter and headed straight for his bed.

Being only a single roomed establishment, however, where the kitchen looked onto a decent sized lounge room that doubled as a bedroom once you pull out the fold down bed, he had to make the extra effort to do so before falling face down onto the unmade, but very welcoming mattress.

Sleep consumed him, freeing his mind of his tumultuous thoughts, replacing them with drifting images of the sky, clouds, and birds. It was as if he were dreaming a children's storybook full of bright colours and perfect skies. He could almost imagine himself spreading his arms as wings and flying through the gentle, caressing air.

*   *   *

He awoke the next morning with a shudder. His bed seemed to bounce slightly as he regained his bearings.

"It's Friday I'm in love!"

He reached over and slapped the top of his clock radio, stopping the offending song.

He blinked a couple of times before making any further effort to move. It had been a good night's sleep. No muscle cramps, no dead arms for having been slept on, just a complete sensation of relaxation.

Yawning, he pushed himself up, realising quickly he was still fully dressed.

Odd, he thought. Normally, even if he were dead tired, he would change and, from the looks of his dirt encrusted and torn shirt he had more of a reason than ever to have done so.

"Odd," he repeated, aloud this time. But it didn't really matter.

He showered and dressed again for work, pulling his trousers and a second shirt from the small cupboard beside the fold up bed.

According to the clock, seven fifty, he had an hour and ten minutes to get to work. Plenty of time. He liked getting there early anyway. Meant all the cleaning could be done, all the odd jobs gotten out of the way.

He could catch the CAT buses (City Automated Transport) to get him there in fifteen minutes or so. Luckily he didn't have uni today or he'd have to drive, paying a fortune for parking. He found most of his income went on parking or petrol these days. It was even worse than his rent. But he got by.

Grabbing his keys, badge and wallet from the counter, he locked up the apartment, both upstairs and down and made his way to work.

*   *   *

"Look at this blood culture."

Doctor Eryn moved away from the microscope, allowing the taller man access.

He moved in to take the doctor's place, looking at him briefly before bending to the eyepieces.

"What am I supposed to be seeing?"

The Doctor was in a state of excitement, even more so than usual, "This is a sample of blood taken from the lad found at the explosion."

"So?"

The Doctor moved forward, his frustration and excitement both obvious as he replaced the first sample with a second on the microscope, "So, this is what normal blood looks like."

There was a pause as the tall man stared into the sterile white piece of machinery.

"Oh."

The Doctor smiled, "Exactly my point. Mister Peerson, do you know what this means?"

The taller man reclaimed his normal height, glaring down at the squat man in the lab coat beside him.

"He's a freak?"

"Not just that! He's an anomaly. And it's quite possible the explosion caused it."

Fire seemed to flare in Peerson's eyes, "And what caused the explosion?"

Hesitating slightly, his excitement waning, but only for a moment, the Doctor moved to the other end of the large examination room.

20

"Well... There was an unexpected contingency we hadn't planned for."

Peerson all but growled, "You told me everything had been taken into account."

"Yes, but not this."

Peerson moved around several large metal examination tables to stand beside his underling.

"Look here," the Doctor pointed down at a computer screen, on it a black and white image of two elevators and a door set in a window application. He clicked the mouse once and the video began playing. A time counter raced by in the bottom right hand corner but nothing happened on the screen.

"I'm growing impatient Doctor."

Eryn smiled smugly, "Keep watching."

Numbers continued to pass in the corner until finally the door to the stairwell opened and a young, somewhat dorky looking individual stepped into sight. Then there was static.

"What is this supposed to prove?"

"Look," some typing, the enter key and a reloading of the screen later and Peerson had a general idea what his associate was on about.

Large pixels filled the window, but the image was still recognisable. A hand and something between its fingers.

"A car alarm?"

"That's no car alarm. We'd taken all of those frequencies into account, with it being set up in a car park."

Peerson leaned closer, "Then what?"

The Doctor stretched back in his chair, turning to regard his employer, "That's what I would like to know. But whatever it was, it caused some sort of chemical reaction in the bomb that in turn affected that boy's genetic make-up."

A possibility sprung to Peerson's mind, "And what about our men?"

"Currently having tests run. I have suspicions they may have been affected in a similar way, what with being so close to the blast, but not so dramatically."

"Let me know when you have any results. I want to find out just what all of this is about."

The Doctor watched as the tall dark suit turned and left his lab, "You're not the only one."

*   *   *

Dim red lights hung from the ceiling, the walls bloodied by their glow. Along one wall, a long tub, inside four trays filled with foul smelling liquids, above was a wire line with pegs clamped higgledy-piggledy along its length.

Along the opposite wall, three enlargers, and a curtained doorway.

From within, a moan of interest.

The curtains were flung aside as Stacey Brownlin entered the larger room; his attention focussed solely on the photographic paper in his hands. In the red light, little of the coloured image was discernible, but when Stacey reached the only other exit in the room, he flicked a switch and the room flashed into brightness. The image in his hand took on a new appearance as his eyes made out the colours and shapes, adjusting to the change in light.

"Interesting… Very interesting."

He put the photo on a table standing in the centre of the room and vanished back inside the curtains.

*   *   *

"Hello Russell."

It was her. It had to be her. He let his eyes roam the shopping floor in front of him, searching for her face amongst the fixtures. Having just stepped off the escalators, he kept moving until he had a clear view of the computing counter.

There she was. Kristen. As beautiful as ever, her eyes positively glowing and her mouth smiling at him. He could feel his own mouth responding of its own free will.

"Come over here."

Interesting, Russell thought, certainly very direct. But he did what he was told.

"What?"

She leaned over the counter, peering deeply into his eyes. He wasn't going to complain, but he did wonder what she was doing.

The expression on her face changed to one of slight confusion.

"Your eyes aren't that blue."

"They change with my moods," he explained, unsure where she was going, "Sometimes they're a deep blue, other times, grey. Why?"

"I saw you on TV this morning. Your eyes were so blue."

He nearly choked, "You saw me on TV?" What was she talking about?

"Yes, before I came into work. I was watching the news. Are you okay?"

"Um… Yeah I'm fine."

"I meant your arm. It looked pretty bad."

He paused, blinked. His arm. Something had happened. What was going on? Almost out of the blue, his arm began to throb ever so slightly. Then it all came back in a flash. The explosion, the police, the reporters, the silvery wisps of wind. It was a dream. Wasn't it? Just a dream.

"Um… I haven't a clue what you're talking about. I wasn't on TV." It sounded like a lie, even to him.

She looked a little disappointed. Not at his loss of star appeal, but at his need to lie. He could tell by the look in her eyes. And such pretty eyes. So rich in colour and life. A perfect blue in a perfect face.

"I...uh... I have to set up confectionery."

She nodded, a smile creeping back onto her face.

He smiled back and moved away from the counter.

He could have hit himself. He cringed as he thought about the lie.

But, if she had seen it, how many others? Who else would recognise him?

He looked over his shoulder at her as he moved behind his own counter.

She was still watching him, her mouth smiling, but her eyes puzzled. She quickly looked away and he proceeded to remove the cloth covers from over the lollies and chocolate bins that made up his counter. If he could, he would have assured her that he was a lot more confused than she was. But right now, he had a job to do.

*   *   *

"I'll have a dollar of Chico babies and a dollar of... hang on. Aren't you the lad on the news?"

He nearly let a groan escape his lips. This was the twelfth customer in less than an hour that had asked. And it was only ten thirty.

Instead, he smiled stupidly before shaking his head, "Sorry, Ma'am. Not me."

The old lady nodded and went back to her order. He was beginning to get a hang of the lying business.

A few minutes later he had a quiet patch. He moved from one end of his counter scooping the lollies forward in their bins with large metal scoops, trying to keep his mind occupied with work, and to look busy in case a manager came wandering by. But, as usual, something else filled his mind.

He glanced quickly up at computers. They were busy. Customers stood around the counter while two guys, Matt and Reagan, were hard at work trying to get rid of them all.

She wasn't there, or so it seemed.

As if on cue, she stepped from behind a column, located just behind the counter, carrying a small plastic container. She was obviously busy.

He continued to scoop the lollies and watch her as he went, until she finally looked over while serving a customer.

He could feel his face go red with embarrassment, but she smiled and gave a little flick of her head in acknowledgment. Russell had become familiar with that particular move. It certainly wasn't the first time he'd been caught out staring. But she would usually smile and flick her head upward in a backward form of nod, like she would if her hair were long enough to get in her eyes. He found it quite endearing.

"Flirting again, huh?"

He spun on his heels, still holding the scoop, "What?"

It was Emma, one of the girls who worked with him in confectionery. Obviously she was just starting her shift.

"You were flirting."

Squinting at her, as if scrutinising her sanity he said, "What makes you say that?"

Emma was an attractive girl. Twenty-four, dark hair tied back in a ponytail, reaching just to her shoulder blades. Her round face seemed so smooth and cuddly, like if it were a teddy bear, you'd want to reach out and hug it. But of course, you would end up suffocating her in the mean time. If she weren't practically married and not interested in younger men, Russell would have asked her out straight away. Then again, he would have done the same to all the women in confectionery. Ironically, they were all attractive women of varying heights, hair colours and statures, but they were also nice people to work with. Not the sort of people you would think of seeing selling lollies.

That all fit into a theory Russell had developed, however. To look at the way people are allocated departments; it would really be hard not to notice some aspects.

Russell himself had applied for a job a year before hand, putting on his form a request for Books, Music or Computers, having had experience and knowledge in each of these fields. They were located at various points around Confectionery. Funnily enough he was put in confectionery with a lot of good-looking women.

Good looking women and a skinny young chap? Quite the opposite look from people who would eat a lot of lollies. Sort of a commercial con job to fool the customers into thinking you can eat all the lollies and chocolates you like and still stay thin and pretty. Not that Russell minded, in so far as it was a good job with a lot of nice people. But he still wished he was in another department.

The truth of the matter is that no one behind the confectionery counter actually ate lollies any more. It became a form of character trait of the job. You worked with the stuff so much, smelt it all day and found yourself wanting to throw up at the mere thought of putting a chocolate bar in your mouth. Even the bright coloured jellies didn't seem as appealing as they did when you were a kid.

But it wasn't only Confectionery. Computing was staffed by young and attractive men and women, sort of contradicting the notion of the stereotyped computer geek being the only people who know about computers. Unfortunately, apart from a few exceptions including Kristen, most of the people in that department didn't know a thing about computers and found themselves lost when asked a more detailed question than, "Does the keyboard come with the computer?".

Books are the same. Older women, seemingly wise and knowledgeable – as if you read books and become a respected and wise member of the community. And music is full of hip and trendy young kids that wouldn't fit anywhere else, except maybe in the clothing departments.

"Rebecca thinks so too. It's just the way the two of you talk." Rebecca was the head of the department. A very tall blonde, who had a lovely personality. Smart, funny and brutally honest. Very popular around the store, and not for her looks. People liked her.

But the point was everyone seemed to be noticing what was going on between Russell and Kristen.

Okay, He had hardly been discrete about it, but he hadn't expected it to be that obvious. He could feel his face going a brighter shade of red.

"I'm right aren't I?" She was actually amazed she had caught him out.

"No." He had to play the obligatory denial card.

She let out a small laugh; "You like her. Does she know?"

Russell didn't even bother continuing his charade, "I don't know. I've tried to make it obvious."

"It looks like she likes you back, though."

'If only,' Russell thought to himself, "It doesn't bother me," what a lie.

"Why don't you ask her out?"

Duh! "Yeah right," Like you can just approach a girl and ask. The annoying thing was that Russell had already had this running through his head. Admittedly it was good to talk to someone about it, but even with Emma egging him on to make the next move, he couldn't do it.

"What?"

Like it wasn't half-obvious why he couldn't. He shook his head, "Look at her. Then, look at me."

It dawned on Emma what he was talking about. "Oh, come off it."

He tried to change the subject. His point was made and he was going to stick by it.

*   *   *

"As I suspected."

Eryn was once more peering into the microscope. Beside it lay three slides. He moved the receiver to his other ear and continued.

"Burns and Lyall were both mildly affected. As for what this means, I still don't know. They're lucky it didn't kill them.

"You mean like the bomb was supposed to do?" Peerson sounded tinny over the phone, his gruff voice no longer sounding as foreboding and threatening as in person. It also helped not having a giant of a man shadowing you as you worked, thought Eryn.

"But that was what I was getting at earlier, Mister Peerson. That device. The boy somehow affected the chemical reaction, effectively mutating the bomb which, in turn, affected both his and the men's biology. If I could some how replicate —"

"I haven't got time for this Doctor."

"But, sir, if I could closely study what occurred; we may have a scientific breakthrough on our hands."

"I don't care!"

"We could make millions, sir!"

There was silence on the other end. Eryn knew he had pressed the right buttons.

"Millions? What are the chances?"

"It all depends on what it is we have discovered. All we'd need do is alter the facts on how we made the discovery and then release it, whatever 'it' is and we could rake in the profits."

Again, silence before Peerson answered shortly, "I think you're limiting yourself. Do what you must."

His voice was replaced by the engaged tone. He had hung up.

Eryn practically whooped for joy. He moved away from the scope and went to one of the three large windows that divided his lab from another examination room. This one was more "inviting", the term he preferred, with its two white padded surgical tables surrounded by all manner of equipment. On each table he could see the two men caught in the explosion. They were alright, for now.

But he may need to sacrifice one; to get a better idea what further changes may have occurred. Peerson probably wouldn't like that. But what choice did he have if he wanted to find out...

Eryn stopped mid thought.

The boy. The cause of it all. The only witness. The only other person affected.

Rather than sacrifice one of Peerson's men, who would miss the nerdy looking fool that had stumbled over the bomb in the first place.

He let out a little chuckle before heading back into the operating room.

CHAPTER FOUR

Greyson's. That was where he worked. Stacey had heard Pam saying it last night. The largest department store chain in Australia. Pam was a journalist friend. They had studied together at university. She focused on print news while Stacey preferred Photo media.

Turning off the engine and grabbing his Olympus camera, he got out of his Colt and made his way to the store. It would be packed this time of day. Lunch time.

He managed to get inside without too many hassles, though he suffered a great deal of path-rage. People walking too slow, not looking where they're going, nor checking their blind spots when they step sideways to avoid someone else. Basic consideration went out the window and down the drain when it came to people walking in the city. Their brains switched off as their eyes led them where the lights were pretty or the sale is good. Like giant moths swooping into a light bulb, head-butting it when they reach it, not being able to tell where things are when it's staring them right in the face.

Stacey remembered working in retail while he was studying. He also remembered the worst part about it was the customers.

Screw "The customer is always right". Not in his experience they weren't. Bloody idiots, was more accurate.

The only problem he had once inside was finding which department this Russell chap worked.

He spotted the information desk behind a wall of customers.

"Perfect," he muttered under his breath.

Lifting his camera from around his neck, he spun around aiming it this way and that, snapping the odd photo when he thought he may have gotten a decent shot, but mainly to make it look as though he was a tourist. He felt the use of a film camera rather than digital helped this, though that was a personal preference. Film gave a better image, truer, rawer. He did use digital at work sometimes, but if it came down to it, film all the way.

He backed slowly toward the information, bumping into people and apologising, his thick London accent aiding him in his guise. Londoners had a chance of getting two responses: one of drunken respect out of the stories you hear coming out of England about them being avid soccer fans or pub crawlers, or absolute disdain for exactly the same reasons. Fortunately in the eight years he had lived in Perth, Stacey's accent hadn't changed a bit and the customers around him eyed him with blatant contempt or stifled amusement. Heck, even the young girls gave way to him without hearing the accent. He was too darn cute to hold back, even if he did say so himself. It was true. He was a striking man. Short, but well built from his soccer training and rowing practice. He was into sport as well as photography; it's just one came above the rest. His own short cropped hair and round face gave him the typical cockney look, but his good spirited eyes could always open doors with the right glance.

Right now, he was using them to keep an eye on where he was heading and make sure he didn't step on anyone whilst simultaneously taking snap shots of the insides of Greyson's, which was pretty mundane. White walls, white panelled ceilings, bright spotlights here and there lighting various fixtures or price points. Then there was the merchandise and the customers. Quite boring really, excepting the customers. There was quite an array. He managed to squeeze a couple of shots off on unsuspecting individuals he found particularly fascinating.

Then he was through. He felt the bench of the information desk against his hip and he quickly turned to regard the two women sitting behind. The noise was awful. Questions were leaping out of brainless mouths all around.

"Where are the toilets?", "How do I get up to the next floor?", "Do you sell car parts?"

One woman was calmly going through her customers one by one, doing the best job she could do under the onslaught. The other was going like a bat out of hell, spewing information to questions that may or may not even have been asked of her.

Stacey decided the latter would be the better; otherwise he'd have to wait in line.

He withdrew an enlarged section of the photo he had developed earlier from his pocket. This showed little more than Russell's face. He shoved it in her face and mouthed the word "Where?"

Mid answer, she spun to him and shouted, "Bras on sale Confectionery for just thirteen ninety-five."

He smiled his thanks and nodded.

If he remembered from his days working here, that was on the other end of this level.

He pushed his way physically from the counter, creating a path way for himself as people pushed against him to catch even a glimpse of the information ladies some of them may never end up talking to.

Protecting his camera with one hand, he shoved out of the crowd and fell into a stream of dawdling customers slowly making their way to God knows which department.

There was nothing Stacey could do, so he found his little niche in the crowd and moved onward.

It was a fair while when he finally made it to where Confectionery used to be and where Men's accessories had set up shop.

"Bloody hell."

Pushing onward, he made it to the lifts. Just opposite them was a sign posted locating all the different departments. Confectionery was on the lower ground.

"Bugger."

He squeezed, barely, onto one of the lifts and made his way downstairs.

When the doors opened again, it was as if the lift released a huge sigh as the people tumbled out again, only to resume that slow steady pace that seemed compulsory when in a department store.

But here, he had to be careful. Surveillance was what he was here for; he couldn't be too obvious.

He once again fell in step with the other customers, finding the gentle swaying back and forth as they waddled somewhat hypnotic and relaxing. He finally caught sight of his target through a line of cards and stationery.

He lifted the camera and zoomed in on the chap.

He looked ordinary enough. A little gangly, but nothing a few gym sessions wouldn't fix.

His camera whirred as it snapped shots and automatically wound on. Stacey had plenty of film in his jacket pockets, but he was hoping he wouldn't need it. It looks too conspicuous trying to reload a camera in a store. Some people may get the idea you're ripping off the film, despite the fact that film was rare in this technological age.

He moved onward, getting closer, but keeping a fair distance between himself and the boy who was hard at work behind the counter. He actually looked a little flushed with his hair falling out of place, still sticking together because of the hair gel, but managing to look a little wild. It was warm also; his face had a slight film of sweat. It would all come out in the photos.

Passing into computers, he tried to hide behind one of the software fixtures. But it still didn't give him a clear shot. None-the-less, he kept aiming and firing.

Taking a step backward, he found his foot coming down on someone's shoe. He jumped around and found himself staring at a pair of well-formed breasts. Well, if he hadn't of looked down ever so slightly he wouldn't have been, but what's a guy to do.

Over one of them was a nametag, "Kristen".

He let his eyes lift upward until he could see her face. An attractive young one, this one. The thought that he wouldn't mind photographing her sometime entered his head. Nude or clothed, it didn't matter, but he knew which one he preferred. She was tall; he'd give her that.

"Can I help you, sir?"

Was that contempt? So much for the rule of the customer being right. Then he remembered this woman worked in Greyson's. She had probably already found out it's full of shit.

"No, thanks. Just browsing," He tried laying on the accent a bit more and, you know, giving her the eye.

Her expression revealed before her response what she thought of his attempt.

Sarcasm dripped from her words; "Some things aren't for sale."

29

He was speechless. He knew he was in the wrong, but he seemed to have hit a nerve with this one.

"I'm sorry."

"Can I help you with anything else, Sir?" She practically spat out the last word.

"No, thank you." He backed away and tried to disappear amongst the crowd, but with her height, he could see she was watching him all the way to the escalators.

*   *   *

"Russell." It was the tone a manager used. Neither a question nor a statement.

"Yes?" He looked up from the register to see Joseph, probably the scariest manager in the store standing in front of him, on the other side of the confectionery counter. He was tall, dark skinned and heavily built. As for his nationality, Russell wasn't sure. African, African American, perhaps. Either way, his deep voice struck fear in the hearts of every employee. Well, almost. Rebecca had made good friends with him, as had a few others. People kept telling Russell that he just had to learn to behave around him. If he insults you, give it straight back. If you have an idea, give it. Stand up for yourself in other words. Not something Russell was particularly good at. But Joseph still seemed to treat him okay.

"Can I have a word?"

Russell surveyed the counter behind him where Emma was still serving. It wasn't busy any more.

"Sure."

He followed Joseph to one corner of the department, away from the counter and the majority of customers. He stopped and turned toward the smaller man.

"Are you alright?"

Russell was taken aback. It certainly wasn't the question he'd been expecting. Alright? Was he alright? Well, it only figured the management would have a concern as to whether their employees were up to working standard or not. That thought bought an image of a slave camp to mind, where the weak were herded and culled for their lack of stamina. He hoped that wasn't what was happening here.

He thought about his answer before giving it, though it really didn't require much thought. The truth would suffice, "Sure. Why?"

"Well, what with your ordeal last night. We had the police contact us, wondering if you needed any counselling."

Russell smiled. Counselling? What for? Were people really that weak minded that they couldn't cope with something out of the ordinary happening? Sure it was a near death experience, but so was choking on a pea. You never got counselling for that, and Russell could remember what an ordeal that had been when it happened only months before. In his own mind, he thought people needed to stop coddling each other, to grow up, stand on their own two feet. Counselling? What kind of weak-minded fool did they take him for? He actually found it quite amusing, even let out a slight laugh.

Joseph looked at him, a look of genuine concern.

"No. I'm fine."

"You don't want to go home early? Take some time off?"

Was this a nightmare? The smile dropped from his face. He couldn't afford to lose the hours. He had a mortgage to pay for the apartment. He had barely managed the deposit, let alone maintained his monthly payments. He still owed his parents for helping with some of the payments.

"No," he nearly snapped the word. Embarrassed, he restrained himself, "No. I'm fine. I've already been through the lunch rush, anyway. I'll be fine."

"If you're sure?"

"Positive."

Joseph nodded, "Well, the detective, Corrigan was his name, wants you to give him a call. He left this number."

A slip of paper was transferred; Russell stuffed it in his pocket. He'd deal with that after work.

"Thanks. And thanks for being concerned."

Joseph smiled as he moved away, "Hey, we can't lose the top man of confectionery."

"I'm the only man in confectionery!"

Joseph laughed, "I know."

*   *   *

He called the detective after work on a pay phone in store. It was five past five. The store was open until nine o'clock tonight. They exchanged words; the detective expressed his concern, Russell, his reassurance that he was okay. Then it was organised for Russell to go to the police station straight from there. What a waste of time.

He swiped out, unable to find Kristen to say goodbye to her, and made his way out of the store. He felt pretty refreshed, all things considered. Slightly hungry, but that was normal. Usually he'd be lucky to grab any food on his break, leaving him starving by the end of the shift. Not this time. Still, he had time to get something on his way to the station. What a walk that would be.

He estimated half an hour to an hour without his car, most of which was through the more unwelcoming areas. The old end of town.

The city had initially been set up on the Swan River. It was still there, but had expanded more to the North and West toward the ocean. What

31

once was a six block by four block Central Business district which focused on retail malls and the commerce side of things, became a twenty-four block by eighteen-block establishment. In terms of size, this was at least four times as large. Unfortunately this lead to urban blight, where the old town became somewhat redundant, excepting its use as a transport thoroughfare to the other side of the river and the location of the Central headquarters of the Police, which was not so central any more. The other buildings that had been located there were either empty or spotted with failing businesses or derelict apartment sites.

During the daylight, it all seemed harmless enough. It would even have been somewhat appealing if he had been a photographer.

As for what he told the Detective, what could he say? He explained about his walking up the stairs, not bothering to worry about the story of his keys, about how he opened the door to the wrong level, and then described what happened when he opened the door to the right one.

"There was a flash of orange light and – Bang! That was it. After that was a blur," a lie. He could remember quite clearly what had transpired in the second floor of that building. But they didn't need to know he was hallucinating.

"All I remember after that is the police, the reporters, the hospital and you." He stopped. That wasn't true, either. But what he was leaving out here was important.

"It was a white van."

Corrigan looked at him a little surprised at the topic change.

"I'm sorry."

"The bomb. It was in a white Mazda van. The windows were tinted to almost black. It was only small, but it packed a hell of a punch. It was parked right next to my car. Damn. I better put in the insurance papers for that."

"Can you tell me anything else?"

He thought for a moment, "No. Sorry."

They had been quite courteous. A cup of tea, which received odd looks. "Why not coffee?" is what they were probably thinking. Can't stand the stuff, was what he thought in return.

Even on letting him out of the building, Corrigan walked him to the front doors, where they stopped at the sight of reporters lined up along the exit path.

"Great."

"Another exit?"

"Yeah," they changed direction, Corrigan leading him down another path, "Have they caught up with you yet?"

"Not yet. I don't have the time to worry about them. Too many other things on my plate."

"I know what you mean. But be careful, they'll be calling you all day and night until you give them something."

"If they don't watch their step, I'll give them something alright," they both laughed, "No, seriously. I'll leave my phone off the hook if I have to."

"Might work."

Russell was snuck out through a back exit. It didn't look like anyone had seen him, thank goodness. It was a major story in the newspapers already. He had seen one in a newsagency along the way. There was a picture on one paper of the burnt out building, on another, one of Russell, dirty and worn. But on another, the one he actually considered buying was an image of him standing in the middle of what looked to be a blast zone. People lay scattered around him. It was rather unsettling. It had to be one of those fake tabloid papers, what with a title like "Bomb Demon Possesses Man", or something along those lines. Probably a fake computer creation. Though it did seem vaguely familiar. He had shrugged it off.

The sun had set by the time he set out for home. The "Dead End" of town seemed like a totally new world. Sinister shadows, skeletal buildings, eerie creaks as foundations and supports eased into the cooler night temperatures; it all congealed to create a most haunting experience.

He rammed his hands in his trouser pockets again and hunched his shoulders, trying not too seem to imposing or stick out in the darkened roads. His white shirt, however, acted like a beacon in the night. He may as well have been shouting "Come and get me you muggers!"

He heard a vehicle approaching from behind, its headlights glaring off broken shop front windows and casting even more shadows on the pavement.

Russell moved toward the shop fronts, trying to blend into the surroundings, but continued walking. He didn't want trouble, but he didn't want to stop either. He wasn't expecting trouble, but being somewhat paranoid, he couldn't help suspecting the worst.

The vehicle seemed to slow. Just my imagination, Russell thought to himself. Why would they slow? There are richer people to mug than him.

Obviously the driver of the van didn't think so.

It pulled up just in front of him.

He stopped and looked up. Another white Mazda. Exactly the same make.

"Shit."

The passenger door opened, a man in black stepped out, a balaclava over his head. A man or a very flat chested woman. He doubted the latter.

He heard the slider door on the other side open also.

Not good.

"This is not good."

He started to back away. Slowly at first, but as they approached he quickened his pace.

From somewhere nearby he heard a loud "click-whirr" which echoed in the night.

The men kept coming, also increasing their pace. There were three in all. Plus the driver who had started to turn the van around.

Russell ran. He pivoted quickly and bolted down the street, dodging a broken bottle and a garbage bin that lay partially over the path, its metal support snapped by some neglectful vehicle, having rammed it.

He could hear their footsteps behind him.

Someone slammed into him from behind and he found himself falling face first toward the pavement.

When he finally made contact, the guy's arm wrapped around his waist in a form of rugby tackle. It was more the shock of jarring his body than the pain of contact. Something was really wrong. Normally he'd be screaming in pain after such a tumble. Bad enough it was concrete, but it was broken in parts and he could feel it digging into various parts of his anatomy.

Instead he tried to roll over, to face the guy who was trying to claw his way up his body. Kind of gross when you think about it.

He managed to wriggle around, breaking the guy's hold on him. He lashed out with his arm, trying to make contact, but found himself punching air. That same silver misty cloud of air he had imagined last night.

The guy was struck by the cloud as it blasted into him, having reacted to the force of Russell's punch. He toppled backward mid grasp, leaving Russell room to wriggle free.

"What the hell?" Russell glanced, only for a second at his hand. What had just happened?

Then he made the most of his new found opportunity.

He jumped to his feet and was about to run again when he realised the other men had him cornered.

But what caught his eye was not the men, nor the van, but the silvery wisps of air that surrounded him. They reacted to the currents blowing by, the slightest breeze sending them into a swirl of life. This was so odd. Could they see this too?

But it was more than that. As he looked into the silvery colours moving by him, he felt something. It was hard to describe; he was lost for a word in his mental vocabulary. Even a made up word didn't sound right. The closest thing he could come up with was "connection".

These silver clouds just seemed to feel right. Whatever that meant.

The two standing men moved closer, the third was getting up from the ground.

Russell reached his hand out toward the mist, trying to touch it.

As he did so, they began to react. The slivers of silver came alive, swirling and heaving in the air. He could feel them as they raced toward him, answering his call, blowing past him, around him, sweeping his hair off his head, gel and all, and creating a bubble of chaotic wind. He could hear it whispering to him, not quite talking to him, nor calling his name, but communicating somehow. A whisper, unlike the normal roar of the wind; somehow hidden to the normal ear by the noisy gale storms, or rumble as they blow on your lobes. This was so much more subtle. It seemed to slide gently over his skin, like water, flowing over every inch of him, catching his clothes in the gales. He watched as the air around him came alive and enveloped him once more in a cocoon. It was exhilarating. It was more than a "connection". It was "completion". He laughed out loud at the thrill of the experience. Nothing erotic, just captivating and exciting all at once. This felt so right to him.

The men had stopped. A mixture of his laughter and the appearance he conjured up. His hair waving wildly in an unseen wind. An isolated gale blowing solely around his body like some sort of ethereal force.

"Oh boy," one of them whispered, his eyes bulging behind the balaclava.

Russell regarded the men around him, one still half way from getting to his feet, stopped mid movement.

And he smiled. He knew what was going on now. He knew what he was doing.

He punched his arms out, hands clenched, toward the two remaining men, sending forth two streams of air that burst forward, hitting the men with an invisible force square in the gut and sending them flying backward a couple of metres.

It was pure exhilaration. He had power. A power he had never even dreamed of. A power there had been mere mumblings in the community about. Freaks of nature appearing here and there. But that didn't worry him. Not now, not with the winds at his command.

He understood it now. Something in that bomb had done something to him. How? He didn't know. What? He didn't know. He didn't care.

Right now, all that mattered was dealing with these guys.

Another "Click-whirr" and Russell spun to regard the van.

The passenger side door snapped open, a dark figure inside leaning over.

"Get in the van! Get in the damn van!"

His friends didn't argue. All three of them, dazed and unsteady, scurried to the safety of the vehicle.

Once they were inside, the engine over revved as the driver slammed his foot on the accelerator, not juggling the clutch properly, before vanishing down the street.

Russell felt the wind around him settling, watching as the strands of silver dispersed into the darkness once more.

He stood still for a few moments. Letting everything sink in. Was this real? Was I hallucinating again? And all he could say was:

"Wow."

CHAPTER FIVE

His phone was ringing when he got home.

"Hello?"

"Mister Paige! My name is Claudia Rinefeld from the Perth Quarterly, I was-"

He dropped the receiver; his head was throbbing slightly.

Not from tiredness or exertion. His wild thoughts were losing themselves in his mind, racing back and forth with imagined storylines in how he would beat gangs and bad guys and questions about what should he do now, how will this affect his life? Had anyone seen him? What would happen if word of this got out?

The phone rang again. He picked it up, ready to put it down again.

"Russell? Is that you?"

"Mum?"

"Russell, why didn't you call?"

*   *   *

The curtains practically burst aside this time as Stacey barged out of the smaller darkroom into the brightly lit black and white stations.

This was amazing. He had caught it with his own camera.

It was a long shot. Two men lying on the road, a third crouched nearby. In front of them, Russell Paige, his arms outstretched and body puffed up with the winds that surrounded him. Of course, they were not visible in the picture, but his bloated clothes, billowing from the gusts were quite evident. Not to mention his hair. He looked absolutely wild. Unfortunately they were taken from behind Russell, so his face wasn't visible. But this was perfect. Pam would love this. But she wouldn't be the only one.

"You ripper!"

*   *   *

"He did what?"

Trent Peerson gawked at his speaker phone, "You mean to say he just knocked them over with a mere hand gesture?"

Eryn's voice stumbled out of the speaker, shaken and meek, the way Trent liked people sounding when they spoke to him, "Well, not quite. Well, actually, yes. That would be pretty accurate, Mister Peerson."

Trent turned slowly to look out the window of his seventy fifth floor corner office. It was located in one of the tallest buildings in Perth. The CP2 or Central Park 2, named in honour of its predecessor, still standing, but more of a historical monument on the other side of town.

The CP2 was over eight hundred metres tall, including the mandatory antennas, satellite dishes and communication relays located on the top. But from his office on the seventy fifth floor, Trent Peerson could see most of Perth. Tiny cars zipping by, only recognisable as whizzing headlights in the distance. Neighbouring buildings were lit up like giant Christmas trees; some with people barely seen still moving around inside. It was Friday night. Late night shopping in the city. Also one of the big social nights in the relocated Northbridge.

Northbridge was located just north of the city and, in the past was known as the big nightspot. But as the city expanded, it was knocked off the map. Then as a new nightspot was discovered, the locals renamed the suburb as Northbridge and petitioned to have it done so legally.

None of this mattered to Trent, though. What mattered to him was that he was only looking out the seventy fifth floor window.

He wanted the penthouse. He wanted to be right up there with the best. He wanted more money than any other conglomerate or corporate body in his own private savings account. And he was going to get it come hell or high water.

He watched the lights, imagining what they would look like from higher; from that top floor window. And his mind was set.

"Mister Peer-?"

"I want that boy," he said it quietly; threateningly. He thought he could hear Eryn gulping on the other end of the line. That was good. He was not happy and when he wasn't happy, no one else would be, "I want him now!"

"We... We don't know where to find him."

"I have people for that, Eryn. Use them and bring him to me by tomorrow mid day!"

*   *   *

Saturday was a bright new day. Sun shining, a few more clouds in the sky as they neared autumn. From a distance, perhaps a little more smog than usual, but unnoticeable to the inhabitants of the CBD.

Late patrons of the night clubs were straggling home one way or another, each one looking more worse for wear than they did when they left home the night before.

The night crawlers disappeared into their holes as the police became more prominent. The cars once more starting their surge inward from the outer suburbs, shoppers and workers alike trying to beat the morning traffic, only to instigate an earlier peak hour session.

The circle of life began once more.

And Russell was a part of that.

He awoke to the sun pouring through his window. Somehow, it had managed to either squeeze past the hundreds of tall buildings surrounding his pad, or to strategically reflect off the glass exteriors and back into his solitary window. He moaned, pulling the covers over his head. He wanted to sleep. Why couldn't he just sleep?

Finding it useless now, He shoved the covers aside and looked across at his clock. Nine twenty four. His phone was still off the hook beside it. It would be days before he even thought about replacing it.

He didn't have work today. But he wasn't about to hang about the apartment doing nothing all day. He had too much on his mind. Last night it had taken him ages to get to sleep with all the thoughts running through his head. Before that, it had taken over an hour to get his mother off the phone. She had been quite worried, what with seeing it on the news and in the paper. It was understandable, but hardly worth that much worry. He was okay. The wound on his arm had already disappeared. It was amazing. He had showered last night and removed the bandage to find it completely healed over. All very strange.

He dressed and went out. Shopping sounded like a good idea. Not to spend money, but to just look around, see what he wanted to buy, what he may one day afford and what he probably never would.

The best place to start was at work. There was a great range of things in Greyson's. Not that it was all good, but there was heaps of it. Music, computers, books, clothes. Anything and everything under the one roof.

Russell frowned. He was starting to sound like an advertisement. Had he been working there for too long?

Regardless, he made his way by foot to the inner parts of the city where there were malls, arcades and walkways aplenty to get him from one end of the city to the other, from one shopping centre to another.

He browsed the windows as he walked. He could also drop into the insurance agents to place the claim on his car.

*   *   *

It could be said that Pam Dauber works twenty four-seven. It could also be said she is an over-zealous feminist. Technically both are correct, but with a few minor terms and conditions included. On weekends, she spent much of her time, or rumour has people believe she does, on her mobile phone, trying to raise a story idea for the next issue of the "Perth Tribunal". Truth was Saturday was her one day off. She preferred to lounge around in her boyfriend's house; they shared rent, and relax in front of the mind numbing repeats of Elvis Presley's movies. She wasn't particularly an Elvis fan, but it beat those lame arsed lifestyle shows they had on like "Better Houses and Garden Pergolas".

Patrick Mulloch, her boyfriend, was currently out at ten fifteen.

There was a knock on the door. Pam let out a long harrowed sigh and wriggled her lithe body off the couch. It was warm, after having stolen Pat's spot, feeling nurtured in the remnant warmth of his body. It made her feel closer to him, to think she had somehow absorbed part of his natural aura, not that she was into any of that mumbo jumbo about auras and astral projection. Her paper printed it, didn't mean she had to believe in it.

Pulling her dressing gown tighter around her, she made her way to the entrance hall. Looking out the peephole, she recognised the grinning face.

With a flick of her wrist, the deadbolt was released and; after a moment's consideration as to whether she really wanted this new burst of excitement in her house on her only day off, the door swung open.

"Hello, Stacey, what is it this time?"

The cockney rushed in, pushing the door shut behind him, "Same kid. New evidence."

As lethargic as she felt, Pam couldn't help wishing she could bottle this guy's enthusiasm and sup on it from time to time, "The Paige boy?"

"Yeah," He pulled a photograph from his pocket and shoved it in her face, "Take a look. I wasn't sure if it was telekinetic or what, but he sure packs a mean punch.

Her eyes scanned the image in front of her and all of a sudden she was interested. She took hold of the photo and marched back into the lounge room, her lethargy left behind at the front door, "Has anyone else seen this?"

He shook his head, but she knew the answer without seeing his response. Stacey was too careful, despite his enthusiasm. She had already used his last photo for the paper, thinking little of the situation. But this second piece of evidence meant things were just a little too coincidental for comfort.

"Have you made contact?"

"No. I went in to his work to see him, but… well, let's just say it was a little crowded."

"Anyone suspect anything?"

She grabbed the remote off the couch and silenced the television as he spoke, "Doubt it. It was lunch rush. In Greyson's you could be a three headed goat demon from the planet Quash and still not be noticed."

Pam gave him a disgusted look; "You're still reading the crap I print?"

He smiled, "I like to see where you're going."

"Most of it is bullshit. You know that. Hell, you give me half of my pictures to draw stories from."

He pointed to the photo in her hand, "But this one's different."

"I can see that."

"So, what do we do?"

"Who are these other guys?"

He moved beside her, looking closely at the image, "No idea, but they're not ordinary thugs. Related to the bomber, perhaps?"

"Probably. So they're making a play for the boy."

Stacey smiled, "Looks like he can take care of himself."

"That's not the point. People know about him. We have to make sure we get to him first."

"We could see if we can catch him at work. You get dressed; I'll be out in the car."

*   *   *

He pocketed the papers from the insurance agents. Hopefully they wouldn't screw him around too much. He was a media spectacle; they probably couldn't risk it. If this was fame, it could have some advantages.

Maybe now he could build up enough courage to ask Kristen out. What with his newfound powers and the media spotlight, he could probably sweep her up into his arms, regardless of what he looked like. All he needed was five minutes with her. Just enough time to turn around and ask her out. That was all. Five minutes alone.

He felt himself subconsciously praying to some higher power to bestow these magical moments on him. He knew it was pointless, but hey, every little bit helped. He wasn't sure if she was working today. Maybe he could just pull her aside and ask. Or maybe he could call her from another extension and do it over the phone.

Oh, yeah. How brave is that? Can't even do it face to face. He sighed. Obviously the new powers had nothing to do with self-confidence.

Still, he was sure if he had those five minutes, everything would be solved.

Greyson's was only a few minutes walk from the insurance agents. He kept his eye on the ground for most of the way, for fear of being recognised.

What if he was? What would happen? Would people hound him, hog his time? Would he become a media spectacle right there in the street? Or would people ignore him? There were plenty of rich and famous people in the world already, what would one measly person on the street be to anyone else? Would they even recognise him? He shook his head. It didn't matter. He was still the same person, powers and all. He didn't feel any different. Same strange sense of humour, same longing thoughts of Kristen, same cowardice to do anything about it, same old face staring back in the mirror or glass. He was still Russell Paige. Nothing could change that. It's just not everyone had gotten to know him yet. Maybe if he succumbed to the phone calls, gave interviews, maybe people would like him then?

But would the phone calls stop? Would he get peace and quiet? Privacy? That went for his powers, too. What if he revealed to the world what he could do? He remembered the rumours of the other freaks. People not quite like other people. Much like the Jewish were treated in Nazi Germany or African Americans in the days of enslavement. They were jeered, hated, attacked. Would the same rules apply for him? Would

40

he go from being a sought after interview to being a hunted freak of nature?

And what if he had imagined it all anyway? Honestly, men attacking him out of the blue? What for? What did he do? Maybe he imagined it all on the boring walk home. He could always test his powers later on, after he finished shopping. There were plenty of places he could go. King's Park, for instance. The most popular nature reserve in the city area. Wide open spaces or secluded clearings. Anywhere would be perfect for testing his powers. Heck, the curb crawlers and beat walkers all managed to find secluded areas for illegal sex, how hard would it be to find somewhere to test his powers, if they existed in the first place. If not, well, a nice nature walk would do him good. He looked up at the buildings ahead of him.

He could see Greyson's just up the road.

He quickened his pace and started eyeing the people going by. No one was looking at him. Not yet, anyway. It seemed safe enough to walk normally.

As he turned a corner to head toward the main entrance of Greyson's, his step faltered.

There she was.

Like some kind of miracle. His wish had been granted.

Kristen. Walking so tall and gracefully out of the main entrance, adjusting her bag on her back. One of those single strap numbers, fawn in colour. The band stretching over her right shoulder and down to her left waist to join onto the pack. A small mobile phone pouch sat empty just over her right breast. She looked up and somehow spotted him in the crowd. Smiling, she approached, even as he walked toward her.

"Hi, Russell."

"Hello. Finishing work?"

"No, just having my break."

"Cool."

He could feel the blood rushing to his face, somehow managing to clog his tongue.

"You're not working today?"

He shook his head and managed to squeak, "My day off."

She nodded, her confident manner consuming his beating heart completely. He couldn't blink, he couldn't breath, and he couldn't speak.

"Well, I've got to get something to eat. I'll see you around."

He nodded. There was a noise somewhere, a "cluck"-ing sound, similar to the one he had heard the night before, or thought he heard.

He watched as she walked away, she turned back and smiled before disappearing into the crowd. He turned his head to scan the crowd. There was a small group of Asian tourists nearby, Japanese perhaps, one held a camera and was trying to organise the other four, his family, to stand in front of a small Australian Memorabilia shop.

He waited a few moments for his heart to slow down before entering the shop, the blood slowly draining from his face.

*　*　*

"In Confectionery," Stacey looked over his shoulder, trying to see past the Weekend shoppers. There were more of them today than the lunchtime before, "Pam? Pam?"

"Over here!"

He saw her hand waving back in the direction of the sunglasses department. A good ten metres behind.

"Just push your way through!"

"The flow's going against me!"

"Hang on! I'll come and get you!"

He swam through the tangle of shopping bags, arms and whining children to find Pam standing huddled against the back wall of the sunglasses counter. She looked practically petrified.

"Why didn't you tell me it was this bad in here? I could have done a story on it."

Stacey lifted his camera, "Don't worry, love, I'll get some shots for you. But we have to get to confectionery. It's the next floor down."

"How are we going to get down there?"

"As I said, we have to push against the flow."

She shook her head; "This is crazy!"

He had to agree with her but: "The kid could be in danger."

She looked slightly miffed, her earlier bout of lethargy gaining a hold on her again, "Aren't they always?"

"Come on! This way!" He grabbed her arm and hauled her into the crowd. It was sink or swim in the shopping world. All they had to do was stay afloat long enough to make it to the lifts or escalators. After that, they could just follow the flow down again.

He felt a tug from a group of shoppers seemingly trying to force their way to the escalators down. Their bright lights seemed like a heavenly stairwell taking people to a subterranean land of wonder.

He hitched a ride on this surge and dragged Pam along with him. He could hear her muttering to herself, but couldn't understand what she was on about.

When he felt the contact of grated metal under his shoes, he nearly cried out in joy. They had made it to the Escalators.

He turned to Pam who was still pulling against him, being dragged onward by the ever flowing ebb of shoppers, trying to suck her back out into the sea of people where she would eventually drown.

But something was wrong.

She was being pulled. In fact it looked as though she was pushing against the people trying to get onto the escalators.

42

And her mouth was moving at a million miles and hour, her words being swallowed by the roar of the ocean of shoppers.

"What?!"

She pulled on his arm, harder this time, using both hands.

He fought his way against the current until he was practically on top of her.

"Look! Over there you dipstick!"

Stacey followed her hand as she pointed upward to the escalator going up.

It was Russell. He was calmly poised on the moving escalators heading for the upper levels. He was dressed in civvies and at the rate the two journalists were going, they would lose him in seconds.

"You take the lift!" She shouted, "Go up floor by floor. I'll move around to the other escalator and try to keep an eye on where he goes."

Together they dove into the oncoming waves of customers, fighting against the pull, trying to drag them back toward the escalators. Once they had overcome the initial undercurrent, they divided and made their ways slowly but determinedly toward their prospective modes of travel.

Pam cursed under her breath. If all these people weren't around, she could do what was necessary to keep in eyesight of the boy. Then again, her logic argued, if these people weren't there, there wouldn't need to be any drastic measures taken at all. She cursed again and moved on.

Stacey was having a bit more trouble, trying to fight for a position on the elevators. As one door opened, scores of people poured out, only to be replaced by scores of others, of which he couldn't manage to be a part.

Even his London accent was getting him nowhere. So he had to do something.

He reached his hand into the next group of people that clambered onto the lift and grabbed a loose arm, which automatically went flailing about. He pulled hard and found there was little resistance. As his captive was pulled out of the lift, He nudged his way in to the gap that was left. As the doors closed, he noticed a little old lady of about eighty shaking her fists at him, swearing profusely. He felt slightly ashamed, but, hey, he reasoned, this could be a matter of life and death.

Pam all but leapt onto the escalator, just in time to see Russell take the next flight up. He was going to level two. She just hoped Stacey would too. Squashed behind a slightly obese man with his shorts riding low on his buttocks and a small group of oversexed teenagers behind, she felt like a hot dog in some sort of kinky sex dinner party. The sweat from both sides was almost unbearable, not to mention the other unmentionable fumes that came from the guy in front. She held her breath and kept an eye on the boy who, for all that had happened to him, looked remarkably docile.

As she rounded the floor to the escalator up to the second floor, she could see he wasn't going up any higher. Second floor it was.

Stacey grabbed the doorframe to the lift on the first floor, feeling himself being pushed outward by the hordes of people alighting the lift. His feet weren't touching the ground, but he held on for dear life with his hands, at least until the new rush of customers began to enter the carriage. He fought for his position by the door and found himself squashed into the corner where the buttons were located. This would give him a slight advantage. He could hold the door open long enough to get out or chose which floors they would go to. He opted for the third floor as he would have had to have passed the first by now, but if he hadn't reached the third, Stacey would be there to grab him. Or at least stop him and ask for directions in order to keep him in one spot until Pam arrived.

The noise and claustrophobic feel of the cramped lift was starting to affect his brain, he feared. His thoughts just weren't coming out as clearly as normal. It could have been the thought of Pam. He'd always had a crush on her, but she's also always been seeing someone else. He shook his head, no. That wasn't it.

A foul smell arose in the cramped elevator. Everyone knew what it was, but only one person knew the origin. Oh shit, Stacey thought, as he was sure everyone else was thinking the same thing. Third floor was out of the question. There was no way he was going to stay in this.

When the door opened on the second floor, Stacey jumped out in relief. It wasn't so busy on this floor. It looked to be Manchester and the like. Somewhere nearby he heard an odd, "cluck". A camera. An old one and it didn't have an automatic wind. Not as good as his own. But taking photos in a department store? Could be an avid photographer doing a study, or a student doing an assignment. There was any number of possibilities. Still, Stacey let his eyes wander the crowd, hoping to catch a glimpse. Sure enough, there amongst a group of women, looking like a small bridal registry organisation, a short man disappeared, his camera, which he had had at the ready, along with him. He was being watched.

Stacey moved toward the group, and the man behind them.

Not surprisingly, he had gone by the time Stacey got there. But he wasn't hard to follow. Stacey watched as he hurried along the pristine white tiles that circled the floor and proceeded to follow him.

Pam had tried to keep an eye on Russell. He had managed to disappear in the meagre crowd, however. She moved from the escalator shaft on the second floor and surveyed the area as she went. That was when she spotted Stacey.

"Stace!"

The short cockney turned briefly to look for her, but continued moving around the periphery of the store. He mouthed something she couldn't quite make out, but pointed toward someone in front of him. Was it Russell? Maybe. So she decided maybe it was best to head him off.

She hurried around to the south side of the store, to where Stacey was heading. She should be able to catch him there. When she arrived in Kitchen goods, however, Russell was nowhere to be seen. Stacey appeared and hurried toward her, his head scanning the crowd.

"Where did he go?"

"Russell?"

"No. The camera guy."

"What?"

"I was being watched. A guy with a camera. I was following him."

"What about Russell?"

Stacey shook his head, "Haven't seen him."

Pam sighed, a little annoyed, "Let's split again. You follow your man, I'll look for Russell."

"I can't find him."

"Who? Russell or the camera guy?"

"Either."

"Then let's just go look for Russell. So what, a guy was taking pictures."

Stacey looked at her; "You didn't see him. Suspicious looking chap, ducking behind people to avoid being seen."

"Maybe he was shy. It doesn't matter. We have to find Russell."

* * *

Someone was following him. At first he thought he was being paranoid. Why would they? Then he recalled the night before. The men and the van. Something was definitely going on. Were they back for seconds? He could hardly use his new powers in here, where he worked, let alone in public view. One was female. That was a certainty. She was the one eyeing him up the escalators and she was too damn good looking to be interested in anything unprofessional. Perhaps she was a journalist, unable to get through by phone, she was stalking him. But why hadn't she asked questions yet? Just yelled them out over the din. That would have been preferable to being stalked. Working in Greyson's gave him the advantage of knowing the reserves, back rooms, and all the nooks and crannies. Though the way he was dressed and without his nametag, that could still be difficult. All the same, he could make up some excuse or other.

He made his way to the linen department, near the elevators, and ducked behind one of the freestanding displays of towels. He tried to think of people he knew who worked in the department, or even on this floor.

There was Anna, in Kitchenware, but she was an odd sort. Not one he could trust too easily. Then there was Jackie. Perfect, he thought. A fresh faced lesbian with the kindest of hearts and the cleanest sense of humour. She had recently turned thirty, but Russell would have sworn she was only twenty-three, not only by appearance, but her manner. She was perfect. If she was working today, that was.

He let his eyes scan the area. She worked generally on this floor, moving from department to department, so she was hard to find at the best of times. With the added bonus of not even knowing if she was working or not, it was darn near impossible. Well, he had time. It wasn't like the woman following him would pull a gun in public. No one would be that stupid, would they? He didn't exactly want to find out.

She was nowhere in sight. Never mind. He could always say he was doing logistics work for Joseph and he'd lost his badge in the reserve, if he got caught. Most people didn't care anyway, especially if they knew they worked in the store. Everyone seemed to take for granted that everyone else was there for a purpose and what that was, it didn't matter. It was only when strangers appeared that people started to worry.

He spotted the small doorway into the towelling reserve and made his way over to it, eyeing the crowd for that woman. He couldn't see her anywhere. So he stepped inside and waited for a few minutes. Maybe she would give up and leave, perhaps try a different floor, giving him enough time to get out of the store.

CHAPTER SIX

"Where is he?"

Eryn shook his head, "I'm sorry, Mister Peerson. We don't have him."

Peerson rose from his desk; Eryn, who stood opposite him seemed to shrink into his neck.

"But... But we do have this," from inside his lab coat, he withdrew a photograph, "We got it this morning. Rickets wanted me to show it to you right away. I'd have to agree to its importance, sir.

Peerson snatched the photo from his underling's trembling hands and froze. His normally angry and imposing disposition melted away for an instant as he struggled for some sort of control on the inside.

"Where did you get this?"

"The photograph says everything."

Peerson sank back into his leather, ergonomic chair and studied the photo for a moment longer, "Leave me."

Eryn didn't need to be asked twice.

*   *   *

They'd lost him. And it wasn't Stacey's fault. Pam would make it out like it was, but that was just her. Anything to boost her ego. Funny thing was he found that endearing about her. An arrogant woman; determined that she is never in the wrong. Every time he was around her, he could literally sense himself becoming stupid, if only for her. Maybe it was because his heart would contract in his stomach and stop pumping the blood to his brain and then that in turn would shrink. He wasn't sure. But when he was by himself, he tended to think a lot more for himself. When she was around, he found himself trying to impress her all the time, and then finding himself failing miserably, like now. Russell had vanished from the floor. Maybe he'd gone to another. Which? It didn't matter. They'd been looking for over half an hour and no luck. He could have left the city by now.

He spotted Pam back in kitchenware. He hurried over and tapped her on the shoulder, not before taking a few photos of her tall, and powerful looking frame. Not that she was muscly, nor that he was a pervert. But he liked photography and he liked her, so where was the harm in working two of his interests together, sort of like journalism and photography.

He knew he was only trying to fool himself, but at least he'd have some decent photos.

"Anything?"

He shook his head. She sighed, unimpressed, "We can't do anything until he turns up again."

"He could be dead."

"Not if he has as much power as you say. He'd stand a good chance in defending himself."

"But what are a few gusts of wind to a well placed bullet?"

She didn't respond immediately, and when she did, she changed the subject, "No point checking the other floors. It would be impossible to find him."

"Agreed. So what about hitting him where he lives?"

She let out a little laugh, "Whose side are you on?"

"What do you mean?"

"Hitting him? You're getting too involved in this whole cloak and dagger stuff."

"Hardly," see, he was looking like a fool already.

"Still, it is worth a try. I should be able to pick up his address from the paper, say I'm doing a story."

Stacey agreed, "I'll case this joint, get a bit of an idea of its layout, just in case."

"Case this joint? You gotta get out more, Stacey."

He rolled his eyes at his own stupidity.

She laughed, "I'll give you a call when I get his address."

He merely nodded and went on his way, heading back toward the dreaded elevators.

She watched him go, a smile having found its way to her lips.

* * *

Along the original and longest business and finance streets in the city, Saint George's Terrace, were a few cultural pinpoints of interest. Some lay hidden and unknown, a secret from the public. There were churches, cafes, even parks. One such park was the Saint George's Square. Part of the original area of Perth, but still caught up in the highflying markets and dollar exchanges. This little garden sits behind two buildings, a small walkway the only access point from the terrace.

Russell believed it to be the most beautiful and, if there was such a thing, magical place in the entire city. A man made and well-tended garden, it was divided into several parts. At one end was a small fountain, an iron casting of a woman, a dog and a chicken sat above it while water plants of varying colours and types filled the catchment. On either side of this are garden benches, wooden and painted green. Uncomfortable, but the view you get when sitting on them more than makes up for the back aches and blisters on your backside. In front of these are four small rectangular grass patches set in a square. Running the width of the garden and dividing two blocks from the other two, was a thin stream of water, ending on one side with a waterfall, disappearing off the edge of the garden, the other another fountain, supplying the stream with fresh water.

The grassed areas are surrounded by knee high hedges and the centre of each is dug in with a symbol that looks almost musical in its pattern, made entirely of tiny rounded beads of gravel. Beyond the squares is a stairway of squared limestone that leads up to another grassed area, spotted with small trees and more comfortable benches. At the far end is a white statue, smooth and rounded of what looks to be two heads, joined together like some indefinable Siamese twin. Around a corner, behind another limestone wall is a third grassed area, most of which is taken up with five large rocks, also smooth and rounded, their shapes seemingly defying the tag of "rock" placed upon it, as if they were striving to be something else, like glass. Their surfaces are pockmarked but only slightly. Weather worn but wonderful.

There is a beauty to these gardens that lasts the year round. Each season bringing forth its own unique attraction, whether it's the blooms and life of Spring, the browning and fading of Autumn or the starkness striving for life once more in Winter or just the blatant beauty in Summer. Any time spent here is time well spent.

And Russell spent much of his free time here. It was his sanctuary, his secret. Though people that worked around here knew of it, had their lunch here, it was still special. People noticed you here, but regardless of who you were, they accepted you. It was like some kind of Garden of Eden. Everyone belonged, everyone was happy, even if you weren't, it somehow created an inner glow that quickly nullified any bad thoughts and brought you back to life.

The moment Russell stepped into the garden that day, everything seemed to brighten up. His thoughts took on a new clarity of vision. Everything seemed so clear. He almost expected all the answers to come to him, though that was too much to hope for.

He sat in the upper area on one of the benches; ham and cheese sandwich in a neat plastic triangular container in hand. He took a couple of deep breaths before opening it and starting on the food. It was almost a religious experience, although he knew he made way too much of the situation. But he liked to think that this place was for him like no other church in the world could be. Pure, perfect.

It took only a short time to finish off the sandwich and to dispose of the plastic in a bin. He then sat back down on the bench and reclined, arms stretched along the backrest and head tilted back to regard the blue sky.

It was beautiful. There was no other word for it. The epitome of beauty. Fluffy white clouds crawled over the blue ceiling above, those now familiar silver wisps of air swirling around in the sky. The leaves slowly falling off the trees, one by one onto the freshly raked grass, which still held the crisp green freshness it had in Spring and would have for the year round. It's newly cut shafts, soft and pliable under foot, like a cushion of air.

"There he is."

The mood was broken. He snapped his head up to look around. There was a noticeable change in atmosphere now. The tranquillity broken.

Two men, in black. One beefed up beyond belief, the other of medium build and height, neither looking happy. They had entered the garden via a set of double glass doors near the fountain at the other end.

The first thought that came to Russell's mind as he stood up was "How dare they!"

He almost said it, but for the realisation of how stupid it would sound.

They moved toward him, not bothered by the beauty in their way, kicking through the hedges as if they were trashcans dropped in their way. That made Russell mad.

"No!"

They hesitated.

"What?"

Russell took a couple of steps toward them. If it meant saving this place, he would do anything. They had no right to tear it up and he had no right to be the cause of their doing so.

"I'll come with you."

"Really?"

Russell thought about it. And was amazed he even had to.

"Of course not, you dicks!"

He turned and bolted back toward the Terrace. Garden or no garden, they had gardeners to look after it, who did Russell have?

He could hear the two men behind him, the sound of their boots on concrete. Then he recalled the pathway that ran the length of the garden, behind the central fountain and along the side of the building. Of course it would be easier to run on than grass and gravel. So hopefully they wouldn't have caused too much damage to the garden.

Taking another sharp corner, Russell charged toward a set of automated glass doors that were already opening for a woman in a dress suit. The entrance was a few metres back from the footpath, but that distance seemed to vanish in seconds. Russell dodged past the woman and practically flew inside and into a corridor directly in front of the door.

A security guard jumped up from behind reception, "Hey!"

Ignoring him, Russell slammed a button on one of the walls, hoping he could jag an elevator.

No such luck. But there was the stairs.

"Prick!" the woman called. With an attitude like that, Russell thought, she deserved what was coming her way.

She too went sprawling, hands first onto the well polished tiles of the lobby, the guard leaping out of the way as the larger of the two men came hurtling into the building.

Russell twisted the handle on the door to the stair well and started climbing, taking two steps at a time. He had made it to the first floor landing when the door below was virtually knocked off its hinges.

Second floor sounded good, if only for a way out of the stairwell. Russell had absolutely no idea where he was, let alone where he was going. As he managed to think about it over his panic, he recalled thinking the worst thing for a person to do in a movie when they are being hunted, such as in Copycat when Sigourney Weaver climbs the stairs at the end, was to go up. There was absolutely nowhere to go if you did. And here he was, being a complete idiot and going up. Now, he could hardly go down. Who knows if someone was waiting for him in the lobby? The only option now was to go further up and he didn't like the sound of that too much.

The second floor had a general floor plan not unlike the ground floor. A corridor with elevators and a t-junction on either end heading toward offices and company leased areas. Again, trying his luck, he punched the elevator call button and was surprised when one of the four shafts beeped. The doors slid slowly open and Russell leapt in as the stair well door burst open.

He punched the 'door close' button underneath the list of floor numbers from 'B' and 'G' up to '12'.

He pushed his back against the rear of the carriage, hoping to hide in plain sight, perhaps, or merely be absorbed by the elevator itself. No such luck.

He slammed the '8' button, hoping to speed up the doors if anything.

Back in the corridor, he glimpsed the larger of the two men as he lunged toward the doors, unable to prevent them closing.

Releasing a breath he hadn't even realised he was holding, he watched the numbers above the door light up in order as the elevator moved. What the heck was he going to do now?

They would be on their way up by now, either by stairs or lifts. Or they would be waiting for him back in the lobby, waiting for him to make his escape.

Then again, there had to be another way out. There always is in places like this, either the fire escape or the below ground parking for executives. True, not all of these buildings had a car park, but there had to be a way out of the basement, other than through the damn lobby.

The Elevator lurched to a halt and the doors began opening again. Russell slammed the 'door close' button and 'B' simultaneously. He would find a way out. It would be down in the basement.

Or was he just being an idealist?

That was a problem he found himself suffering from. Idealism. Not something to be too proud of, especially in a realist world. Generally he was a realist and it wasn't a problem. But the moment things went a little awry, Pop! In came the idealist notions of how it should be. Rather than dealing with what is, there was always that inner hope of this is what could be. Like viewing life as a big game. Almost like a role-playing game, the likes of Palladium's Rifts series or as primitive as Dungeons and Dragons. There is a games master somewhere, perhaps even God, even though Russell wasn't sure he existed, who gave him a set scenario. And it was his job to get out of it. But what Russell failed to see and he knew that when he looked back on it, was that what he did had its consequences. Life isn't a game and in a case like this, if he died, he couldn't go back and role up a new character. It was game over. No extra lives or second chances as in a computer game. No save options to load up, even if it meant going over the same old ground over and over again. What is done is done. But Russell's idealism seemed to wipe all of this out of his head. Even with love. In a perfect world, Kristen loves him and would ask him out in a couple of days or so. Yet, in reality, he just wasn't sure if he was wasting his time or not, or if she was even remotely interested. And in those occasions, nothing else seemed to matter; not food, not money. Just love and Kristen. Again, no thought of what is, just what could be. Ridiculous. And now, he found himself in the same predicament. Idealism was in control once more and there was no stopping it.

The doors 'dinged' open onto the basement and he stepped out. It was huge. Obviously he had been fortunate enough to get in one of only two of the four elevators that went all the way down as there was no corridor on this floor. Just a big open car park that looked to spread for a fair distance underground.

It actually looked like it could cater for another building or two, and perhaps did stretch that far. There was only one way to find out.

He took off from the lifts and ran across the hard pavement. There were at least forty cars parked here and there, giving a fair supply of cover if necessary, but it didn't look like he'd be needing it. There was no sign of the two thugs. He slowed down, taking a more cautious approach. On the opposing wall, he could see a line of three elevators and a door to a stair well. Obviously another building. To his right, toward the street, was a large roller door, closed. He had two choices. The street or the building. He chose the latter. That way it would be harder for them to follow, rather than him simply appearing on the terrace, he could hang around inside the other building a moment longer and make sure the coast is clear.

He had to admit, it was all quite thrilling. Being chased, having to make possible life and death decisions, though he wasn't sure if these guys would actually go that far. Then again, they did plant a bomb in a car park. Anyone and any number of people could have been killed or injured. Fortunately they hadn't been. Well, excepting himself as far as he could tell and even then, he still wasn't sure of the effects of the explosion. They had obviously done something to him to give him the powers, but it seemed highly unlikely anyone would plant a bomb in the hopes of mutating people in such a way. Unless of course they were some sort of mad experimental scientist hoping to play god. But that was less likely than a terrorist organisation who just wanted to make a point. But what had been the point of the explosion in the first place? Was there a ransom involved? Possibly. The detective hadn't mentioned anything, but it seemed he was more in the dark than anyone else. So what was the point behind it all?

Perhaps these new powers could help get the answers. Russell thought about it as he moved toward the lifts. Perhaps he could start looking into it. If it was such a big deal that they would try and hunt him down, the only real witness to the event, then there had to be something highly suspicious going on and he wanted to find out what.

There was a noise behind him followed by a loud Bang that reverberated through the basement. A window exploded inward in a car beside him followed by the windscreen blowing out over the bonnet.

Gunshot?

He ducked for cover behind the car and peered through the window toward the stair well he had been in only a few moments before. Someone was back there, hiding. He had managed a brief glimpse of one of the men disappearing behind another vehicle. But was there only one of them?

All the same, it would be pointless staying where he was.

He edged backward; staying crouched and hopefully out of sight. Trying to keep a car body in between him and the thugs. Obviously they had changed their tactic. Before they had wanted him alive, now they were shooting at him. This was serious.

"Duh," he muttered to himself. What kind of an observation was that? "This was serious"? How bloody stupid would you be if you hadn't realised that the moment the bomb went off.

Something moved to the right. One of them?

He ducked behind a car and attempted a quick glance over the boot. Still no one in sight. But they had to be coming after him.

Another loud gunshot echoed through the car park and he fell to the floor, back against the tyre.

He turned just in time to see a chunk of wall beside the elevator rupture and spray the floor.

The lifts were not an option. They would shoot him before the doors closed, or even before he got to the damn things.

What he needed was cover.

He concentrated; focusing his mind, hoping this was how it was done. Sure enough, he began to see the silver wisps of air again. Not so many this time and not as mobile as they had been outside. Perhaps the tight and closed quarters he was in was affecting them. Stagnant air.

All the same, he could use it to his own advantage.

He didn't know how to describe the way he did what he did. He wanted the air to do something and it did. Like he was mentally asking it to do it, but it took a bit more concentration. Practically willing it to move.

He felt a warm breeze, mixed with the stale exhaust fumes that managed to linger in the car park, start to pick up. He cajoled it, convinced it to blow harder and faster toward the building he had just come from. But if he wasn't careful, he'd run out of ammo. Not because he'd run out of air, but it would all end up down one end of the basement. He knew physics, he also knew that he needed to circulate the air, let it diffuse around and back, so as he can send it off again. He concentrated harder, forcing the air into a spin, two circles blowing down the middle of the car park and then dividing, retreating back up to the other end down either side and back through the middle again. Harder and faster, the silver clouds dancing wildly as the spun and drove onward and around building in intensity and strength until each circle became a veritable cyclone.

He got up onto his feet and ran, still crouched over, toward the roller doors. His way out. Strangely, he could only feel slight affects of the wind, as if it were avoiding him, trying to keep him from harm.

Some one yelled behind him. But he couldn't make out what was said over the wind. It was howling, screaming even between the cars and around the basement. He didn't look back until he reached a small panel with a white button on it. It looked to be the door release for drivers to press when they wished to leave. He hit it hard and ducked behind the machine, glancing around it, back toward where he thought the thugs were.

Sure enough, his powers were having the desired effect. Both men were huddled in the opposing corner, practically trapped by a wall of wind; their short hair and their clothes billowing in the wind as it rushed past them again and again like a gigantic wash cycle.

There was a tremendous rush of air as the roller door began rattling open. The fresher gusts of wind intertwined with the recycled, but ferocious blasts that were already at work in the basement, causing an even greater upsurgeance of tumultuous wind.

The very ground began to shake as cars began to scrape sideways against the pavement, dragged and pushed along by the gale-force winds. It suddenly occurred to Russell that perhaps things were getting a little out of control. The wind had done its job, he was able to escape now and maybe the men would think twice about following, but if the storm kept up, he could end up doing more damage than the explosion had, to the point of affecting the building above.

He refocused his attention. Concentrated on slowing the wind down. The silver threads had been all but lost in the frantic activity, but he could still sense them. So he reached out with his thoughts and tried to hold onto them, pull them back, and slow them down. At first they wouldn't respond. So he concentrated harder, tightening all the muscles in his head, hoping it would make a difference, straining against the drag of the wind. And it began to work. He felt a sweat break out on his forehead as he literally grasped at the wind with his mind, slowing it down, easing it back. He could see the effects it was having. The cars had stopped moving for one, for another, the silver wisps were also slowing, returning to their normal casual dance rather than racing about on an ethereal sky circuit.

The two men in the corner were still huddled against the wall; their black jackets pulled up to protect their faces.

In a short while the wind would have settled, but Russell didn't have that time to watch it. Instead he bolted up the driveway, through the roller door entrance and back onto the street. As far as he could tell, the two men weren't following.

CHAPTER SEVEN

"Oh come on, Harold. It was front page news yesterday."

"No," Harold's camp and pompous accent was endearing, but his attitude was definitely getting on Pam's nerves, "Yesterday's news was for yesterday. The boy is of no concern now."

"But what if there is a real story behind it?" She knew she'd made a mistake the moment she said it.

He turned on his chair, away from his computer and stared at her in amazement, his eyes practically bulging out of his head, "Real?"

"You know what I mean?"

He stood up, bearing down on her. He was tall if nothing else.

"I know exactly what you mean! You think I don't take my job seriously. You think that I print garbage for the mere sensationalism that it seems to be. You think that I'm some old has-been too caught up in the swirl of the supernatural to care about the line to draw between reality and fiction."

He was close, but Pam thought of him more of a "Never-was" than a "Has-been".

"Now, Harold. You're over reacting."

He raised his hand, "No! Maybe you're right. Maybe I don't draw that line so clearly. But I know for a fact I deliver the news people want to read. They want fresh meat on the table every week. They don't want the same story recycled over and over again."

"This isn't recycled! It's new. It could be a story worth digging into."

"When I was younger, Pamela, there were plenty of stories worth getting into. I would have published them all. There was a great one involving my neighbour at the time and a fortuitous black out that seemed to be the work of God, delivering unto him the fate he deserved. It would make a fine story, but it, like yours, is old news. Old news is just not good news. I'm sorry."

She'd heard that story before. He liked bringing it up, but he was using it to push the wrong point. And now she was going to use it to her own advantage, and she shivered at the mere thought of it.

"Maybe people would like to hear that story, Harold. Maybe you should publish it. Who knows! You might find a niche audience out there starved for the tales that lead us to where we are. Or people of your generation who want to look back and think that things were as dangerous and awkward back then as they are today. Have you thought about that?"

He was silent for a moment. He was definitely considering this. You could read Harold like a book. So obvious in every way, what he was thinking, doing, whatever. You just had to look at him and he'd give himself away.

"You might have a point. Just a page. Like a historical section. I think you've just hit on a perfect idea! And with Australia Day this week, we could do a special report! Pamela! I could just kiss you!"

She raised her arms in defence, "No. No need. I just want the boy's address and the chance to check him out."

Harold smiled, "Anything for my best reporter."

She returned his smile, hoping he couldn't read the falseness behind it. He was so predictable, so pliable. At least she had achieved what she had come for. And she might even get a raise for it.

*   *   *

Pam had sounded pretty sarcastic on the phone. She had managed to get the address out of Harold, obviously, but it was also obvious she had had to endure his normal pathetic whinging and whining.

Stacey thanked god he didn't have to work directly with the git. Being a photographer, and freelance at that, meant he could work with anyone he chose or through anyone. That's why he stuck with Pam. He knew her and they had a good working relationship; if you took the personal aspect out of it, that was. There had been a time when he was scraping for cash, but as his experience increased, so did his skill. He had managed to hone his abilities to the point he was quick to act if necessary. If something was going down, he was always ready for it. That was why he tended to carry the camera around his neck most of the time. He also usually kept one hand on it, for support, not to mention security, and in the odd chance something should happen, it was just a case of hoisting it to his eye.

The last couple of days had been good.

He still had the camera around his neck as he approached the door to Russell's apartment. He hoped that there hadn't been many reporters around already, to the point of totally getting on the boy's nerves. But that is usually looked upon as invasion of privacy. In this sort of story, the best angle would be to organise an interview prior to showing up rather than harassing. In the case of the latter, you faced the possibility that the talent, as Russell was referred to, wouldn't want to talk to that particular paper or program at all, or ever again in the future if there were further developments. Most newspapers couldn't afford such a reputation anyway, so they stuck to the old 'call before you come' policy. Again, being a freelance photographer meant Stacey had a bit more leeway, not having to represent a particular paper and worry about their ideas of ethics and policy.

Besides, he wasn't here on journalistic terms.

He found the door without too much trouble. He need only follow his nose next time. The smell from the patisserie was almost overwhelming. But he stole himself away and knocked on the door to Russell's apartment.

"Can I help you?"

Stacey turned to regard the man speaking to him.

"Russell? Russell Paige?"

The boy, well, man, but he looked like he was only sixteen, despite his actual age, spotted the camera and backed away slowly. He hadn't been close to begin with, obviously not trusting the man at his door. Stacey couldn't afford to let him get away.

"Wait. I'm not a reporter. Well, I am, but that's not why I'm here."

Russell's left eye brow raised slightly, "Then why the camera?"

Stacey looked down at the beautiful piece in his hand, a true work of art it was. Forget the photos it took, it was fine enough to look at on its own, "Habit, sorry."

"What do you want?"

Stacey stood his ground, trying not to seem too imposing. It was hard anyway, being a short man for a start, "Simply to talk."

"What about?"

"I can see you're a suspicious one. Don't blame you, really. Not after everything."

Russell took another step back, his eyes almost accusing the cockney with a simple look, "What do you know about 'everything'?"

"I'm sorry?" this actually confused Stacey a little.

Russell's eyes widened in realisation; "You're with them!"

"What?"

"You tell who ever it is you're working for to stay the hell away from me. Your two friends from earlier can vouch that I'm more than capable of looking after myself."

Two friends? What was the boy talking about? Then Stacey made the realisation.

"No. You got it wrong. I'm not with them. I know about them, but I assure you, I'm not involved that way."

"And I'm supposed to believe that?"

Stacey thought about it, "No. Not really. But I'd really appreciate it if you did."

"No doubt."

"Look," Stacey took a deep breath, fighting with his inner conscience. He was about to do something he would never consider doing in normal circumstances. When he continued, his speech was long and drawn out, fighting to finish the sentence, "I'll give you my camera."

"What? What would I want that for?"

"Let me finish. If you just let me talk to you for a couple of minutes, I'll give you my camera as, like, a form of insurance."

"Forget that. Why would I care about a bloody camera?"

"Watch your mouth, boy!"

That totally riled Stacey. Anyone could see the camera was practically worth its weight in gold. Nobody dissed the camera, especially when it was hung around his neck, or they would have to answer to Stacey's temper.

Russell looked a bit surprised. This guy had to be crazy. Or damn possessive about his camera. He certainly wasn't someone to trust.

"Stacey, calm down."

A woman spoke from behind him. Russell turned and backed against the patisserie window, making sure no one else could take him by surprise.

"Russell Paige? My name is Pamela Dauber. Call me Pam. We need to talk."

She was a damn attractive woman, that's who she was. Russell's eyes nearly bulged out of his head. For one thing, she was wearing a black, tight top, which left little to the imagination. She also wore a dark jacket over the top that did little to conceal her 'womanhood' and the curvature of her hips was more than evident in her tight skirt. She wore tall black boots. A very sexy look that suited her to a T. She was perfect. Toned, yet supple. Her dark eyes, though outwardly kind, were something else when you looked into them. There was an inherent sanguinary quality to them that suggested she would rip your heart out if you ever got on her bad side. This sense was enhanced by her long black hair which added an almost animalistic quality to her as it hung straight down either side of her face and over her breasts, Russell wasn't sure if the colour was natural or not. Her make-up was impeccable which implied she was direct and knew her business and it was more than clear this woman was not to be messed with.

Russell managed to blink and nod at the same time, but his words were caught in his throat.

"Pam?"

The man called Stacey was gawking.

"Surprised?"

"That is one new look I'll never complain about."

Pam smiled, her brilliant red lips never parting, adding to the mystery of this seemingly complex woman.

Thankfully Stacey knew who she was. It was the kind of thing Pam would do, but never as dramatic as this. He raised the camera to his eye and quickly got off a couple of shots. There was no way he was missing this opportunity.

"Stacey."

"Sorry."

"Now, Russell. Is there somewhere we can go?"

"Are you alright out here?" It was Mrs Rites, the patisserie owner. She was standing in the doorway, wiping her hands on her apron.

"Uh, yes, everything's fine. Thanks. Though I would love three of your custard tarts."

Mrs Rites smiled, "I'll just get them for you, Russ."

Russell looked back at the two strangers as Mrs Rites re-entered the store, "First I need something to eat, then we can go upstairs."

*   *   *

"You're a hard man to find."

They were sitting in the living room slash bedroom of Russell's apartment. There was a sofa where Stacey and Pam sat, Stacey leaning back, his arm along the backrest and Pam sitting forward, obviously a little uncomfortable in the skirt, and Russell sat on a sofa chair. They each had a mug of tea; Russell cradled his in his hands.

"I've a silent number."

"We know."

"But who ever is after me isn't finding it so difficult."

"You mean they've come after you again?"

"Yes. Two guys this afternoon. I don't know how they found me. Probably followed me from Greyson's."

"That's where we lost you."

Russell found this all uncomfortable; "You've been tailing me, too?"

Pam, who'd been doing most of the talking, took a sip of her tea before answering; "We've been trying to get in contact with you. We were lucky we had someone to get your address off."

"Who?"

"My employer."

"Where do you work?"

"A tabloid newspaper. It doesn't matter."

"Was that your paper with me on the front, the 'Demon Bomb'?"

Pam smiled, a little embarrassed, "That was my article, and Stacey's photo."

"I don't think it was a Demon Bomb. It was set up in a van."

"We know. I just based the article on the photo. Some of it was fact; most of it was fiction. That's the sort of paper it is, though my boss tends to get a little too caught up in it all."

"So what do you want with me?"

Stacey pulled the second photograph out of his brown leather jacket and threw it onto the coffee table.

"We had more proof. You aren't just a once off news item."

Russell started to get up, annoyed, "You said you weren't here as reporters."

Pam put up her hand to stop him, "We're not. It's a little more complicated than that. You're in danger."

"So?"

"We're here to help."

Russell sat down, letting out a laugh, "And what are you going to do? Keep stalking me?"

60

Stacey hopped forward on his seat; "We were only trying to get close to you to talk."

"I know. But you're obviously not the only ones. Those other guys did a lot better job of it."

"It's because of Greyson's. They don't know where you live, but it seems common knowledge where you work. They'll be targeting you there from now on I suspect."

The realisation kicked in, "Great! What am I supposed to do? I work there. I need to work."

"That's why we're here."

"You keep saying that, but what? What can you do?"

"Keep an eye on you for one thing."

"Perfect! And when they come after me again, you can watch from the side lines when they kick my head in."

Pam smiled at him, lowering her mug to the table, "Not quite. We're a bit better equipped than that."

"You sound like all talk. That's all you've done. You've shown me no real proof that I can trust you. I don't even know why you're interested. It's not like its human nature to go out of your way to help someone else, especially if it means risking your own backsides for it."

"Look," Stacey lifted his hand, pointing his finger into the air. Russell followed with his eyes, looking toward the ceiling. There was nothing there.

"What?"

"No. Look."

Russell looked back at Stacey's hand and nearly jumped out of his seat.

Extending from the tip of his index finger was a thin tongue of flame. It licked into the air, dancing mildly, but apparently not fuelled by anything but the air. It stood about four inches high, though as Russell watched, it dipped and flared and lashed about before dying.

"You guys. You're..."

"Very much like you," Pam finished his sentence, "Yes. That's why we're here. There aren't many of us, and when people find out about us, the reception is far from friendly."

"But, how?"

"It's different for everyone," The mug on the coffee table began to rise, literally floating on thin air, and moved into Pam's open hand, "Stacey and I were born with our abilities. You, as you well know, had a catalyst that set yours off."

"The explosion."

"Right. Which is another reason why we're here."

Stacey spoke up; "We need to find out about that bomb, how it did what it did to you and who was behind it in the first place. Someone wielding that power can be dangerous, the effects could be disastrous."

"So let me get this straight, "You two have powers. His is what, pyrotechnics and yours is telekinetics," Pam nodded, allowing him time to comprehend it all, "And you both pose as journalists at a weird-arse newspaper as cover as well as to allow you a possible medium for finding others like you."

"Like us."

"Whatever. Isn't that all a little too clichéd? Like in comic books. Spiderman, Superman. Reporters for newspapers."

Stacey laughed, "Leads me to the idea maybe the writers of those books might be just like us. Why else would they be preaching such tolerance? It could be a case they've taken our job just that little bit further and made a political game of it."

"So what now, then?"

"We don't know. We were hoping you could perhaps fill us in with any information you have."

"I don't know anything."

"What did you see at the explosion?"

"Nothing. A van, just like the one from the night you took that second picture, but that was all. No people, no bomb, no anything."

"Sounds like the bomb was planted inside the van."

Pam nodded, "Have you any idea who these people are?"

Russell shook his head, "No. They just wear black and they're starting to send big bruisers after me, not to mention they don't seem to care whether I'm dead or alive any more."

"How so?"

"They were shooting at me."

Pam glanced at Stacey, "Not good."

"You're telling me. I had to call up a storm to lose them; nearly lost control of it. Could have damaged the whole building I was under."

"You might want to watch that," Stacey replied, "Don't try doing anything too drastic with your abilities just yet. You have to ease into them, not use them full force. Learn self control."

"Like I have a choice when I'm being shot at."

"Which could be a problem. But it also means we need to get to the bottom of this as soon as we can."

Russell moved forward on his seat, "Well, what do we need to do?"

*   *   *

Kristen's room was still pink. She hated the colour, but she hadn't gotten around to painting it. All she wanted was a simple white. Not the girly look her father had done up for her when she was five. Still, she'd done her best to cover it up with posters, memorabilia and the like. She was very much a fan of music, but no bands in particular. Instead of bands or solo singers, she had posters advertising the latest Ministry of

Sound or Gatecrasher CD launch, not to mention the Touring Posters for the associated Disc Jockeys and photos snapped at the concerts she had gone to.

Music was her life. Well, apart from work, which seemed to be taking up way too much time at present. She'd just accepted a full-time position in the computing department and that drastically cut back her free time. Music had always been her passion though, so in her free time she had it blaring on her stereo or she was busy on the computer burning discs for later use.

It was like a drug in itself, not that she'd ever done drugs. Drinking, yes, sometimes to the excess, but never drugs. The music was usually enough. The euphoric feeling of the beat pulsing through your body, the bass vibrating through the floor, up your legs and through your spine as the melodies washed over you from above, totally swallowing you in music, like a protective bubble sucking the worries of life away. It was the closest you could get to perfection.

"Kristen!"

She slapped the stop button on her disc player. How long had he been calling? He tended to get annoyed if he had to repeat himself more than twice.

"Coming!"

She went to her door and unlocked it. Her father stood on the other side.

"As to why you have to lock your door."

"Privacy."

"We give you privacy."

She smiled, "I know, its just… you know."

He nodded, somehow knowing without needing to have it explained. He was good like that. Mind you, they were close. She knew she could be referred to as a Daddy's Girl, he even called her that some times, but she had no need to feel ashamed or embarrassed. They got on well, they were family, was there anything wrong with that? Not in her eyes, besides, what everyone else thought couldn't compete with the love between her and her father, though she'd never say that out loud.

"How was work?"

She'd had a full shift today. It was a busy one, too, but mainly because of all the mistakes her co-workers made. It happened all the time. On one occasion, one of the older men working in the department sold a computer to a gentleman, explaining it was a new model, never been out of its box, when in fact it was a demo model that had been on display. It was the third computer complaint that day and Kristen was about ready to throttle someone. Fortunately today they were simple mistakes, easily solved.

"Great. And yours?"

That was another thing they shared. They both worked long hours. She figured that was what made them closer when they were together. They hardly saw each other throughout the week.

He nodded, smiled, "Good," He paused, as if thinking, "Listen, Kristen. I was just watching the news."

"Yeah?"

"There was a follow up to that bombing, down the road. There was mention of further terrorist activities down town."

She wasn't sure where this was leading, but she continued to listen, "Really?"

He nodded, then looked her straight in the eye, "That boy, the one they found at the bombing, he works with you, doesn't he?"

"Yes, But-"

"I don't want you having anything to do with him."

This was sudden, "What?"

"It could be dangerous. What if he gets involved? Who knows what could happen?"

"He's not involved. He said it wasn't even him."

He managed to turn that back against her, "You see, he might be covering up something. He might be a part of it."

It wasn't that he was being hard on Russell; he was, in fact, remaining calm. She knew he only wanted to protect her, but, still, she was big enough to look after herself.

"Please? Kristen?"

She looked at him and nodded, "Okay," not that she meant it, "It'll be hard, seeing as that we work just opposite each other, but I'll try."

He smiled, moving forward to hug her, "That's my girl. I just don't want anyone being hurt."

"I wouldn't be, dad."

"Just to be on the safe side, Kristen."

After he left, she turned her music back on. But the rhythm just didn't seem to feel right. That was the first time her father had done something like that. He was protective, yes, but that was just ridiculous. She shook her head and tried to ease back into the vibrations of the bass.

CHAPTER EIGHT

The second explosion came on the Sunday morning. The city was pretty much empty, excepting the morning joggers and the few delivery services that still operated on that day of the week.

The people with inner city living, Russell included, awoke early that morning as the world was shaken again. It was nine o'clock exactly when Russell jolted awake to a loud boom and to hear his windows rattling from the force.

He jumped out of bed, managing to tangle himself in his sheets, fall over and scramble his way to the window. The sky over the buildings opposite was a perfect blue. What he saw in the reflection of the windows, however, was something totally different. Smoke was billowing over the top of the skyline behind him, how close to his apartment, he wasn't sure.

Hurriedly, he dressed and made his way down to the street. There was already a crowd moving along the pavement, trying to find out what was happening.

He ran down the street, around the corner and nearly tripped over his feet when he saw what had happened.

It had been an empty building. Two blocks down from his apartment. Just sitting on the corner, unobtrusive, more of a landmark than anything else. Three stories of empty space had been completely flattened; the street around it was strewn with bricks, mortar and flames. The rubble on site was a raging inferno and the emergency services were just turning up.

Russell, along with half the neighbourhood, pushed his way down to the scene.

From the television footage and reports in the newspaper, this was nothing like the first explosion.

For one thing, the car park had only been mildly affected. One floor of cars had been destroyed, but the damage went no further. There was also talk of the flames crawling down the sides of the building. Odd behaviour, especially as people described it as being a cold flame.

This occurrence, on the other hand, was much different. As everyone could see, the building had been levelled. For another thing, the flames were burning furiously and the heat from them was very much a factor as Russell drew closer.

It didn't take long for the authorities to corner off the site and get the fire under control. It also didn't take long for Russell to start contemplating the coincidence that the explosion, this time, was so close to his apartment, rather than being on the other side of town. Did they know where he lived? Was this a threat?

His mind shut off the questions in an instant when he spotted something.

He was glancing around, eyeing the crowd. Were any of these people involved? Paranoia he figured, all the same, you can't be too careful, when he spotted a van. White.

He pushed through the gathering crowd, struggling to get away from the scene and toward the vehicle.

It was familiar. As he got closer, he could discern the make, Mazda. It was them again. The same people.

"Russell?"

Someone was calling his name. The Cockney photographer.

"Stacey?"

"Over here!"

Russell managed to catch a glimpse of the small man being pushed along by the crowd. He was only a couple of metres away.

"No. Get over here! Have you got your camera?"

"Always!"

The small man disappeared from sight; Russell struggled to see where he was. Perhaps he had been trampled by the crowd.

"What is it?"

Russell jumped. Stacey was standing just behind him.

"Follow me."

The van was still there. Were they standing by to gloat? He wasn't sure. The two men pushed onward, regardless.

When they finally broke free from the masses, Russell kept a slow pace. Stacey moved up beside him. "What is it?"

"That van."

Stacey raised his camera and started getting shots. He zoomed in on various aspects, such as the windows, hoping to catch a glimpse of someone inside, and the number plate.

"That's the same one from the other night," He reported.

Russell looked at him, "When I was attacked? How do you know?"

"Same number plate."

"And you didn't tell the police?"

"Did you?"

No. He hadn't. He'd been attacked and hadn't even bothered telling the police. But that was mainly because of his lack of any explanation. How did a lone man like him get away from a bunch of thugs? He could hardly talk about his powers, could he? He grizzled to himself inwardly. It was a difficult business, this super hero gig. Still, he decided to change the subject, get the focus off him.

"If you were there Friday night, why didn't you help me?"

"I had a feeling you'd be able to take care of yourself."

"Still, we may have been able to find out who's behind it."

Stacey continued taking photos, also keeping an eye out for the driver using his zoom, "That wasn't our job. It's really a police matter. We can only get involved if there are sufficient 'suspicious and super-natural' influences to warrant our presence."

"Says who?"

Stacey looked at Russell blankly, "Actually, that's a very good question."

"Look."

Two men, dressed casually, having foregone their blacks for a more subtle approach, were approaching the van. Russell couldn't be sure but one of them looked like the smaller of the two from the day before.

"This way," Stacey grabbed onto his shirt and hauled him away from the crowd. For a small man, he was sufficiently strong.

"Where are we going?"

"My car. Unless you have a better option?"

Of course he didn't, excepting notifying the police and getting the heck away, but, strangely enough, that certainly wasn't the most inviting.

The colt was parked only a few metres away. Stacey hopped in first, unlocking the door for Russell who clambered in, pushing a camera case, satchel and a few scattered newspapers onto the floor.

This wasn't very surprising. Russell had noticed the tendency for the cars of single people to gather enough junk that you could end up with the impression someone may just well be hidden underneath it all. It could also explain the occasion you see people driving along; talking to themselves, having convinced themselves into believing someone is under all that mess.

It was a feisty little machine. It roared to life and Stacey kicked it straight into second gear, pushing quickly into the street. The van was already on the move.

"Watch out!"

"Don't worry, I'm a good driver."

People were practically diving out of his way as he dodged through the crowd.

The van was only going a moderate speed; it wouldn't take long to catch up. But if they got too close, they might recognise Russell in the rear-view.

"Hold back a bit. We're tailing them, not ramming them."

Stacey cast an annoyed glare his way; "I'm doing the driving, okay?"

The van turned at the first intersection, having caught the green light, Stacey kept close behind, "You haven't done this before, have you?"

The cockney grumbled, "And you have?"

"No but I read enough books and watch enough movies-"

"Oh and you think this is all books and movies?"

Russell was starting to see they were going to have to work on their attitudes toward each other, "No. I was merely saying-"

"Well don't. Okay?"

The van pulled up at the next intersection, waiting for the lights to change. Nothing strange there. The rear windows were tinted so Russell had no chance of seeing inside. He hoped that the driver wouldn't be paying too much attention to who was behind.

The lights changed and both vehicles were off again. It wasn't until they made it onto the terrace again that the van started picking up speed. They were heading back toward the older side of town. Not surprising considering that was where the last two attacks on Russell had occurred.

"These guys could have a base of operations set up in any number of those older buildings down that way."

"Hopefully we'll be able to find them sooner rather than later," Stacey replied, glaring out the window as if trying to harness Pam's abilities, or perhaps some other talents out of reach.

This brought another thought to Russell's mind. How did the journalists find out about their powers? Born with them? Does that mean ever since he was a boy, Stacey was spitting out fire? And did Pam levitate her toys instead of using her hands? Was it as much strain on them physically as it was for Russell? What did their parents think? Why did they opt to keep it secret? And why is there a real need to keep them secret?

Is it people? Are they so paranoid and scared of what's different? Is that really what people are like? Ready to ostracise someone for a simple difference.

Obviously there were acts of racism, sexism and every other ism in the book, but, really, was it so bad that such a group of people as Russell had just found, needed to conceal their true identities from the world.

Wouldn't they be looked upon with awe, as Superman or Iron Man? Kids these days still play super-heroes don't they?

"I'll be Iron Man and you can be Spiderman," that kind of thing. If kids can do it, why can't the adults?

Who wouldn't want the power? Okay so they were great. But there was also the need to be in control of your powers, to make sure you use them for the right purposes. But Russell was starting to enjoy what he had. Think of everything he can do. Controlling the very wind. It's something people have only dreamed of in the past or watched on television or in comics. But it was real. Really real and Russell could do it. It was amazing. Even the sensation of doing it, the feeling that he is part of the wind and vice-versa. He still had a long way to go before being confident in using his ability, but, hey, when that day came, there would be no stopping him from standing out there and declaring to the world, "I am..."

Hmm, he thought to himself. A name. A title, like Spiderman. Something cool. He'd need one. Then again, did Pam? But they were subversives. If he was to go out there for the greater good, he'd need a title.

But what?

The van made a sharp left, swinging out wildly into the other lane; the driver managed to keep control.

Stacey was fast enough to brake a little before attempting the turn, losing ground on the corner, but making it up in the recovery.

"They're onto us."

"Obviously," Stacey seemed a little perturbed, though Russell wasn't sure where exactly his hostilities lay.

Their speed crawled up the speedometer as they kept up with the Mazda. It wasn't like they wanted to crash into it, or even get close. They just needed to keep it in sight.

From the looks of it, that was going to be a task they'd have to work at, or at least Stacey would.

There were cars on the street ahead, the van dodged from lane to lane to pass, Stacey followed suit. Fortunately there were two lanes in either direction; otherwise they could be in deep trouble.

Unfortunately, the driver of the van seemed to be reading his mind.

A sharp turn into Murray Street and the outlook changed considerably. This was a two-lane street.

It was better than a one- No. Maybe that would give them ideas, Russell thought. He knew he was being childish but it was getting quite exciting. The prospect of dying in a car accident was not very appealing, but it seemed to be getting further and further from his mind.

What was the point of being a reluctant hero?

Mind you, he found himself, more often than not, pondering the merits of being a super powered individual. Risking one's life to save a world of ungrateful people. Well, not everyone would be ungrateful and hopefully some of them would be worth saving, like Kristen.

He hadn't had very many good experiences with people, but there were certainly enough of the more decent kinds out there to warrant keeping the world safe from harm. Take the Rites. A lovely young couple, full of life and new love, both working hard at having children. Decent people. Kind, considerate. Russell hoped they were like the stereotype of the typical family, though he knew that was more wishful thinking than reality. Still, their existence pointed out that despite all the, well, not so good people, there were still a heck of a lot of nice ones to save.

Besides, if it meant he could strut around in those very revealing lycra costumes, hey, he was up for it, he mused to himself; he'd have to work on his physique first, though.

The van slowed, just beyond it, Russell could see an old Holden Barina slowly swerving from one side of the lane to the other, like a gigantic beetle after a hard night of drinking. He couldn't help thinking, 'aha, we have them now.' Though it sounded so clichéd, and if movies were anything to go by, they were bound to slip through their fingers anyway.

Without indicating, the van swung out into the oncoming lane and roared onward and past the Barina. Stacey, after checking the coast was clear, managed to complete the same manoeuvre.

The van had begun to lay on the speed. Russell could picture its speedo passing the eighty kilometres an hour and still continue to rise as it pulled further away. But Stacey wouldn't have any of that escaping business. He floored the accelerator and closed the gap between the two vehicles in mere seconds. For an out-dated hatchback, this machine had guts. Russell looked over at his driver and thought he could see a hint of a smile. Was it pride for the vehicle or the thrill of the chase? It didn't matter; Russell was really starting to get caught up in it all. He was tempted to wind down the window and feel the windblast in on him as they sped through the streets.

Often the streets in Perth were like wind tunnels, roaring down from the skies and rumbling across the pavement so fast and strong, sometimes it felt you could literally lean into the oncoming wind at a forty-five degree angle. The small Colt wasn't having any such problem heading down the streets with its small and somewhat angular frame, but the van was starting to feel the strain. It was becoming increasingly apparent that the driver had to fight to keep control of the vehicle as it began to swerve erratically, yet only slightly across the lane. Obviously the wind was not so forgiving on the large box on wheels doing ninety plus down a thirty zone.

They would soon be running out of straight road. At the end of Murray Street was a large cathedral, the one next door to the hospital Russell had found himself in only days earlier. At that point, the road curved sharply to the right and then sharply to the left and around the cathedral, creating a hook like road. They were going to have to either turn off one of the side streets or wait for the road to reach that hook at which point they would have to slow considerably or risk capsizing. And from the look of it, they weren't going to be turning any time soon. Instead their speed continued to rise, and with them, Stacey kept pushing also.

"Uh… Stacey."

"I know."

"They're not slowing."

"Trust me, I know."

Russell wasn't sure if Stacey had caught on, or even realised what he was talking about. Maybe he was just being cocky; all the same, they were looking at a major accident.

The road narrowed slightly on either side as the footpaths began to jut out into the street, forming small alcoves for cars to park in. Still, the van moved onward. They were almost on top of the corner when they suddenly applied their brakes. The red indicator lights on the back flashed on as the brakes locked and the tyres tried to grip the pavement.

Even with the windows shut, Russell could smell the burning rubber as the Van continued to glide forward, losing traction as the tyres failed to find purchase. The driver tried to spin the wheel, taking them around the corner, but the height of the van worked against him.

As it rounded the corner, the top heavy vehicle's right side wheels lost touch with the ground, bringing it up on the other two wheels and threatening to topple sideways. It was looking fifty-fifty as to their chances, but Russell finally lost interest in them.

"Stacey!"

Without a word, the Cockney twisted his steering wheel slightly before applying the hand break. With a sudden jarring heave, the Colt went into a seemingly wild spin, throwing Russell hard against the window so his face was slammed against the cold surface, leaving him worried whether he'd have any teeth left.

His eyes open, he watched as the landscape around him rotated at a hundred miles an hour, though it was much slower, and did his best to keep his dinner from the night before down. In the blur he lost sight of both Stacey and the van, his eyes bulging and head spinning, he knew he was going to be feeling sick for ages after this stunt.

That was until, beside him, he heard the handbrake release and the engine rev up again. Stacey floored the accelerator and sent Russell flying back into his chair, feeling what could only be G-forces. Through the grogginess in his head, Russell managed to spot the van again. They were actually moving past it as it lurched forward and sideways, finally losing its battle with gravity and sending it into a sideways roll.

With its momentum, the vehicle continued to roll several more times, colliding with the large rock fence post that held the main gate to the cathedral. There was a shower of sparks and rocks as the two met, the van jarring to a halt.

Stacey eased on the brakes and pulled into one of the parking bays on the side of the road. This guy was one hell of a driver.

"Where'd you learn to do all that?"

Stacey smiled as he undid his seat belt; "You'd be surprised what you learn on assignment. I didn't always work for the tabloids, you know."

Russell stumbled as he got out of the car, grabbing hold of the door to maintain his balance. Stacey on the other hand casually strolled around the car to stand beside the younger man.

"Sorry, I should have warned you."

"'Sokay. I should have seen it coming. You're amazing, though. I can't believe you did that."

Stacey shrugged, not one to take too many compliments easily, he started to move toward the van, "We still have work to do."

They weren't the only ones to move onto the scene. Hospital staff had already mobilised. The hospital was only a couple of metres away and the stretchers were already coming out the door.

71

Everyone stopped, however, when a strange rumbling started from within the van. The slider door, that was now the ceiling of the vehicle as it lay on its side, began to bulge, almost balloon as something from inside attacked it.

It was odd. Surely no one could do that with their feet, and a gun would probably poke holes in the door before having that effect.

The rumbling grew in intensity as the metal of the door continued to bulge uncertainly, seemingly deflating before growing an extra inch or two in diameter.

"What the hell is that?"

Stacey shook his head; "I have no idea. Be ready."

Russell knew what that meant and started to focus, allowing the silvery wisps of air to come into focus.

He nearly lost sight of them, though, when the door finally exploded. There was a rush of heat and air as the metal popped like a giant balloon, exploding upward and outward, showering the ground with metal, glass and what looked to be human-

Russell almost gagged, but avoided looking at the larger chunks. There were screams from some of the nurses and from early churchgoers who had started to make their way out of the cathedral to see what the commotion was about.

Finally a hand emerged, thin, but covered in the black coverall and jacket. When the rest of the body appeared, Russell recognised him from the chase the day before. He was the smaller of the two men who had followed him into the building.

The little man launched himself upward and managed a somersault before landing on the grass. Behind him a second man, also from yesterday, stood up, his massive shoulders barely managing to squeeze through the hole. He too launched himself up and over the side of the vehicle, not attempting any acrobatics, but threatening to tip the vehicle back to its correct position.

"I know these guys."

"How?"

"They followed me. They're the ones who were tailing me yesterday."

"Great. You beat them then, we'll do it again."

Russell wasn't so sure. Something was up.

The little guy muttered something to his companion and pointed toward the two "heroes".

The larger man laughed. Without warning the little guy's hand pulsed with a deep green energy that seemed to grow in his hand before ejecting itself toward Russell. It was a literal pulse of energy.

Russell ducked for cover, allowing the projectile to fly over his head. There was a small explosion behind him, but Russell knew he couldn't afford to look away.

"Oh, Bugger," Stacey whispered.

"How did they get powers?"

"Same way as the rest of us. There could be any number of explanations."

The larger man began to charge; his physical stature enough to scare a fully-grown bull away.

"Split up. I'll handle Dufus here. You take Pipsqueak."

Good idea, Russell thought. Stacey handles the big guy while he handles the guy that spits bolts out of his hands.

He hurried out of the way as Stacey swept his arm forward, spitting out a stream of flame from his palm, forcing Dufus to stumble to a halt, almost falling onto his backside with the sudden change of trajectory.

There were more screams from the public as some made their way back inside.

Russell focused on the wisps of air and coaxed them to life. He called them back to him hoping to gather a little momentum before sending them upward and straight back toward Pipsqueak. He wasn't sure if anyone else could see the Silver strands, but it still looked impressive to him as they charged, like a spear head toward his target, threatening to skewer him where he stood.

Pipsqueak was completely shocked when it struck. Obviously he couldn't see the strands; he had no way of knowing Russell was attacking. Russell felt a smile touch his lips in pride. He had a very subtle, but very powerful ability. His enemies couldn't see it coming.

Pipsqueak was thrown backward against the van, jarring painfully before sliding to the ground, stunned.

Stacey was fairing almost as well. Dufus wasn't able to get close enough to make contact; his brute strength was useless. Or so Russell thought.

Annoyed rather than tired, Dufus stopped moving. He clapped his hands together with the force of two trains colliding and lifted them above his head. In an instant, he brought them down again, the effort he placed behind the swing evident in the clenched muscles in his face.

When his fists made contact with the ground, it was as if an earthquake had hit.

Russell fell backward as he lost his footing, still slightly groggy from the drive. Stacey, however managed to keep his ground, at least until he saw what was happening.

From the point where Dufus had made contact with the ground, the very earth was vibrating like a tuning fork along a straight line. In mere seconds, the tension on the rock below began to take its toll, tearing the stone apart like tearing paper. A rip began to form in the earth traversing so quickly along the tremor lines which led right between Stacey's feet and beyond.

It didn't stop there. Stacey continued to struggle for his footing as the mini quake approached, unable to find enough ground to push off of to jump out of the way. The gap continued to grow, opening inches in mere seconds.

Russell sat up, watching with amazement as it widened at points beyond a foot. There was no telling how this could affect the Earth's tectonic layout, if it would have effects somewhere else. Sort of like the chaos theory or whatever it was, that a butterfly flapping its wings in South America could create a tornado-

Russell almost choked on the thought. What if his own powers were having the same effect? Could he, in fact, be the cause of a future disaster.

When he spotted Stacey, however, that thought spun out of his mind. His colleague was in trouble.

He focussed again, drawing all of the silver air together and around Stacey's body, the effects noticeable with his clothes billowing out around him.

He eased the air to form a cocoon of sorts around the man and tried to lift him up.

Amazing himself, Russell watched as the wind he was controlling did just that. He levitated his colleague about a foot off the ground and shoved him gently away from the fault line Dufus was creating before bringing him back down again.

The surprise was almost tangible as Stacey gulped at the air around him, trying to remain calm enough to deal with the problem at hand.

Dufus looked up, expecting to see Stacey in his original position, but he almost baulked when he saw his prey had escaped.

Russell was about to follow up with a gust of wind to knock the big fellow off his feet when a sharp pain stabbed through his right shoulder. The residual glow from the pulse blast was a telltale that Pipsqueak had just attacked.

The smaller man was up again. It seemed he had to same constitution Russell had developed from his run in with the explosion.

The explosion. Could it be these two were even more closely linked to the car bomb than he thought? If he had acquired his ability of controlling the winds when hit by the bomb's concussive blast, perhaps these were the two that had set it in the first place. That would explain everything. Well…almost everything.

Russell collapsed to the floor both in pain and in a motion to dodge any further attacks and rolled away down a slight grass embankment, hopefully out of eyesight. He felt as well as heard the second bolt fly by his head as he landed on the ground, his shoulder aching every time it made contact with the earth. Thankfully it hadn't been a powerful blast, then again, how powerful could they be?

All these different powers left him with so many questions. But the one that came to mind most often was: What are the ramifications these powers have? This in turn led to other thoughts and questions such as:

Are they environmentally safe? What does it mean for human kind? If there are genetic changes at birth, is this a step along the evolutionary ladder, or is it just a case that we're using too many mobile phones? As far as he knew, there was no one to answer Russell's questions.

What he did know, however, was that getting further from Pipsqueak was not going to aid in the fight. Nor, really would getting any closer. But there was a definite need to do something.

He had an idea. Copying what he had done to Stacey only moments before, he drew the air around his own body. He could almost feel it cushioning his body like a warm blanket. Even between himself and the grass, he could feel it pushing its way in.

Then he focussed on lifting himself into the air. Not as slowly as he had done to Stacey, more of a jet stream, throwing him up. But to do this, Russell had to concentrate even more. He pictured where he wanted to land and urged the wind to form a second blanket, more like a cushion, to catch his fall.

With that set in his mind, Russell let fly. He felt his body get thrown into the air, like being forced out of a water spout, where he felt the wind around him, steadying him, directing him like a tunnel, caressing him like he were part of it. He was almost lost in the thrill of it. Until he saw the van about fifteen metres below. He had over shot the mark a little. Never mind. In an instant, he compensated, forming the pillow of silver directly in his trajectory.

He wasn't sure how he managed it, but he twisted his body mid-air, similar to a somersault, but only to make sure his legs would make contact first and not his head.

It was amazing. Time seemed to slow down for him as he began to float down toward his destination, gently comforted by the very air he was passing through and land easily on his feet, back on the grass, now standing within the cathedral's yard. Between him and Pipsqueak there was a massive wrought iron fence, held together and in place by large rock pillars spotted around the perimeter.

Pipsqueak was almost out of sight, excepting his head, which was staring straight into the sky as if hoping to catch a glimpse of a bird flying over head.

Now was Russell's chance. He heaved down on the currents above, bringing them to bear on Pipsqueak, hoping the effect would be like that of dropping a tonne of water over someone's head.

The result was rather similar as far as Russell could tell.

When the attack made contact, it was almost a comical sight to see Pipsqueak's short, though slightly boofy hair collapse under such tremendous force, followed by his whole body vanishing out of sight, giving way to the wall of air Russell had just let loose.

What Russell didn't see, however, as he silently cheered his own effort, was Stacey's wildly aimed fireball Dufus had managed to dodge. It wasn't until the ball struck the undercarriage of the van that Russell knew anything was wrong.

It still took him a while to comprehend the implications of fire on Oil, petrol and other liquids within the vehicle. But it all clicked together when the fireball managed to superheat the petrol tank.

The van went up like Hiroshima, though on a much smaller scale. Shards of metal and glass were sprayed upward and out over whoever had remained to watch the spectacle, not to mention at those involved in the debacle.

He sensed the blast before he saw it. Something about the feel of the air tingled at his skin, warning him something more was coming. Russell turned on his heels and dove for cover, hoping to get as far from the explosion as possible.

Flame licked out in every direction across the grass, reaching deep into the yard and indeed playing over Russell's head as he pushed his body further into the ground, wrapping as much cool air as he could around him.

"Holy smoke."

As the fire died down to only encompass the vehicle, Russell managed to stand up and try and survey the damage. It was quite extensive. Car fragments had landed on nearby parked cars, fortunately, as far as he could tell, Stacey's Colt was unscathed, but the crowd was cowering under the hospital's emergency entrance parking cover, on top of which burning items of van smouldered away, threatening to catch the building alight. Several windows had been smashed across the street and the pillar against which the van had leant was practically no more. There was a stump of rock with twisted strands of iron, curling away from the blast and its ferocity. The grass surrounding was black from the heat; some patches were sizzling away, glowing a faint red even in the sunlight; or what was visible of it. Smoke was billowing up from inside the van, the initial mushroom cloud having dispersed across the sky creating an eerie night feel.

Then Russell turned to regard the cathedral.

He found the remains of the stone pillar. The massive double doors had been crushed inward by a large rock. Another had punched a car size hole in the wall a few metres above. The stain glass windows on the front of the building had also been shattered, as to whether the blast was at fault or the shrapnel, Russell couldn't tell. What he could see was a large black car seat hanging from one of the lower parapets, burning fiercely with several of the wooden beams nearby starting to smoke.

What had Stacey done?

Stacey.

Russell turned again, calling out his colleague's name, "Stace-"

A second green bolt connected with his stomach, sending him flying backward and onto his back.

That one had hurt. It wasn't so much the energy contained, but the physical force behind each blast, Russell deduced. All the same, that hit knocked the wind out of his guts. He gasped for air, trying to use his new abilities to coax a small breeze in to fill his lungs, but most of it turned out to be smoke, which sent him into a fit of coughing.

Rolling onto his side and into the foetal position he fought to regain his breath.

It seemed the air around him had become smoke. The wind had changed, drawing the black clouds toward the chapel, thus enshrouding Russell in its acrid odour that stung his eyes. Through the tears, however, he could see a shadow. It had to be Pipsqueak. Somehow, even with such close proximity to the explosion, he had survived and was back with a vengeance.

Even now, Russell could see his hand start to glow with that same green energy, ready to send forth another bolt, perhaps to finish him off.

That was when Russell heard the music. It was only faint, almost like listening to the Mr Whippy van's "Green Sleeves" a couple of roads away. That was a blast from the past, Russell thought before his mind started to flay in several different directions.

Where was the music coming from? What had happened to Stacey? And in general, what the devil was going on?

Beside him, he heard something fall. Only softly, almost imperceptibly. If he hadn't been lying so close, he wouldn't have been able to tell.

But the smoke took on a strange bluish hue, as if reacting to a nearby neon light. But this was no light.

Managing to focus enough to draw in some clean, fresh air, Russell rolled onto his back to stare up at a not so tall, though he was from this angle, man completely dressed in black. He couldn't make out much of the detail, but he could tell something around the man's head was glowing an icy blue colour, like a halo.

Russell almost choked again. Was this an angel of God, come down to protect his haven? Or was he here to claim my soul, he thought.

The answer came shortly.

Without moving anything, a stream of electricity shot forth from this newcomer's eyes and disappeared into the smoke.

Then came Pipsqueak's scream of pain as whatever it was struck home. Russell tried to lift his head to have a look, but saw little in the dark cloud. He did hear, however, a slight 'whoosh' as the smoke flared blue again and the man beside him disappeared.

Sirens flared in the distance, the smoke, once more changing direction, began to ease as Russell finally managed to stand again, to see what devastation had occurred. Surprisingly, Pipsqueak and Dufus had made their get away, Stacey having faired better in his own battle.

"Russell! This way!" Who was he to argue? He lumbered over the wreckage, avoiding the van as best he could for fear it may explode again, but Stacey helped him over and back to his car, "We have to get out of here before the police arrive."

"No kidding."

Once inside the Colt, Stacey moved back onto the street and casually drove away.

It had been a practical waste of time. The whole fight. Violence for violence's sake. No information gathered. No bad guys stopped, excepting whoever else may have been in that van and Russell didn't really want to think about that too much right now. He still felt a little queasy from the smoke.

"So, what do you think?"

Russell looked over at the driver, "About what?"

"Our little confrontation."

"How can you be so blasé about it all?"

Stacey smiled, but it wasn't full of humour or mirth. In fact, Russell swore he spotted a little regret in there, "You have to be. You realise, with all that you've become, you're hot property. This may not have been your first real encounter, but I can almost guarantee it won't be your last."

"But what if this isn't for me. What if I don't want to do this kind of thing?"

"You might not have a choice. They know who you are. Now, so do the people at the hospital, at the church. They may not know your name, where you live. But they know you exist. And that's all they need. There will be rumours and news stories. Not just in our little tabloid, but in the real news. Of course, they'll all try and deny it, pass it off as the effects of a faulty canister of laughing gas making people at the hospital hallucinate, but there will still be that underlying truth. Not to mention the doubt and fear."

"Fear? About what?"

"You read the comics?"

Russell nodded, knowing what Stacey was talking about. He hadn't been much of a comic collector lately, but as a kid, he'd spent most of his pocket money on the light-hearted stories involving the wonderful world of Superheroes. He had picked up a couple every so often since, just to see how they were progressing. What had struck him as odd was how the context had changed. In the past, there was humour in it all. Way back in the Uncanny X-men comics when Jubilee first appeared, there were issues when the X-women went shopping or the X-men were attacked by a massive alien force which was wiped out in the time it took to play a game of cards. Jokey things. But lately, the colours were darker, more sinister. Like the first Star Trek the Next Generation movie in comparison to the series. A darker mood with much better and scarier lighting. Not that Generations was scary or anything. The X-men faced harder challenges that were almost realistic. The emotion behind it all, too. It was no more that light-humoured banter between Henry McCoy and Bobby Drake, but the difference between life and death between Scott Summers and Nate Grey.

Could any of that resemble what happens in real life? Was Art imitating life or vice versa? Had the geniuses that came up with the concept of mutants prophesised an event that was only now starting to manifest itself?

But in it all, there is that underlying fear and hate from humanity, which is to say those that don't have super powers. As said by Yoda in Star Wars Episode One: "fear leads to anger, anger leads to hate" except it keeps going. Hate leads to violence, which leads to people getting hurt, regardless of genetic make up.

People getting killed in the name of self-righteousness.

'What am I getting myself into,' Russell thought. Or what have I been thrown into. It wasn't exactly his fault he'd been at the bombsite. Nor the effects of the actual explosion. But did it all mean he had the same obligation as those fictitious X-Men to defeat the bad guys and lie low when not. Hide in the shadows to make the rest of the world feel safe. There shouldn't be a need to. But what was an idyllic thought doing in a world where the hard reality was always too sad to think about?

Russell was no longer feeling the thrill of the battle. It had been surpassed by an unsinkable feeling in the pit of his stomach that seemed to be growing every moment he thought about what had happened and may end up happening. This wasn't what he planned for life. He wanted to finish studying. Graduate university and follow through with Commerce. Not to mention get a decent job, settle down, get married, have kids and all the things a normal person would do. But right now, it looked like there was a long way to go before he could see any of that happening.

CHAPTER NINE

"What do you mean, 'whipped your arse'?"

Peerson was livid. That much was clear, "You're telling me that two small freaks of nature managed to defeat you?"

Reg, Pipsqueak to others, felt his face flush with anger. It was bad enough finding out he had received these odd abilities, but to be insulted to his own face by his boss was more than a little annoying. He'd put up with that kind of crap back in high school. Besides, it was this git that told him to plant the first bomb in the first place. He and Jack had done everything by the book. Made sure everything was set right. Even the doctor, Eryn or whatever his name was, said nothing could go wrong. Then the damn thing went off early and both Reg and Jack were caught in the blast.

Instead of demolishing the building, the damn thing somehow 'reconfigured the genetic structure' of both Reg and Jack as well as some little git who managed to be in the building at the same time. As far as Reg was concerned, that git was a waste of thought and didn't know why Peerson was so obsessed about him. Until Eryn explained that it was that little git that was responsible for Jack growing an extra two feet, not to mention tripling his body weight. The poor guy had always had problems with his weight. Then there were the green lights Reg kept seeing every time he got a little fumed. Well, more specifically the one that seemed to emanate from his hand.

Sure, he'd been impressed by the new powers, but still; he was being referred to as the Freak by his old work mates, not to mention his own boss.

"You didn't tell us this guy could spit lightning."

"You're the one who discovered his wind based powers, and you're accusing me of neglect?"

He had a point. Normally he wouldn't argue with Peerson, but ever since he'd gotten his power, He'd found that he had gained a little leeway in their discussions. He wasn't sure if it was because Peerson was a little fearful, which he doubted, or if it was a sign of respect, which was also a little too far fetched.

"No, but you can't expect us to know what to do with our own powers in retaliation. They are only new to us. We still need a little time to practice, get used to it all."

Peerson paused for a moment. He even looked them both over as if passing judgement, "Fine. You can use the gymnasium facilities out at the Carapace Industries Site. I'll give you security clearance and make sure it's all kept under wraps. But you better be promising me some real effort. I want that boy, dead or alive, I don't care."

Reg pulled on Jack's elbow, feeling like a little kid pulling at his parent, trying to drag him toward the toys, "Let's go, Jack."

They walked out of the office and toward the lift, "That kid is stronger than we thought. Not to mention his friend."

"They work well together," Jack added.

Reg was almost hurt by that. Jack and Reg had been a team for years. They'd always worked together, whatever the job. They'd practically signed up together, "Hey, and what are we? Abbot and Costello?"

"According to Peerson, the two stooges, not to mention chopped liver."

"Well, I happen to like chopped liver. And that's how we'll be delivering that little git to Peerson. I have an idea."

*   *   *

He'd been called into work. Helen had called in sick, and no one else from the department was able to come in, so Russell had been called. Fortunately he'd been home. Stacey dropped him off a couple of hours earlier, giving him time to shower and dress. He felt a little dirty after the fight, not just because of the smoke, either.

But when he got to work, he let it all go. This was work; there was time for worrying about that other stuff later. He set to serving the customers. Sabrina, an attractive young half Asian, half Irish girl worked beside him on the other register. They bantered a little when the custom was slow. It was fun. They always managed to find something to argue about, in a friendly sort of way. Something controversial like sexism or racism or one of those other isms. Normally spurred on by Russell's mock emphaticness about one of those topics. He didn't always believe what he was saying, but it made for an interesting conversation. They got on well, but she was no Kristen. And, of course, Russell found his eyes darting across to the computing counter every so often. She was working over there. Sometimes, he could see her behind the counter, or serving a customer by the computers. No matter where she was, or which way she was facing, he felt his heart beat skip a couple of times.

"I need to take my lunch."

"That's cool," Russell replied.

"Will you need cover," Sabrina asked, having broken out of the conversation they were involved in.

Russell nodded, about to help another customer.

"I'll see who I can get."

She disappeared from Confectionery and Russell put through the transaction. Then another, when finally someone arrived to help. He looked up to see who Sabrina had found and nearly choked.

"Good afternoon, Russell," Kristen chimed. It wasn't patronising, but she always had a little singsong voice when she greeted Russell. Maybe she used it on other people as well.

"Oh," Russell tried to act disappointed as a joke, "She got you."

81

Kristen smiled, "I could go back if you want."

Russell sighed, "No. You'll do I guess."

That was the end of the conversation for a while as the customers started to pile the chocolates on strong. It was easy to see why Australian doctors were starting to worry about the number of over-weight or obese people in the country. Everyone was buying chocolate. Either in the small lolly bags, which Kristen and Russell had to get as a complimentary service for the customer, or in the full boxes of chocolates that ranged from Duc'do to Lindt and even Almond Roca.

Most of the chocolate in Greyson's was of the more expensive quality, but that didn't stop people from buying it. Especially the Lindt Lindor variety. They came in several sizes and colours, even sold individually for eighty cents. They were absolutely delicious. A nice round shell of chocolate filled with a soft creamy centre of more chocolate that seemed to burst as you bit into it. It was truly delectable. And very popular.

Finally the line dropped a little until both Russell and Kristen stood idly. He leaned back against the till while she surveyed the crowd. Not hard to do with her height.

This was his chance. It had been ages since Kristen had worked over in confectionery, and it could be a lot longer until the next time. She used to come over regularly to cover for lunches. But she had grown in importance in her own department, meaning some of the more recent casuals were sent over instead.

This was truly his chance. No customers, no other work colleagues. No one to feel embarrassed in front of. But he couldn't just blurt it out, could he? What if the answer was "No"? What if he ended up looking like a bloody idiot?

All he wanted was to ask her out. Once he got the answer; that was it. If yes, great! If no, at least he would know he was heading along the wrong path.

They were just standing there, not looking at each other, as if they were both too nervous to look. It was probably just Russell's reading in that, but it was possible.

No. That was it. No more stuffing around.

"At the risk of sounding like a complete idiot…" There. He'd started. And was about to go on when his heart finally reacted to his nerves.

It leapt into his throat, along with a gallon or so of blood that rose to his burning face. His whole body was thudding at fifty thousand beats a second, in time with his heart.

He was choking, not literally. But the words had caught in his throat.

"Never mind." He gave up, but his nervous reaction hadn't.

Kristen finally looked at him. He could feel her eyes boring into him. What must she be thinking? Russell knew he was as red as a beetroot. He knew he was practically vibrating like a guitar string. Kristen had to know what was up.

"What?"

"Don't worry about it," He couldn't say it. He'd started to, but common sense or something else got in the way.

Kristen laughed slightly, "No, you can't just start like that and not finish. You have to-"

Russell leapt at it. His head felt so light as he let the words flow, his body still in the throws of absolute nervous tension.

"I was wondering if you'd be interested in seeing a movie some time."

Silence.

Kristen looked away. Russell could feel it. It was going to be bad.

He prepared himself for what was coming. It was like slow motion. That very first word came out and Russell thought his legs would give in.

"No," But it wasn't over, "You know I work six days of the week, plus uni so I don't have much time."

He wasn't going to give up that easily, "So do I, practically, but sometime after work."

"Okay."

Okay? 'My God!' Russell nearly collapsed, the blood flooding his brain and face seemed to drop, like a tidal wave to the rest of his body. Okay. Great!

The customers started to come again. Both sales assistants began serving, but Russell's mind was elsewhere. He was happy, finally. He had half expected the 'No' to stand, but it was one of those Yes-No's. When it hinted at an affirmative, only disguised as a negative, as if she actually wanted to, but considered it an impossibility.

He shook his head, clearing his hair from his face and trying to shake the thoughts from his mind. This was work. He could think about it all later.

*   *   *

As he left work, he was on a high. Who wouldn't be? Russell kept thinking about the conversation he'd had with her, like a dream he didn't want to let go of, wishing he had a mental camera he could just rewind and play over and over again. He headed out the first floor entrance of the store that led to the train station walkway, allowing pedestrians to safely cross the busy street below. It would have to have been one of the most used and oft-times over crowded footpaths in the entire city. Even now, as the city began to close down, there were hundreds of people scrambling to get to a train in time.

Russell ignored them, not out of arrogance, but out of a blissful reverie. He really didn't care about anything else. Except her saying "Okay."

He pulled his jacket tighter around him, not that it was cold, but the warmth of it made him settle a little deeper into his thoughts. It was amazing that such a pretty girl could even consider saying "okay" to someone like Russell.

He was jarred out of his reverie as the ground beneath his feet began to shake. Earth quake? Big train pulling into the station?

Being on the first floor was not the most secure place to be in the prior occasion. People began to squeal as the bridge began to heave a little, pressure cracks appearing in the tiles.

The vibrations increased in intensity and the glass wall, which acted as a weather shield on the bridge exploded in either direction, showering the street below and virtually attacking the crowd cowering beside it. Russell could already see some people were injured by the glass, not to mention some of the debris that had started to break away from the ceiling.

The very floor beneath his feet was starting to undulate and the people around him began pushing their way along the walkway, panic obviously building as they went.

There were screams on the bridge as some parts of the flooring gave out, revealing considerable holes dropping the twenty or so feet to the concrete and cars.

He knew he needed to act. He didn't even know what was causing it, though a few options were springing to mind.

He called up his powers for the second time that day and compressed the silver strands into a wall of air at the centre of the bridge. And pushed.

There would have been at least thirty people jammed on the bridge, fighting to stay on there feet and make their way off the structure. But due to the violent shaking, they weren't getting too far. So Russell helped a little, giving them all a push and a little support, almost cushioning the people caught in his wind-wall, while still moving them forward. Soon the pedestrians were clambering to relative safety within Greyson's or further along the walkway.

He felt the sweat on his brow. After the work out this morning and the effort of maintaining the wind-wall, he was beginning to feel the dredging effect on his stamina. Obviously he had his limits.

That was when Dufus stepped up to the bridge. He looked like a giant caricature of a cowboy ready for a gun-slinging showdown. His massive bulk on his arms somewhat hindered their ability to dangle straight by his sides, giving him the crook arm appearance. But the beefiness of his chest gave the impression of a massive bull ready to squash you in one charge.

There was nothing for it. Russell stepped up to the challenge, standing casually on the opposing end of the bridge. Neither one making a move, simply staring the other down. Of course, Russell had the advantage there as he could still conjure up his abilities without the need to move more than an eyebrow. But Dufus' power was completely physical.

It was time to speak, "What's up with you?"

"We seem to have a little problem."

The voice came from behind him. It had to be Pipsqueak. Russell turned and backed up slightly, as to keep both men in sight. Sure enough it was the smaller man. He was casually strolling up the walkway toward him.

"And what would that be?"

Pipsqueak smiled, "You."

Dufus started to make his way along the bridge, being careful to avoid the holes and the cracks. Obviously his weight was a little too much for the bridge now it was shaken and weakened. It began to creak slightly as he moved.

Russell continued to back up. But both men continued to approach.

"I don't know why I should be a problem. What did I ever do?"

He needed to get as much information as he could. Even if it meant staying in danger a little while longer. Sure, he could handle these goons for a bit, or enough to get away, but he also needed to find out what the devil was going on.

"Well, there was that little incident this morning."

"You started that. The whole bomb thing."

"Which brings us to the other thing; you're interference with the first accident."

Obviously he meant the bomb in the car park. The way he said it implied the quotation marks some people would signify with their hands.

"I didn't do anything. I guess I just happened to be in the wrong place at the wrong time."

Pipsqueak's smile grew wider. His almost weaselish face looked to be near splitting in two, "You have a habit of that it seems. Now, you can either come peacefully, or, well, not."

"Hmm. Let me think," Russell turned and bolted as he shouted his response, "Not!"

The two men began to run after him, obviously predicting his move. What they didn't predict was the security guard from Greyson's.

Russell had a lot of friends at work, some of which were there for store security.

The glass entrance had already been opened by the bystanders watching the three men. But as Russell began to run, one of the security guards broke free from the crowd and tackled Pipsqueak to the ground.

The small man collapsed under the onslaught, slapping at the guard who had taken him down. That was when Dufus arrived. He bent down and took hold of the guard's shirt back and heaved him away, virtually throwing him like a rag doll back toward Greyson's. The guard landed hard, too stunned to get up straight away.

"Get after the little git!"

Pipsqueak jumped to his feet as Dufus followed the order and began lumbering along the walkway. Well, it looked like a lumber, but he did it with incredible speed.

Russell was nearing the end of the walkway. If he were to jump over the edge he had a forty foot drop into a vacant block that was being developed as a supermarket and specialty shop arcade. The other option was to grab onto the top railings of the skinny stairs that lead down to street level and head down that way. It would slow him up considerably was his only thought.

It was, however, the safest option.

He lashed out with his hand and yanked himself on a wide arc, using the rail as a pivot before bolting down the stairs. Some were loose due to lack of maintenance, but Russell had to slow anyway for the mere size of the steps. He could hear Dufus' clodhoppers resounding closely behind him, and getting even closer as he tripped over every odd step. The chances of getting away were getting slimmer and slimmer. Finally, his feet made the bottom step and he launched himself up the road, unable to hear his pursuers due to the roar of the cars along the road beside him. He could tell from the expressions on the drivers' faces as they drove past, however, that Dufus or Pipsqueak were gaining.

A sharp pain drove into his back as the air around him flashed a bright green. The force of Pipsqueak's bolt sent him floundering for footing, sending his upper half toppling over his feet.

The ground came at him faster than the cars beside him would have and his arms sprang up protectively. The bones in his arms jarred as he made contact and grazed as his body continued with the momentum. He could feel the blood oozing out of the wounds that now ran the length of his forearm and elbow.

No time to worry about that now, however. He heaved himself up again, finding his knees and shins in a similar predicament, but also discovering the pain was merely a dull throb. Normally he'd be screaming in pain, but now, it barely registered.

Russell continued onward, slower than normal as his clothes rubbed aggravatingly. A second bolt of force connected with his shoulder, once more toppling him forward. This time, he managed to roll as he fell, nearing the curb and the speeding tyres beyond that.

Behind him, he spotted the two men. They weren't far and Dufus was making brilliant time.

Once more jumping up he stood, eyeing the street. Car after car went flashing by, making it nigh on impossible to cross.

So there was the other option.

Carefully judging the distance between himself and the other side of the street, he reached out toward the currents streaming past him with the car's momentum. He could almost feel their presence as he called them up and coaxed them to recreate the stunt he had performed back at the cathedral. In moments, he had launched himself into the air, like a bird almost, arms outstretched as if diving into the clouds, though not so high. Below him, the cars continued on their course, unaware of what was happening around them.

Four lanes in total passed underneath and Russell started to make his descent again. Once more he tucked himself into a tight ball and somersaulted, bringing himself around to land on his own feet in a cushion of air.

If he'd been at the Olympics doing gymnastics, he most likely would have scored a perfect ten, probably out of the sheer fantasticalness of the manoeuvre. He crouched low and turned to look between the bodies of the cars. In the flashes he caught glimpses of his opponents, trying to peer over the top of cars to catch sight of him.

Staying down, Russell turned back along the road, back toward the walkway and ran, hoping the cars would give him cover. If they didn't see him, he'd be able to make it back to the train station and safely away from the two predators.

No such luck.

He had made it within twelve feet of the entrance and the walkway when he heard brakes squealing behind him followed by thud after crash as vehicles collided.

Looking over his shoulder, he saw what was going on.

Dufus had stepped onto the street, irrespective of the cars coming at him, and had continued to walk across the road. There was a cacophony of horns blaring and metal screeching as he continued, not physically damaging anything himself, but wreaking havoc with his mere presence. With his size, any driver would rather hit another car than his mass. The damage bill alone from the confrontation between man and machine would be tremendous, not to mention if he wanted to press charges for damages; which would be ridiculous as he would have been the cause of it all, but the way the law worked, he'd still probably be found to be in the right.

Time to stop the skulking, Russell stood up and pushed himself into a sprint. He was already weary from this morning and this activity wasn't making it any better. He could feel his heart beating in his chest like a massive drum. He wasn't sure if it was nervousness, fear or just the fact he was unfit. Though, again, he considered the fact that before the 'incident' with the bomb, there was no way he could keep up this kind of physical exertion. The bestowing of these powers, accidental or otherwise was a massive blessing. He felt little pain, he had a greater endurance, not to mention the fact he could do things out of the ordinary. But all the same, if it meant going back to a safer more peaceful life, he'd probably do away with the powers.

No you wouldn't, his mind chided himself. Do away with all this? And go back to being a lazy Student working casually at a department store? There was way more to life than that and he was proving it with every moment.

He ducked behind a column, hoping he was out of their sight. But when a large chunk of concrete exploded, showering the ground around him with fine white dust, he knew he was mistaken.

Taking up the challenge, he continued into the train station. It was far from empty. Each platform, twelve in total, was choked with people. Prams, teens, mothers, grandparents, all walks of human life. And getting through them all would be hell.

Another of Pipsqueaks bolts narrowly missed him, darting past and colliding with the bottom of an escalator, tearing out most of its foundations. The people riding on it screamed in fright as the mechanical steps began to buckle in half, bending under the weight. The support from the upper level began to give way and Russell found himself faced with a bigger problem. The fall for those on the upper steps was considerable enough, not to mention the debris that could come away with it.

There was a burst of air as he pulled it through from the street. On it rode the fumes of exhaust, but that didn't distract him. In a similar move to the one he'd used to cushion his descent, he gathered the compressed air beneath the structure and eased it down to the ground, the people on it still yelling for help. The concrete above moaned with the strain before snapping away, tearing with it massive chunks of the upper level. Fortunately the people above had avoided the unsteady ground, possibly having found out about the walkway.

Russell shut his eyes, concentrating harder on keeping the people on the escalator safe as it moved. The actual effort required to make the air pillow adjust so slowly, while still giving it sufficient force to keep it from collapsing was intense. He felt the veins on his temples throb as he forced the air to hold its position, allowing it to circulate, but only within the compressed area, as if he had erected an invisible balloon around it.

When the concrete finally touched ground he felt himself swoon. His head felt light and he almost forgot his own predicament.

"Touching."

Pipsqueak was right beside him, somehow having managed to cross the road with Dufus.

But Russell wasn't out of tricks yet.

The wind he had called forth as a support was still lingering in a dispersed air bubble he'd kept hold of. Now it was time to take the offensive.

He felt the air caress him as it blew past, but he knew the speed and force he had put behind it would be more than enough to put the smaller of the two attackers out of commission. Sure enough, Pipsqueak howled in frustration as the wind took hold of his body and launched him backward toward the street, once more narrowly missing the cars as he landed beside the curb.

Enough was enough, Russell thought to himself.

He wiped his brow and turned around to see Dufus standing right in front of him, distracted by what he had done to Pipsqueak.

"Want some of the same, big fella?"

Russell didn't see the hand coming. It sort of appeared out of nowhere, colliding with the side of his head and sending him spiralling into darkness.

CHAPTER TEN

He awoke, sitting on the cold metal seat he had also been tied to. It took a while to register all this.

And when he got beyond that, he took in the square room he was located in. It was grey in colour, dreary, almost dirty looking, though it was only the colour of the material used. Thankfully there was nothing unsanitary in here. He assumed there was a door somewhere behind him, for he couldn't see one in front of him. And the padded walls didn't seem to reveal any sign of a hinge or outline to represent an exit.

He could, however, hear what sounded like breathing. Over a microphone, perhaps. Or it could have been some sort of electrical device in the distance, rumbling loudly.

"Before we get started, Master Paige, we would like to ask you a few questions."

Someone was in the room, behind him. A man. He sounded quite tall from the angle of the voice. It was also one of distinct purpose, deep in pitch and resounding, even in this padded room.

"Started on what?"

Someone else giggled.

"I will be the one asking the questions, my boy."

Boy? Who did this guy think he was? Boy? Russell almost grunted his frustration. He had always been referred to as kid, boy or youth. He was near on twenty-one and yet everyone thought he was sixteen or so. He'd discussed it with one of the men from Home Office. They had dubbed it the 'Youth Gene'. Like a miracle gene that kept people looking younger than they really were, like Michael J. Fox. Russell was sick of the kind of treatment he received, however. The being asked for ID even when he was two years over the drinking and gambling age. Entering bars, clubs, everywhere that required you to be a certain age. "Can I see your ID?"

There was no point arguing this time, though. Where would it get him? All the same, he couldn't help himself.

"What did I do? Why am I here?"

"Master Paige. I told you, I would be the one asking the questions. Persist in your insolence and you will be sorry."

Russell shut his mouth.

The man behind him took a deep breath. The other man giggled once more, at least until Russell heard a loud "crack" and he started whining, "Sorry."

"Now. What happened when that bomb went off?"

What was this? The secret police? He'd already answered this for Corrigan, "Are you the police?" he knew they weren't. But why were they so interested in finding out what had happened. Perhaps it was like the X-files. Scully and Mulder. Only these guys liked the more violent approach rather than the soft-spoken subtly the characters in the TV series sometimes displayed. Of course, Russell was never fond of that show. Russell had seen better acting in a local amateur production of South Pacific, and that show was bad enough.

"I warned you Master Paige."

A searing bolt of pain shot through Russell's body and he was forced to cry out against it.

"I don't know! Nothing happened!"

"You did something. You somehow affected the bomb's reaction. What did you do?"

"How do you know it was me?"

Another bolt erupted into his body, tearing at his nerves, sending him into a fit of pain.

He squirmed against the chair, fighting against the lingering effects that tingled uncomfortably over and under his skin as the sensation ceased.

"We have you on camera. And the device you used. What was it? Where did you get it? What does it do?"

"I don't know!"

He screamed before he felt the pain this time. He knew it was coming. And sure enough, it coursed through his veins, into his eyeballs, his ears, into every part of his body.

"Lies will get you more pain."

"I'm not lying! I don't know what you're talking about! I didn't do anything!"

Russell forced his eyes open. Still straining against his bonds, he had to think of a way out of here.

And that was when he saw them. The silver wisps again. He could see the air around him, somewhat stagnant, but ever present.

What the hell was going on here?

"It sounds like he's telling the truth."

"Have you gotten anywhere with your studies so far?"

"Almost. A few more test and I'm sure we'll have something."

There was a pause as the deep voiced man considered this.

"And you found nothing on his person?"

"Not a thing, except his wallet."

There was another pause before Deep-Throat spoke again, "Where are your keys, Master Paige?"

Keys? They should have been in his pocket.

"In my pocket."

"Think carefully before you answer again, Master Paige as you know what will happen if you lie. Where are your keys?"

They were in his pocket. Weren't they. He moved his left leg a little, trying to feel the weight in his trousers. Nothing. His keys were missing. Had they taken them?

"You've got them."

91

He practically screamed as the energy ripped through his muscles and into his bones.

He forced himself to yell over the pain, "I don't know! I don't know!"

The pain stopped and Russell slumped in his chair, letting his head lull to one side, exhausted from his earlier efforts and wasted from the continued onslaught of electricity or whatever it was this evil Deep-Throat was throwing at him.

"I...uh... I tend to believe him, Sir."

"So do I," the man lowered his voice as he spoke to his assistant. Russell didn't have the strength to even bother straining his ears to hear what was being said. He just wanted to go home. So much for Stacey and Pam keeping an eye out. They didn't even respond to the damn bridge situation. No one did. He'd been left alone to fight those two mismatched thugs and had his butt kicked.

So much for trusting those damned reporters. Where did it get him? A fight at the cathedral in front of scores of innocent bystanders, almost injuring some of them. Then having to save more innocents from a disabled bridge and the escalator. If none of this had ever happened, he'd be fine, everyone would be fine. They wouldn't be targeting him and thus putting ordinary people in danger. It was his fault that their lives were put at risk. All because he... What? Russell's brain stopped thinking for a moment. What? It repeated. He hadn't done anything. All he'd been doing was walking into that damn car park, walked up the stairs playing with that damn key-ring-

The keys. That was why they had asked for his keys. Somehow, they had something to do with all of this. Then his mind flashed backward to how he had been toying with the button on the key ring. That little black button. Had that been the cause of all this turmoil? This violence?

It had to have been. It had somehow set off their bomb early and obviously done something to it, thus giving himself powers. Instead of flattening the building, it had mutated somehow and, in turn, mutated Russell. Talk about what goes around.

Then where were his keys? They should have been in his pocket. Maybe they fell out in the morning scuffle.

No. He'd used them at work to open his locker. He always kept his jacket in the locker if he wore it to work as he had done today. Then maybe the second fight. But he thought about it. No. Even when he was running along the walkway, he hadn't felt them bouncing against his leg. His wallet had, but not his keys. Odd. He should have noticed it. Then again, he was being chased by homicidal maniacs, so he had a small excuse. Even still, if he did have them, then these creeps would have them now, and would be using it for whatever means they wished.

But where were they?

Then it struck him.

He could almost see them now. Dangling from his pad-lock which in turn hung from his locker. He'd left them at work. It wasn't the first time he'd done it. One time he had stuffed his jacket inside, locked the door and gone onto the floor to work, only to receive a call from security telling him where they were. And he'd done it again. But this time, he'd left the store without them.

Which had to be a good thing. These idiots weren't going to get their hands on it.

Fortunate, or coincidence, he thought to himself as the two men behind him continued to mumble. Had he developed some other power, perhaps a second sight, like premonition? He laughed a little at that, knowing full well he had no such extra powers. Or did he?

"What do you find amusing, Master Paige?"

"Nothing," he covered.

"I don't believe you."

"Just thinking, that's all," Oops. Bad move.

Deep-Throat finally moved from behind the chair, his sharp angular face almost hawk-like in appearance bent forward to within a couple of centimetres from Russell's. He could smell his breath. From the look of the man's suit, he should have been able to afford toothpaste at least, or even a pack of gum.

"May I ask what?"

There was absolutely nothing polite about this man's manner, but he seemed to love the pretence in his voice.

He had to come up with something innocuous, "About how that smaller fellow went sprawling. He looked like a rage doll."

Deep-Throat reclaimed his full height. He was very tall. His build was pretty good too, but from where Russell was sitting, this man was a giant, "Most amusing."

"I've seen you somewhere before, haven't I?"

The man's eyes widened for the briefest of moments. Almost a cliché action; before narrowing down to tiny slits.

"Most unlikely."

It was odd. The man was familiar for two reasons. From two different places, but he couldn't pick either. He was wealthy, yes. Maybe he'd been on the news regarding some investment thing, or, more likely, a law suit or criminal action. Yes. That was it. Russell recognised him from the news. But it was too long ago, something he'd seen back at high school in his media class. But the second place, he couldn't put his finger on it.

It didn't matter, anyway. What was more important was what they wanted with him, not to mention would they be letting him go any time soon. From the look on this man's face, however, he knew the answers to both questions weren't going to be favourable.

"However, since you seem to be most uncooperative, I'm sorry to say, my friend here will need to run a few tests."

93

"What sort of tests?"

There was only a slight buzz now as Deep-Throat pressed a little controller in his hand and the chair radiated a shock of energy. Obviously, his last question was somewhat acceptable.

"That will be up to Doctor Eryn, but let me tell you now, they won't be pleasant."

With that, he left the room.

"What, no good byes?"

"I'm still here."

"What a comfort."

The second man, Doctor Eryn, moved into view. He was a squat man, slightly chubby, well groomed, more out of professional requirement than choice. Although the man's giggle and behaviour earlier implied he was a bit of a small-brained weirdo, his manner portrayed something more. This man wasn't as stupid as he seemed.

"It's time for you to sleep now," The Doctor bent down and took hold of Russell's arm. In one hand the man held a syringe and it didn't look very inviting.

Trying to yank his arm free of the man's grip, he wriggled about, feeling the grazes on his arms and legs scratching against the rope, re-opening the wounds. But that didn't matter. There was no way this mad scientist was going to…

He felt the needle jab into his arm and within moments the energy to struggle seeped out of his fingers as the walls started to go askew. The face of the man before him elongated before shrinking away into nothing.

*   *   *

He came to once again somewhere totally different. Laying on a hard bench of some kind, dressed in only his underwear and a hospital gown of sorts. He felt somewhat violated by that notion, but the cold metal beneath him kept his mind from wandering too far. It was an open backed piece and only ran to his knees. The actual material was thin and the table was absolutely freezing.

Looking around, Russell could see he was in some sort of operating room. A bright light hung over head, beside him a small trolley laden with items he couldn't quite make out from the angle he was strapped down at.

To his right, a door slid open on an automatic system and two people walked in covered from head to tail in surgical clothing. The masks and caps gave an almost condom like look to them, but Russell found nothing humorous in that thought.

He had to get out of there. He wasn't sure if they had planned for him to wake up for the surgery or whether his new physiology got rid of the drug earlier than usual or what. All the same, he didn't exactly want to be operated on.

He tried to focus, letting the sharpness of the cold beneath him help direct his energies.

He wasn't sure how well it would work, but in moments, he began to see the slowly drifting silver currents, reacting to the motion of the doors that had allowed a further in rush of air.

There was air here, something he could use.

Concentrating hard, he gathered the currents above the table, letting them coalesce and interact with each other. He could feel the resulting breeze from the activity in the air above. Obviously so did the two doctors. They faltered mid step and stared toward Russell's wind swept body. Hopefully, Russell thought, the gown wasn't playing up too much.

From the moment they realised something odd was going on, to the point when Russell threw the air ball at them, they had very little time to react. Maybe turn slightly, hoping to escape whatever was about to happen. But no such luck for these two.

The ball sent the two flying toward the doors once more, tossing them like flies in a storm head first through the glass even before the door's motion sensors could react to their presence.

As if realising its mistake, the doors slid open, jarring both bodies against the door frame; acting like an iron cage as they struggled to get free, which in turn kept the motion sensor active thus keeping the doors wide open.

Now, to get out of the straps.

Russell pulled at both of his wrist straps, hoping to wriggle them loose, instead finding the hard leather was cutting into his skin.

Then he had an idea.

It was simple enough to redirect only a slight portion of the power he had used against the two surgeons. All he needed to do was angle it slightly and bring it back toward the table, and the small tray sitting beside it. Give it an up lift and-

With a crash, the tray lifted into the air and tipped on its side, spilling surgical equipment over the table, some falling down to the floor with a clatter. Grasping for anything, Russell felt around, being careful not to cut himself.

His hand found purchase on a small knife-like scalpel. What they had planned to do with that, he didn't want to know. Deftly, he twisted it around and proceeded to saw at the strap, finding as he did so, the pressure his straining put on it leant itself to the tearing of the material.

After quite a few moments he had one hand free. Enough to get a faster action happening on his other restraints.

He jumped off the table, finding the flooring was as cold, if not colder than the table he'd been lying on. Scuffling his feet to avoid stepping on broken glass or any of the spilt surgical equipment, he moved past the

still struggling men who, surprisingly, hadn't been calling out for help. As Russell drew closer, he saw that the doors had luckily caught the men just under the tip of their sternums, effectively keeping them both somewhat winded as the mechanism jarred open against their bodies.

Outside the operating room, or vivisecting room, whichever these loons had tagged it, was a small washroom, like you see on those medical dramas. Scrubbing tubs were situated in the centre, similar to the control set up in Doctor Who's TARDIS.

There was a door to the left which seemed to be the only exit. With no other choice, Russell continued to scuffle out that way, finding himself in a locker room. It was only small, but at one end there were showers and toilet cubicles. On the other were eleven tall lockers. Hopefully, some were stocked with clothing.

He moved along each one. Finding personal effects and changes of clothes. It wasn't long before he had organised a neat little wardrobe for himself, consisting of a t-shirt, a dark puff jacket and black jeans. To top it off, a pair of nicely polished boots, laced up to half way up his shin. A little odd for size, but more than suitable for wear.

At least he'd scored something out of this little adventure; though now he had to buy another pair of trousers.

Strangely, however, he considered the fact there was only one entrance to the operating room.

It surprised even himself that the thought niggled at his mind. But why would they have only one, especially through a locker room. Would they normally cart a patient through a locker room? And if he was such an important 'guest', or was he just being egotistical, then why weren't their security measures, such as cameras? They couldn't have solely relied on the anaesthetic.

Something was smelling fishy, here, and it wasn't his feet.

Instead of proceeding out the other exit to the locker room, he turned back to the scrub room. When he re-entered, he saw something that didn't surprise him in the least.

The men were gone. Rescued? Escaped? But where to?

Someone was playing a game and Russell was the pawn.

Well, he thought to himself, they still have to learn I'm not one to mess with.

"Ooh, I'm shaking in my boots," he said out loud, more in response to his false bravado than their challenging him.

It was times like these he found himself wishing he had telepathy instead. Smiling, he began searching the walls to this room. Running his hands over the smooth tiles, hoping to discern a crack or join in the wall that may very well have been another way out. Sadly, there were none.

So it was back into the operating room.

Another seemingly dead end. Like the middle of a maze the rat is supposed to find his way out of.

The walls in here were metallic. Reflective like mirrors, but much stronger.

Let's see how strong.

Russell heard the howl of wind and the slamming of the locker room door as he called forth the air from all three rooms. He stood back, allowing the strong currents to rush past him, caressing his body like an invisible seductress before storming forward.

The sheer force of the wind was incredible. He could feel it building in intensity as he sucked the air completely from the other two rooms and forced it into a veritable hurricane inside the operating room. He could see the silver strands lashing out against the metal walls, ineffectual in their intangible form. But as the loose equipment was swept up into the storm, he directed them as an attack. Chips and scratches soon pockmarked the walls as he pushed harder, the sweat breaking out not only on his forehead but under his arms. The control he was forcing was immense and required every ounce of strength in his body. It was as if he had clenched every muscle. He could feel cramps rising in his biceps and calves, but he kept pushing. The tray and its stand were shortly swept into the fray and they too danced and bounced against the wall.

But they still weren't enough to cause suitable damage. So, there was one other option.

Pushing even further, he felt his legs start to buckle. His knees wanting so much to give way with the strain he was placing on his very body, as if every molecule was being taxed for its energy. It was incredible. Liberating almost.

He felt at one with the power filling the room. A transient sense that was awash and aglow in the silver strands that belted around the room like lightening. It was both painstaking and invigorating to wield such power, like it was a release of all the pent up anger in his bones. He would liken it to standing in the middle of a massive meadow and screaming at the top of your lungs. A complete and utter abandon, yet, it required such control to make sure he didn't get too carried away with his onslaught against the wall. He wasn't even sure why he was attacking the wall. Maybe it was all those detective movies with the two-way mirrors. But these aren't mirrors, he tried reasoning. But even as he thought it, his mind countered, 'But what if they are'. And it spurred him on to push harder.

With that, the table was finally swept into the air. He was speechless when it took flight, not that he had anyone to say anything to, but the notion that he could lift such a massive and weighty object. A large steel table he wouldn't have dreamed lifting by himself with his bare hands, and now, he had it swirling in the air. It was under his control.

And with that control, he redirected the air currents, taking them off the circular spin he had set them on and pulled them back toward him, letting them, along with their load of glass, surgical equipment and furniture, pass around behind him toward the door before lifting them high above him and sending it all crashing forward toward the offending wall with such force, he felt the floor beneath his feet quake.

There was no way the wall could have withstood the attack, metal or not. The cumulative debris and the force behind it all punched a hole through what Russell could now see as a durable, though thin metal divide.

He let the silver strands disperse into the air and the rooms seemed to sigh in relief.

On shaky legs, he moved forward to his newly created exit. The edges of the hole were peeled open, like the exit hole in a tin can after having been shot through by a bullet. Beyond that was another room, too dark to see anything, but he could hear someone.

The glass was still tinkling as it settled after their wonderful aerial adventure, but over that, Russell could hear muffled moans. Had he hurt someone?

Lifting himself up through the hole, his arms slightly unsteady underneath him, he hopped down into the dark area beyond. The light from the Operating room barely made a dent in the pitch black in here. There had to be other sources of light, or had they been damaged when the wall gave way?

Russell edged deeper into the dark, keeping his arms out, hoping his eyes would shortly adjust, and giving him even a slightly better ability to see.

Sure enough, with the light spillage, he started to make out various shapes.

There appeared to be chairs knocked over, even tables. Nothing was completely discernible, but Russell was able to make a general map of the result of the explosion. Obviously the wind power behind his attack had followed through into here, the change in air pressure becoming a wall of physical force, sending everything flying away from the new exit, similar to the effect Russell's power had had when it first manifested at the car park. A blast wave.

"Hello?" He said it warily. Okay, it would draw attention to himself, but if someone was stupid enough to respond, it would give him an idea if he had actually killed anyone or not. That was one thing he didn't want to do. Russell wasn't completely sure, but he had the inkling that someone had died in the van crash. That had, in part been Russell's fault, but more so who ever was driving the van. They had been speeding. Stacey, though he was following them, had only increased his speed after they had. He was not the cause, nor really was Russell. And if they hadn't blown up the building, there wouldn't have been a need to follow them in the first place.

But right now, Russell was certain he didn't want to be responsible for someone's death, not through deliberate or accidental means with his bare hands or with his new powers. He didn't want that sort of action on his conscience. Ever.

Someone responded to his call. Another moan in the darkness.

He started to move toward it, to see if they were okay when the room was flooded by a bright wash of light.

From every corner, a floodlight flared against the dark, effectively blinding Russell. He sheltered his eyes with his arms, already blinded. He could see the bright red underneath his eyelids where his eyes had been affected. He could also hear a door slam open to his left and the sound of footsteps, not to mention feel the rush of more fresh air.

Which he would use.

They weren't going to get him again.

He shot out his arm toward the sound of their boots and pushed with all his might.

The men yelled expletives as their feet were knocked from underneath them. He could hear as they fought against the wind, scrambling on the floor.

Doing his best, Russell forced his eyes open to try and get an image of where to go and how to dodge the captors.

Against the lingering blur of white, he only managed to grab scraps of the sight before him. It was going to be a tight squeeze. So, using what little energy reserves he had left, he called back the air and encased himself in a cocoon, similar to that he had back in the building only a couple of days ago, hoping it would be sufficient shielding against these men.

And he ran.

Blinking furiously in the hopes of clearing his sight, he was still able to find the direction of the door and pass through it. The men grabbed at him, their blows deflected by his force field, though as it was not tangible, they were managing to push through it. He could feel them reaching at him, breaking its surface as if the air itself was communicating everything it sensed back to him, though he knew that wasn't the case, or did he?

He managed to get past them and continued running. But he couldn't see where.

The corridor was still bright, mainly ahead of him. He wasn't sure where the light was coming from, but he just kept running.

Maintaining his cocoon, he pushed onward, his legs weak after so much action and running from earlier that day, not to mention everything he'd been through since.

The light kept getting brighter, as if he were running toward heaven, or a very bright spotlight.

When he broke through a pane of glass, he had a feeling which one he'd be reaching first.

Glass exploded all around him and once more, there was a tremendous back draft. The floor disappeared from beneath his feet and Russell found himself floundering for a handhold, foothold, or absolutely anything.

Where the hell was he? The cocoon around him dispersed in the panic that began to set in as he felt gravity start to work and he began to fall.

Thoughts punched through his brain. How far, how long? What, when, why, how? Nothing coherent until he shut his eyes once more, not that he could see anything in the first place. But as he shut his eyes a calm settled over him. He felt at home, like he was surrounded by family and friends once more. He wasn't sure if it were a life passing before his eyes experience or just that in these final moments he was going insane.

The sensation of falling passed, stopped. Was this death? He felt so light, as if he were suspended by strings and made simply of cloth.

He opened his eyes, and he could see once again.

And the world was there for him to see.

He hovered above the city, the activity of the day hustling and bustling below him.

The earth stretched around him as far as the eye could see, every horizon visible from this vantage point, excepting, of course, those hidden by the massive sky scrapers nearby, including the one he'd just stepped out of.

Drifting on air, the very silver strands he'd come to associate with his abilities were wrapped around his body, like a suit of armour. No more dancing or swirling. They simply held onto him, stopping him from falling. It was still draining what reserves of energy he had left. He found it funny he thought of himself as a battery now, but he was very close to being a dead one.

Ever so simply, he turned and regarded the window he had just fallen out of. It was a few metres up, he wasn't even sure what floor it was, but was over half way up the building itself. The CP2.

Carefully, he eased himself upward and backward away from the building until he was in line with his second makeshift exit. Framed by the broken glass was Deep Throat. As familiar and as collected as before. His arms folded. The faces of the men behind him, however, were awash with amazement and stupefaction. That was sufficient to make Russell smile.

With that, he turned once more and drifted back down to the street below.

CHAPTER ELEVEN

When he was only a couple of feet above the crowded street he started to hear the gasps and shouts. Kids were doing the 'look mum!' and the 'it's Superman!' thing. But Superman has nothing on this hero. For one thing, this one was real.

If Russell had had any hopes of anonymity they had been blown up in the van, not to mention with the bridge episode. He didn't want to brag about his powers, he just wanted to go home. But first, he needed his keys.

He landed on the south entrance of Greyson's, otherwise known as Murray Street, the one they had driven down only that morning, though at this end it was cut off from traffic and was now a pedestrian thoroughfare.

A crowd had already gathered by the time he touched ground and Russell could hear whispers of "micro-jetpacks" and "test-drive". He merely smiled, trying to push his way through the crowd and into the building.

What he found was that he had a small crowd following behind him, like a procession march. It shouldn't be too hard to lose them in Greyson's however.

He pushed through the Ground floor cosmetics department which was already filled with bodies, male and female alike, trying to get beauty tips from a spruiker doing demos as well as the floor staff giving advice and even demonstrations on eager customers.

With the store being open on Sunday, and most of the suburban centres being shut, it meant Sunday was one of the busiest trading days. Russell decided to use this to his advantage to lose the followers and keep from being spotted by any of Deep Throat's goons if they happened to be around.

It took him fifteen minutes to get to the top floor, where his locker was located. By that time, he'd lost everyone and felt sure he was not being followed, watched or anything else.

So it was with a general ease he strolled into the back reserve for sports wear and greeted a number of fellow employees coming out of the massive locker room. He had a certain anonymity in the store due to the fact it was so large and no one ever really got to know everyone else. But you had a lot of good acquaintances.

When he got to his locker, he found his keys, still hanging from the lock. Luckily no one had taken it upon themselves to take them to security or put them in their own locker.

Russell quickly grabbed the keys and tucked them away in his new jeans. Then re-considered.

They wanted these keys. Well, the key ring at least. He couldn't walk around with them in hand.

He took the keys out again and filed through them. He only really needed two of them any more. His locker key and the house key. He removed those two and put them into his pocket. The rest, and the key ring, had to be put somewhere safe. But where?

"Russell?"

He turned, almost jumping out of his skin, "Pam? What are you doing in here?"

She smiled, "Security isn't the best here. Where have you been, you look awful?"

"Thanks," He looked around and moved to her, taking her elbow in hand directing her back to the floor, we need to get out of here and find somewhere safe to talk.

She spoke as she moved; now taking hold of his hand, "I know a place."

*   *   *

There was a building. Dark orange in colour, with a large arch set in the middle, the entrance.

Eight windows seemed to join with the footpath, indicating a basement of sorts, above those were eight larger windows and above those once more, nine, including one over the door. They were arched; the architecture above suitably shaped with a complimentary gothic style to add and draw character, developing a nice, yet trendy façade to the building. All the windows, however, were blacked out and a large black gate was erected in front of the door. It looked to be abandoned.

When Pam removed a set of keys from her own pocket and unlocked the gate, Russell knew differently.

She shut the gate behind, re-locking it. Then came the front door and the entrance hall.

On either side of the hall were doors, six in all, set widely apart but directly opposite each other. The hall itself was about twenty-five meters in length, indicating the building to be very deep. The designer obviously preferred to take up more in horizontal planning then vertical. Starting half way down the hall was a staircase that led up to a wall and disappeared to both the left and right on a mezzanine level.

She led him down to one of the doors furthest from the entrance, opening it and indicating for him to enter.

"What exactly is this place?"

"Stacey and I prefer to think of it as our home away from home."

Sure enough, the room he stepped into was very much like a small apartment. There was a lounge area and a small kitchenette. Off to one side, there were two doors, marked with the male and female indicator signs for toilets. It was like a small staff room one would expect to see at high school.

102

"Take a seat; I'll get you some tea."

"Thanks," He sat squarely in the middle of the large couch that took up most of the space in the lounge section of the room. It was very comfortable and seemed to swallow him in its cushions. He took a moment to let the place sink in. It must have been huge; "You lease this place?"

He could hear her tinkering away in the kitchenette, "No, some, well, I guess you could call them friends, own it. They let us use it from time to time. It's more of a refuge than anything else. A safe house.

"From what?"

"You're not the first person we've come across with a few problems, just one of the more difficult."

Russell laughed, "You're not the only person to call me that."

She came back with a tray, two teas, a milk jug and sugar bowl. Setting it on the table in front of the couch, Russell sat forward to pour his own milk and sugar before asking Pam about hers. Once they both had their drinks, Pam seemed to decide it was time to get down to business.

"We heard a little about what happened today. Not much. Something about a mini tremor, a security guard being hospitalised with a few breaks and dislocations and then the talk of a jet pack I heard while I was inside trying to find you. I figured it had to have something to do with you."

Russell couldn't help but feel responsible for the guard. Aiden was his name. Nice bloke, probably one of the few that actually took his job seriously. He had only seen a little of Aiden's heroics, when he caught glimpses over his shoulder. He made a mental note to go visit him in hospital.

"As you may have guessed, they found me. They took me up to the CP2. I have no idea why, but…"

Russell proceeded to explain everything that had happened, getting a little too excited about his new found ability to fly but keeping it simple more or less. But he focussed mainly on the idea they had his wallet and therefore ties to pretty much everything in his life from his savings, to his address, to his DVD rental membership.

"First things first. You won't be going back to your place anytime shortly. You can stay here for the time being, relax, and get some rest. Then I'll call Stacey and we can do a little research into whoever it was that is responsible for all of this. And then we will see if there is anything we can do, either in getting your wallet back or in stopping these goons once and for all."

She was being very optimistic about it all, but Russell was starting to feel the drag of his exertions and his normal negative thought flow coming back.

"I can't just stay holed up forever."

"You don't need to be. As I said, we'll work out what we can do. Until then, you won't be going to work without one of us there as back up.

From now on, that is the only place they will be able to get to you. Unless, of course, you call in sick."

"I can't afford to! Besides, I'm not going to screw my whole life up because of this. I haven't done anything. They're the bad guys; they should be the ones cowering in the shadows, not me."

She nodded, understanding, "I know. It was just a suggestion."

Then a thought struck him. Kristen. He'd asked her out. He couldn't not follow through with it. How was he supposed to-?

But it'd be too dangerous. He'd be risking her life. Or would he?

If he called her at work. Arranged it over the phone, then met somewhere away from work, they wouldn't find him. He could lay low, keep a low profile, but have the date all the same. Besides, he had powers enough to keep her safe long enough for her to get to safety. But he wouldn't have a chaperone. He didn't exactly like the idea of Stacey watching over his shoulder.

He discussed the idea with Pam. She was clearly stifling her amusement at the idea. Russell knew he looked a little, if not a lot, desperate, but this had been a long time in the works. He couldn't blow it all now.

At first Pam disagreed, but seeing how adamant Russell was about the situation, she finally caved.

"Just as long as you treat her with a little respect."

"Why wouldn't I?"

"I was just being facetious. Now, I'll show you where you can sleep and you can get some rest."

He followed her back into the hall where she took him up the stairs and up to the first floor. He noted that despite the external appearance of the place, it was reasonably well kept. Not a speck of dust on the banisters, no gathering of dirt in the corners of the steps. Even the walls were devoid of stains, marks, holes, tears or anything like that. It was a simple layout, a simple building, but whoever owned it treated it like it was a palace.

Choosing to go right at the mezzanine and up to the first floor, Pam led him into a hallway. Looking back, he could see that a similar hallway was positioned on the other side of the stairs.

This hallway had more doors dotted along the walls.

Indicating the first two doors on either side of the hall, "Bathrooms. Male and female."

"And here is where you'll be staying," Pam took him to the third on the left and let him inside.

It was a bedroom. Probably as large as his own, though the dimensions were different. It was a long narrow room. At the end was the bed; beside it was a small side cabinet. There was a cupboard, a table with three chairs; for company, Russell presumed. There were a couple of paintings on the walls also. Probably old prints framed and put up to add a little life.

In all, they weren't bad living quarters.

Still it felt awkward. Russell had never been a fan of sleepovers. And the idea that he would be alone in this big building was rather daunting. What if they had followed them? What if they knew where he was and were going to come and get him.

Stop it, he thought. Paranoia was just going to make things worse.

Pam said her good byes and left Russell to make himself comfortable.

Among other things in the room was a small television in the corner beside the door. It sat on a small table. He turned it on for some ambient sound and proceeded to check the place out thoroughly.

Opening the cupboard doors, he found it empty and dark.

There was a rack for hanging and a shelf above that. A good hiding spot for his key ring, but too predictable.

He closed the doors and moved to the bed. He bounced his backside on it several times to test how comfortably he might be sleeping, if he could manage to sleep in a strange room. Pretty springy, giving a fair bit of resistance and support. From there, he moved to a little window just above the bed. But it wasn't a window. In actual fact, if there were a window there, it would look straight out onto a big brown wall. This window was lit by the dying sunlight, still giving an indication of the time, but it was redirected by a system of mirrors or something in a chimney like tunnel. As far as Russell could tell there was something actually magnifying the light, yet softening it so it was brighter, but more of a warm feeling than you'd get from an artificial light source. From the entrance of the room, it looked like a perfectly normal window.

And then he moved back to the table and chairs. Metal chairs with cushioned backrest and seat and a nice wooden table that could be a makeshift desk if necessary for study or even conferencing. Either side was expandable, adding to its length.

All in all, decent quarters. But not something he'd call home.

Then something on the television caught his attention.

"...Supernatural activity. Witnesses all described the same localised earthquake sensation and some even claimed some form of invisible barrier pushing them to safety."

The image on the screen, which showed the bridge outside Greyson's cut to a series of Vox Pops. One woman was wide eyed and breathless- "It was like a gigantic invisible pillow. It seemed to lift us up and lead us to safer ground. It was incredible. Like God was looking out for us."

Russell almost choked on his laughter. 'God?' Why did everything have to be religious? This was more scientific than religious, though he supposed someone could read a little destiny into everything that had happened. Like this having meant to be. He was perhaps prophesised by some man speaking in tongues over in Afghanistan. And he was meant to save the world.

"Yeah right," he chuckled to himself.

The news report continued for a couple of seconds more, asking for further information or for the person responsible to come forward.

He was about to go lie on the bed when the anchorwoman began reading the second story.

"This recent spate of Super-natural or Super-human activity has attracted the attention of the government. Members of Parliament have proposed legislation for research into the cause of these occurrences and tighter laws pertaining to those responsible."

"This should be good," instead of lying down, he sat on the end and watched.

"Following the explosion at Saint Paul's Cathedral on Murray Street and the virtual demolition of the Wellington Street Over-pass, local Government officials have opted to take a harder stand against the cause of these inexplicable events. Labour Senator Johanna Cartwright says she believes the perpetrators should be brought to justice."

A female appeared on screen, sitting snugly in front of a window, a lovely nature scene behind her, yet she was looking oh so arrogant, but still managed to be so concerned. Typical Bureaucrat. Her voice was sickly sweet, as if butter wouldn't melt in her mouth.

"We can not," she actually used both words, "just sit by and allow these acts of terrorism go on unpunished. Someone must be made accountable."

Cut to the reporter, "But what of this Hand of God theory? Can you be sure someone is responsible?"

"According to information gathered by Police and passed on to me, there are already a number of leads in these cases. Witnesses on both occasions have come forward to give information," She looked to the screen, addressing the viewers directly, "And we ask anyone out there who knows anything to please come forward."

"What would happen if you caught those people responsible?"

"They will be put through the appropriate motions."

"You mean a court proceeding to see if they are guilty or not?"

The senator nodded, "That's right. And if it's found that there are people out there with abnormalities such as these, we will need to look at further developing methods to control them."

Control? Clip their wings? Or actually lock them up and throw away the key. Even Russell wasn't sure that would work with most of the people he'd encountered. They'd certainly have one heck of a time keeping that Dufus fellow chained up.

'But what about me,' Russell thought. And Pam and Stacey? The good guys? The ones who have done nothing wrong? Would they be punished too, for the misguidance, or down right stupidity of a couple of thugs?

Nazism or not, this whole situation was starting to read like one of those X-men comics. Hopefully this woman was alone in her stance, or she was full of hot air.

Whatever the answer, Russell didn't want to hear any more. He turned off the television and the lights. Lying on the bed, it took only moments to drift off, his muscles finally relieved of their burden.

*   *   *

He awoke late the next morning. Checking his watch, it was already eleven thirty four and he still didn't want to move. Some of the ache that had gathered in his muscles had died somewhat, but it was as if they had become harder to move. Even the simplest of movements was a real chore.

Ten minutes later he finally managed to stir. He rubbed his eyes, yawned and stretched, hoping to ease some of the lethargy he felt in his very bones.

No such luck.

So, heavily, he wandered down the stairs to the kitchenette to prepare himself some tea. Pam had already washed up last night's tiny mess and the cups were sitting beside the sink. He just grabbed one, snapped the electric kettle on and leant back against the counter. Looking around with dreary eyes, he spotted the phone.

Phone.

Kristen.

It was as if the sleep vanished from him altogether, though his movement was still somewhat hampered. He hurried as best he could over to the phone, picking it up and dialling work.

Hopefully she was working. Hopefully she'd be free. Hopefully-

"Hello, this is Margaret, how can I help you?"

"Hi, could you put me through to computers, please?"

"Certainly. Just one moment."

Her voice was replaced by music for a brief instant before she spoke again.

"That line is busy, would you mind holding the line?"

"Sure, that's fine."

Good. Meant he could keep it short. They wouldn't have to talk much. In actual fact, Russell loathed phones. He didn't mind customers on the other end. It was people he knew he hated talking to. It was almost impersonal. Or something like that. He just found it hard to communicate coherently over the phone.

"Greyson's Computers, Erin speaking."

"Hi, could I speak to Kristen, please?"

"Sure, just one moment."

The phone was clunked onto the bench and Russell heard Erin speaking to Kristen. There was another short moment before the phone was juggled around and Kristen spoke.

"Kristen here, how may I help you?"

His knees nearly went weak. It was so childish, he knew, but he couldn't help it. His heart had been thumping like a manic drummer was playing for his life in some drumming competition the whole time he'd been on hold. He hoped she was interested. She had to be. She had said 'okay'.

"Hi Kristen. It's Russell."

Her voice changed. No longer as proper as when she speaks to customers, "Oh, Hi. How are you?"

"Great. And you?"

"Oh, you know, slacking off here while everyone works hard."

They both laughed. It was an on going joke they had. Russell had started off talking to her by calling her a slacker. In fact she was very hard working, but it was something amusing to say. She seemed to think it was funny anyway and it had just gone on from there.

"I was just wondering if you were doing anything tonight. I know it is late notice but…?"

He let it drift off. Hoping that would be sufficient. He'd said it so fast he wasn't sure if she'd understood or not.

There was only a slight pause before she answered. Was that good or bad?

"No that's fine. No. I'm not doing anything."

"Well, how about we go see a movie?"

He thought he could hear the smile in her voice, "Sure."
"Great!"

He organised to meet her outside one of the large chain cinemas in the city at six o'clock. Giving her time to get there comfortably after work. When he hung up, he almost whooped with joy, before he realised the kettle was doing it for him. He watched as the switch clicked over and the boiling died down before getting himself a tea. Now he had to find something to wear.

CHAPTER TWELVE

Stacey returned from his apartment with some bad news. They'd already been there. They hadn't trashed the joint, as Russell had feared, but they had left a calling card. It was one of his video membership cards attached to a 'with compliments' slip. It was probably easy to trace where it came from, but why bother. Russell already knew where to look.

Thankfully Stacey had good taste. He'd grabbed a few handfuls of clothing and most of it was suitable to wear out. Russell didn't have much in the way of clothing to begin with, but he liked to think some of it matched.

It took him over an hour to get ready; he wanted to look just perfect, which left him with another hour to wait. He decided to go to the cinemas early and wait inside. There was a small café where he sat drinking a bottle of Coke, fidgeting in his seat and worrying whether or not the night would be half-decent or whether she'd be interested in doing it again.

"You're being stupid," he told himself. It hadn't even begun yet and he was being stupid.

He watched the time go by on his watch by two-minute jumps, panicking as each second passed. Would she like him? Would he make a complete fool of himself?

He wanted to slap himself for a couple of reasons. One for being such an idiot, and the other to freshen himself up. He was getting stagnant sitting in the chair moping over the plastic bottle. He decided he needed to take his mind of things and started to contemplate the bottle itself. He began to write a mental essay on the curvature of the bottle, debating whether it was symbolic of a female's body shape or just stylised for the 1960's. He recalled the old glass bottles. It was probably the worst move in history for both milk and Coke to go from glass to plastic. Sort of like money. Every time something went from one form to plastic, it ended up being a dredge on society. Like credit cards. How many people were now deeply in debt because they didn't really think about the need to repay everything you spend on those tiny little cards. How many people had overdrawn their limit or extended it to buy that one extra item and discovered they couldn't really afford it. In Russell's opinion people would be better off saving their money and using the real thing instead of plastic, guaranteeing they could definitely afford it because they would already have paid for it.

He looked at his watch again. Five minutes to go. Finally!

He quickly got up and headed outside, hoping she wasn't early. She wasn't. The night was slightly chilly, and Russell knew he shouldn't do it, but he conjured up a small amount of romantic magic by persuading the warmer air to come down from on high and stick around for a while.

Even though it took the nip out of the air, he couldn't help rubbing his hands together in anticipation. He knew he looked like a fool, as if he were about to receive the biggest cash donation in the world. He liked to think of it as being on par to that. Kristen was definitely worth a billion dollars. She was sweet, funny, kind, everything anyone could ever want to be and she was...heading this way. He nearly baulked at the sight of her. It wasn't that she had dressed up for the occasion, but she still looked wonderful. That was the good thing about working at Greyson's. The uniform was semi-casual, semi-formal and most people tried to look their best, and boy did she look good.

She started; "Hi."

"Hi."

Pause.

She started again; "Shall we decide on a movie first?"

"Sure. Is there anything you'd like to see?"

She smiled. He wasn't sure if she found him amusing, or if she was patronising him or what. He couldn't read her. Most people Russell thought he could, but Kristen, she was like an enigma.

"Let's go look," they walked inside and dodged through a small crowd. Being a Monday night, most people weren't out at the movies. A work and school night meant there would be less of a raucous crowd to put up with. They surveyed the time board above the cashiers. There were a number of movies on. Romance, drama, action, the latest drug fest, a great range, none of which Russell had seen.

"Anything you like the look of," he asked.

"A couple," she seemed lost in the options, "I wouldn't mind seeing Halt. Or that new one, Hippy."

There had been a spurt of single word movies lately. Russell wasn't sure if it was lack of imagination or just a trend. The first of her options was one of the latest drug related, fast paced movies in the tradition of 'Go'. Even the title was related. The second was an adaptation of a book. So far it had done reasonably well at the box-office, but nothing spectacular. Russell hadn't heard much about it.

"I don't really mind. I've told you before I'm not that good at making decisions," and now it sounded to Russell that he was practically saying he was a dim witted fool.

She dug into a pocket, "We'll flip for it then. What do you say? Heads for Halt, tails for Hippy?"

"Sounds good to me."

She flipped the coin and Russell made a mental note. This was a damn good way to make a reasonably simple and inconsequential decision. It was kind of cool as well. Trendy. But that was Kristen. Trendy.

She grabbed the coin in mid air and flipped it onto the backside of her wrist. She looked up at Russell and grinned. He could almost imagine a wink. But she moved her hand away and declared the winner, "Halt it is!"

"Okay. Well that starts in forty-five minutes. How about we grab something to eat first?"

"Sure. What would you like?"

She did that on purpose. Torture? Poking fun? Why were there always choices to make?

But he had an answer for this one, "Let's go to the Carillon," pronounced 'Carillion', "We can decide what we want from there."

The Carillon was one of the most reputable food halls in Perth. It had been around for years and everyone still went there. There was such a huge variety of food from Italian to Chinese. From Health Food to Junk Food. Hungry Jacks, Red Rooster, Wendy's Ice Cream to Aroma Café. A huge variety of everything.

The 'couple' walked around the Carillon's extremities, eyeing the range of food, some of the owners and workers shouting lines at them such as 'What would you like?' 'Can I help you?' 'Yes, Sir?' even when they weren't showing any interest. It came across as almost desperate.

Finally Kristen stopped in front of one of the Chinese stores and began to order. Strangely, and perhaps coincidentally, Russell had decided on the same thing. He had had Chinese from here before and found it well worth the money paid, both in quality and quantity. They literally heaped the plates high with a great range of wonderful tasting foods like noodles, rice and omelettes.

Russell was about to fork over money to pay for Kristen's meal, hoping to be chivalrous, but she beat him to it. Sheepishly, he waited for her to collect her plate before ordering for himself.

Maybe she was just independent. Maybe she would have thought he was being sexist. Maybe it wasn't the kind of thing you did on a first date. Then again, maybe this wasn't a date. He nearly kicked himself. Of course it was. Dinner, movie. It had to be.

They moved, along with their plates, to the back end of the Food hall. It wasn't busy. There were less than fifteen people sitting down, including Russell and Kristen, so it was to be a quiet meal.

As they ate, they started talking. From talk about dreams and aspirations to what their parents did for a living. Kristen wanted to study photography, Russell thought that was ironic with the number of journalists he'd run into, not to mention his own interest. But she's always working which made that kind of step too complicated, at least for the time being. One day she hoped to work for a magazine. Russell spoke of how he had wanted to become a journalist, until he realised what sneaky, conniving and pushy people they actually were. He also explained how he wasn't sure what he wanted to do, maybe delving in psychology, though he had no formal background and it would be more like a hobby than anything else. Then Kristen explained how her mother was a psychiatric nurse. Her father was a relatively successful businessman, but

111

she didn't know exactly what he did. He was hardly ever home so they tried to speak more of interesting things and forget about work.

"What are you doing for Australia Day?"

The question came after the conversation had lagged a bit. She spooned another load of food into her mouth and looked at him expectantly.

Australia Day, he thought to himself. That was... He checked his mental calendar. Two days away. Wednesday.

"Nothing. How about you?"

Australia Day was a mediocre public holiday. Nowhere near the intensity of Thanksgiving or Independence Day. Most people took it as a day to lounge about. There were a few celebratory functions, such as the night fireworks with an aerial display, the Aus. Day Concert at one of the bigger theatres in Perth and some families still felt the desire to celebrate with a good old Aussie Barbecue. To be honest, Russell didn't think much about it. He'd never had pride for the way the government in Australia works, and he wasn't too happy with the way the Eastern States believed themselves to be the superior end of the continent whilst those living in the West were backward and inconsequential. But if it were West Australia Day, Russell would have been up there with the flags and banners with the rest of them. The state and the city of Perth itself had to work hard to develop as well and as quickly as it had. To be considered the largest city in the world, though still not the capital of Australia, was quite an achievement, especially against the ever present New York, Tokyo and the other runners up.

"Dad wants me and mum to spend the day together over in Rottnest. Sounds nice, but not exactly my idea of fun."

Rottnest was a small island off Perth's shoreline. A small holiday destination that hasn't quite developed as well as Perth, mainly due to the Historical Society and the Conservationists trying to protect the war memorials and the Quokkas, small marsupials similar to Kangaroos native to and found only on Rottnest Island. Some holidaymakers liked to play a game termed "Quokka Soccer" which was very much frowned upon by anyone in their right mind.

"You'll miss the fireworks."

"No, someone told me you could see some of them from over on the island. Supposed to light up the night sky with hundreds of different colours."

"Sounds like the same effect a nuclear bomb would have."

"True. Still, it's supposed to be nice."

"Maybe you'll have fun...?"

"Oh, Mum will make sure I don't."

In general, they talked about most things from philosophy to work to current affairs and movies.

When it came time to actually sit in the theatre, Russell was so nervous he was afraid to move for fear of bumping her or making her uncomfortable or stealing her armrest or anything. But, all the while, he wondered if he should try to hold her hand. Soppy? Sure. Romantic? Maybe. Successful? Nope.

Russell moved his elbow, ever so carefully, onto the dividing armrest. Her own elbow sat more to the front of the thin strip, but he managed to nudge her 'accidentally' ever so slightly. So she moved it further away.

The whole length of the movie left Russell wondering whether that was a good sign or not, or whether he was trying way too hard, or… so many possibilities ran through his head, he started to see those familiar, yet somewhat stagnant, silver strands. Was he focused that much on making this a good date, or making a good impression? Why did he have to try so hard anyway? Didn't she like him for who he was without being over the top?

What if he was wasting his time?

The movie ended and Russell offered to walk her to her car. She accepted. They talked again, discussing the merits of the movie. Fortunately Russell had seen enough drug movies to get an idea what this one had been like, he added that knowledge to what little snippets he managed to let slip through his self involved thought streams and continued the conversation until he found a way out.

"But there is no way it could beat the classics."

Kristen looked at him as they walked, "What classics?"

"You know. Never Ending Story. The Muppet Movie. Labyrinth. Dark Crystal. THE classics."

She nodded, quite serious, "Let's not forget Princess Bride."

Russell almost slapped himself, "How could I forget. That show was brilliant! They don't make them like that any more."

"And that was so long ago, wasn't it," She jibed.

"Well, you know what I mean. But I did hear they intend to make a prequel to the Dark Crystal."

"It had better be better than the sequels to Never Ending Story."

"Totally. They couldn't afford to screw that one up."

They arrived at the lift that led up to her car. There was a pay station she had to insert her ticket in first and pay before collecting her vehicle. She slipped the ticket in and the sign flashed 'five dollars'. Again Russell raced to his wallet, "I can pay if-"

"Don't worry about it."

She then called the lift.

They stood in silence for a moment. Him unsure what to say, what to do. Her, he had no idea about.

The doors opened and she stepped in.

"I'll walk-"

"No. That's fine. I'll see you at work."

"Okay. See you."

The lift doors shut and with them so did any sense of ego Russell had left. He had only one thought running through his head.

"What the hell was that?"

CHAPTER THIRTEEN

Russell moped all the way back to the 'safe-house'. He took the long way round, nearly going home by mistake, so lost in his thoughts. He was so confused. He wasn't sure why he let it affect him so much, but what exactly had the night been? Was it a date? Or was it merely a friendly night out?

Why were things so complicated? Even when he had his own life to worry about, he goes and lets romance interfere and make it worse. Maybe he should have just shut his mouth, never picked up the phone and let her forget he'd ever asked. Maybe she wished he had. But she had accepted to go out. So did that mean there was something there? Is there always a kiss on the first date? At least he'd spent time with her in the first place. Which was more than he had before, which was probably why he had been so careless when he walked into the car park, setting off that blasted bomb.

But that could have happened to anyone, whatever mood they were in. He was just being stupid now and he knew it.

Maybe it would be better if the bomb had done what it was supposed to and wiped him off the face of the planet.

He found himself sinking deeper into sour thoughts. Not quite suicidal, just borderline pathetic whining.

He used a key Stacey had given him and slammed the gate behind him. He could really do with a Custard tart from his old neighbours.

What he was about to find out was that his night could go from bad to worse. Though he wasn't entirely sure why it had been bad in the first place, having had a good time and all.

He stepped into the lounge to find Pam and Stacey sitting, obviously waiting.

"What's up?"

"We've done some research. First of all, we had to find out which floor to look up. That was simple, just finding out which window needed repairs and who filed the damage to the Structural Advisement Committee in charge of CP2," Pam was being very efficient. The seriousness of her expression coinciding with the way her hair was tied tightly back gave her a strikingly severe look that had obviously caught Stacey's attention.

"The company that lodged the damage claim was one Peerson Corporation. CEO, one Trent Peerson."

With that, Stacey tossed a sheet of paper and a photograph onto the coffee table where Russell picked it up. Although it was one of those atypical dark sunglasses, 'trying to look inconspicuous' photographs, it was fully recognisable as Deep Throat.

"That's him. That's Deep-"

Pam looked at him, quizzed as to why he had stopped speaking.

Russell tried to push a little more with his mind but, "Nope."

"What is it?"

He dropped the photo back on the table, "I told you he was familiar. Like off the news or something. I nearly had it just then, but it slipped right through."

"You have absolutely no idea?"

"Zip. Nada. Squat."

"Not too helpful," Pam said, "All the same, we know that his offices are located several floors above where you were and we have the means to get to them."

"What are you saying?"

"They're not going to fix a window on a sky scraper's sixty-eighth floor in one day. Well, they could, but obviously they hired some shoddy contractors."

"So…" he questioned without actually asking. Both Pam and Stacey knew what she was getting at but Russell only had an inkling and he didn't like where it was going.

"So that's where we make our entrance. You told Pam yourself that you can fly. Cool. She can use her own telekinesis on herself and on me, taking us both up there with you. From there we can nip into his office, have a steal around and find out what we can, hopefully picking up your wallet in the mean time.

"You say that so casually."

Pam nodded, "He acts like an old pro at this sort of thing. Don't worry. It's sheer bravado."

"Hey, no giving away trade secrets."

"It's not half obvious, Stace."

"Yeah, but the kid didn't know."

Russell let himself fall back into one of the arm chairs, exhausted even though he'd been sitting in a food hall and a cinema for over two hours.

"Oh yeah, how'd the little date go?"

Pam's eyes lit up, "Date? You didn't tell me."

"Nothing to tell. I'm not even sure if that was what it was."

Stacey hung back, a little confused. It wasn't the reaction he was expecting. Pam, however, pushed on, "What do you mean?"

"Well-" Russell went on to explain the evening. Both of his companions listened intently. Neither said a word until he'd finished his tale.

When he had finished there was a small silence as if they were waiting for him to finish. Exactly the way Russell felt when the doors closed on the elevator. Maybe he was just being selfish.

"Nothing wrong with that, is there?"

Russell didn't want to be rude, but he ignored Stacey's question, hoping Pam would give a more precise and helpful response.

And she merely shrugged, "You could read that in so many different ways. Maybe she's not the touchy feely type."

Russell nearly blushed. That wasn't how he saw himself. But, all the same, neither response was all that helpful. What he needed was to change the subject.

"So, what are we going to do about this guy?"

Stacey leaned forward and pulled out a set of floor plans, "I got these from a friend of mine in league with the city council. They're only a drafted copy, but more than sufficient," He handed the schematics to Russell. He automatically tried to see where he had been held. Sure enough, he could see the corridor down which he had escaped, the window having been marked in by someone as having been broken. From there, he could easily trace his movements. The floor plan itself was so convoluted and twisted it was like a maze.

On a second page was a more symmetrical and organised layout, more in tune with what one would expect to find in an office building. There were a series of corridors with adjoining offices, one of which, situated in the North East corner was marked as Peerson's.

"What about security?"

Pam spoke up, "Most security in a building like that is located at the exits and the extremities. The window, having been broken but being located so high up the building probably hasn't been seen as a security risk."

Russell shook his head, "Not by the ordinary people. But they know I can fly. They saw me do it. They're bound to predict that's the way I'll go again."

"Not necessarily," Stacey countered, "It could be they are expecting you not to take the most obvious way in."

"Either way, I'm expected. The video card they left was proof of that. And whether we enter from the window or some other entrance, they'll still be waiting for us."

"No. They'll be waiting for you."

"Well they know about Stacey as well."

"Yes, but not me. We still have a few little surprises for them. It's now just a case of working out the details."

"I don't see why we don't just burst in guns firing and do as much damage as we can."

"As a journalist, Stacey," Pam all but chided him, "I'd expect you to be watching the news."

"You mean that politician? She has her wires crossed."

"Yes, but if we were to take such an offensive, cause such destruction, Peerson would blame it straight back on us and despite our little paper, he's most likely to have more pull in this city than us."

She had a point, and Stacey knew it. He drew back and listened to her idea.

"In light of the fact they'll most likely have that window covered, I say we take them from the inside out. Use the main entry. They won't be expecting three of us, we can use our media cards as our way in, claiming research or interviews or some such story. We could even clarify it with Harry. Thus get easy access to the fortieth floor that way. I wouldn't think they'll be expecting that."

"Or," Russell added, "We could still go from the outside, just not through that window."

This intrigued them both, "How so?"

"Who's going to notice another broken window? Or, who even said anything about another broken window. Your Telekinesis could 'unstick' the glass, we could make a quiet entry, using our powers only in defence, if we get discovered, nip in, look round, pop out and there we go. Finished; least amount of fuss."

There was silence for a bit. Stacey looked at Pam, who returned his gaze.

And they both nodded.

"Not bad," Stacey said.

"It's a pretty decent plan."

"Well, how about it?"

"Okay, sure. We could try it."

"We can do it," Russell corrected, "So. When do we go?"

*   *   *

It was three o'clock in the morning. Russell was hardly in any peak physical condition and with all the latest strain; a late night wasn't the most idyllic situation. They had all dressed appropriately in black. That way they'd be able to blend better inside, not to mention against the night sky as they made their entrance.

They were standing one block away. Distance enough to avoid any external patrols, if, of course, there were any. Russell was conjuring images of television shows where the bad guy had a huge compound with hundreds of armed bodyguards. Like Beverley Hills Cop. Kill one and hundreds more take his place. Not that he wanted to kill anyone. Nor that he'd have that many people in his employ for that specific job description, nor would the building actually allow him that sort of man power.

Basically, Russell was letting his imagination get too carried away.

He stifled a yawn as Stacey made last checks on equipment. They didn't have much. Torches, a small tool kit, just in case, gloves to prevent leaving fingerprints.

He gave his okay and Russell started to imagine what they must look like from afar. Three black clad figures huddled in the street like some sort of saboteurs or conspirators. If a police car was to go past, they'd be picked up for sure.

Pam looked over at Russell, "Are you ready for this?"

He nodded, "I think so." He was slightly anxious about using his powers to fly again. Sure it had been a thrill the first time. But was it altogether safe?

No. He couldn't afford any doubts. The winds hadn't failed him yet. They hadn't given him any reason not to trust them.

But what if his powers were only temporary?

What if the effects of the bomb were about to wear off?

Don't think about it!

Pam lifted into the air. She did it so casually, with such ease it was amazing to watch. Like a slow motion backward dive. She held her arms by her side, almost like a streamlined set of wings, more for effect than anything else, Russell figured. But hey, it was a beautiful effect at that.

Stacey went next, getting caught up in Pam's TK field. He was a little more unsteady about it, not being used to the experience and all. But he didn't make a sound. Merely followed her lead.

Then it was Russell's turn.

He could feel the night breeze already, now coaxing him to follow suit. He'd have to convince the winds to do what he wanted, or that was the way he saw it as being done. It was almost as if they were alive, responding to him in some sort of empathic connection. It would explain to some degree the way he felt a final completion to himself every time he really let loose with his abilities. Maybe that was the way it all worked.

But tonight, the currents were reading him. They kept pushing at him, sliding over his body. It wasn't long before he felt them lift him from the ground, replacing the solid earth with what felt like a solid landing of their own. The silver strands once more forming a kind of disco suit for him as it carried him higher and higher with such ease.

And he let it take him. Why argue with such a wonderful power. He'd always been fascinated by the elements. Earth, Fire, Air, Water. Earth was pretty standard, boring. Fire was exciting, the way it danced and moved, some people claiming it was actually alive. Maybe that was true. Maybe they all were. For, from Earth came life, such as trees. The same from Water. And the way the other two behaved at times, you could imagine them both being physical beings with minds of their own.

Was that the way Stacey saw his own power. His control of fire was intense, the way he could conjure a fireball as he had on Sunday. Did he sense the same connection as Russell? He was going to have to ask him later.

Most of the lights in the building were off. Everyone having gone home for the night. It didn't take long before the trio reached the missing windowpane. It was covered in semi-transparent plastic, no doubt hiding someone or something behind it, in wait of their next move.

But it didn't come in the way those inside may have expected.

They continued to rise and moved around the building, circling it until they reached the North East corner.

Russell crossed his fingers, hoping Peerson wouldn't be in. The lights were out, but that wasn't to say there wasn't anyone inside.

Carefully, they approached the glass, its surface revealing only a reflection of what was outside. If the lights were on, they'd be able to see, but that wasn't how this worked.

Once they arrived, Russell heard a small squeak coming from behind the glass and nearly panicked before he realised it was Pam at work.

There were four large metal screws, or clamps, one in each corner. Slowly, one by one, she was unscrewing them. They turned as Russell watched, barely able to see with what remained of Perth's late night-lights. Once she had them out, Stacey stored them away in a small backpack. All that remained was a sealant around the edge. That was where Stacey came in.

Pam moved him up to the window and he took a quick look at the substance. He then lifted his hand, pointed a finger and shot forth a tiny red-hot stream of fire. The sealant began to bubble and ooze, melting and some of it actually evaporating under the intense heat. It took him less than two minutes to do the whole way around the pane. When he had finished, Pam took control once more. With a barely audible whoosh as the air pressure inside changed, adjusting to that outside, she lifted the pane free. The strain of maintaining both her own and Stacey's height and now that of the heavy glass plate was beginning to show, but she soldiered on, turning the glass around so it was now on its side. She then moved it, base first, into the office.

Leaning it against the other windows, the three finally made their entrance.

No one was home. Russell sighed with relief.

It was a pretty big office, though. Hopefully he'd be stupid enough to leave the wallet in his desk draw.

But that wasn't the plan just yet. First, Stacey ran to the door and put his ear against it. He waited a few seconds before looking back at his companions and shaking his head. Then, he opened the door, slightly, peering out the gap before exiting into the secretary's office outside.

He was their first line of defence. Keeping his ear out for trouble, not to mention fending off the bad guys with his powers.

Inside, the other two got to work.

They both avoided the desk to begin with. Too obvious. Pam started running her hands over the other two walls, hoping to make out any secret compartments or hidden safes. Russell started checking the few cupboards. They were filled with pieces of art. Some things he'd never seen before. Others, he had seen in books when he was in high school doing sculpture. There were a few paintings on the wall as well, but he could only see the outlines.

Every so often he'd pause, wondering if someone was coming. Did he hear something? Was it just Pam checking or Stacey pacing? Had he been seen? Or mugged? Maybe they had taken him by surprise…

He didn't even bother scolding himself for being so pessimistic.

As far as he could tell, the draws to the cupboards were empty. The shelves only occupied by the art.

Then there was a small filing cabinet on one wall. Obviously most of his files were stored elsewhere, probably for his secretary to find. What Russell found were files labelled with some of the larger, well known companies in the city. He didn't know what they were all for and he didn't care. All he wanted was his wallet. He flicked through each one, hoping to find any references such as a loose card that had been dropped or hidden individually or the wallet itself. No such luck. This left only the desk.

Pam had finished her own search and met him by the chair. There were drawers on either side and that was where they started.

The first draw proved exciting, but fruitless. Like in all the movies, he kept a small gun in his upper right hand draw. Easy access for easy defence. Russell avoided touching it, wondering how many times, if any it had been used. Underneath were more files, probably current or recently finished.

"Russell. Look at this."

He stopped his search and looked up. Pam was holding one such file in her hand. Labelled 'D-day'.

"D-day? Deposit Day? Deposition?" He knew he was avoiding the obvious.

Pam pushed Trent's keyboard out of the way and opened the file on the desk.

Inside were photos, diagrams, and letters.

Unable to make any details out, Russell reached over to a small desk lamp and switched it on.

It lit up most of the desk surface including a small, framed photograph just below it, which caught Russell's eye. And his heart leapt to his throat for the nth time this week.

He finally knew why Peerson was familiar. It was so obvious. He hadn't thought about it before. If only he had put one and one together he wouldn't have found himself contemplating four.

It was a family portrait. All three individuals were tall, almost the same height, though one was sitting. The daughter. Kristen. Kristen Peerson. The daughter of the megalomaniac who had tried to kill him.

"Bugger me blue and paint me green."

Pam looked up, her confusion more than evident, "I beg your pardon?"

"That's her."

"Don't you mean him?"

He shook his head, "No. Her. Kristen. The girl I went out with tonight. I work with her. She's his bloody daughter."

"You're kidding me?"

"Look," He grabbed the photo and practically shoved it in her face.

She pushed it away, "I wouldn't know. I've never seen her."

He dropped it onto the desk, "Bloody hell."

"We don't have time to worry about that just now. This looks bad."

Trying to push the whole idea of dating this bastard's daughter aside, Russell looked at what she was talking about; the file.

Some of the photos were recognisable. The Entertainment Centre's stage. Except it was being decorated. Several workmen and women were seen hanging set items, rigging lights and sound or just standing around. From all indications, these were images of the Aus. Day concert. There were Australian flags, gum trees, life-size kangaroos, though only stuffed toys. All atypical items people for some weird reason associated with Australia, though most people never encountered any of those things in their lives, including the Australian flag.

"There's another bomb."

"At the concert. That would explain why Peerson wants Kristen at Rottnest," He couldn't help it. She was still slipping into his head.

"What?"

"Never mind. Where is it?"

Pam shuffled through the pages, trying to find any useful information, "It doesn't say."

"Guys. Someone's coming."

Stacey had stuck his head back through the door.

"How long?"

"They're at the lift. Two minutes max."

"Not enough time!"

Pam shoved the papers back into the file, "Look for your wallet. I'll keep looking around."

Russell started to check the other drawers, "Maybe on the computer."

"It'd take two minutes to load up. We don't have enough time," She continued to look over the documents, the photos, hoping to get any information.

"Got it!" He found his wallet in the bottom right hand draw, amongst some office items such as boxes of staples, elastic bands and paper clips. He quickly rummaged through it, checking it was all there. Licence, memberships, twenty dollars, bankcard and eighty cents in change. All there, excepting the one they had left at his home. Now he could pay Stacey back the fifty he borrowed for the date.

"Almost here."

"Go," Pam called, "I'll hold him off."

She pushed the file back into the drawer as Russell headed toward the window. Stacey came into the room and followed suit.

"Go. Don't worry, I've got you."

Trusting her completely, which Russell admired, Stacey stepped out into mid air and hung there, waiting.

Russell followed suit, drawing the silver wisps around him once more.

"Come on Pam."

The window came first. Sliding along the air like it was on rollers. Then Pam.

She literally ran out into the air, allowing herself and Stacey to drop below sight of the office. Russell once more copied as she adjusted the angle of the pane and slid it back against its housing.

Stacey then removed the bolts from the pack and she took them with her mind.

Russell couldn't help wondering what it would be like to have her powers. It was all so fascinating, how everyone was so different. Did they all act the same way, the powers? Did she actually feel the objects she was holding with her mind? Hers was, of course, a psychic ability. How far did that power stretch? Did it give her access to other levels of human consciousness, not quite telepathic, but Astral. Like in Astral Projections. Could she do that?

He was going to have to sit down with these two one day and find out what the deal was. Ask them all the questions he could, find out all the details.

These people, like him, were unique. Even more so than the average person, because Russell liked to think everybody was somewhat special. He wanted to know more about them.

Pam had three of the bolts in when Russell realised he could still see inside the office.

"The lamp! It's still on."

"Damn it."

"Can you turn it off?"

There was an instant flash of darkness from inside as the lamp switched off and the office lights went on.

"Did they notice?"

"Sshh."

Pam stopped her work on the window. There was nothing she could do while someone was inside. They were bound to hear.

A shadow fell upon the window and all three moved back against the side of the building just below, hoping it would give them sufficient cover.

It was slightly nerve wracking hanging hundreds of feet above the street with nothing supporting you but air, all the while hiding from someone standing only inches away.

Russell couldn't help himself. He craned his neck and tried to see who it was.

Peerson was standing directly in front of the window Pam had painstakingly removed and replaced.

His face was shadowed from the back lighting, but Russell could still make out the hard expression on it. He wasn't happy about something. In fact, with the added bonus of shadowing, he looked down right pissed off, to be blunt.

He stood there for only a short while longer before turning abruptly and disappearing from sight. The lights within went out and Russell was able to breathe again.

Pam hurried with the last of the bolts before the three lowered to the street below, making sure they were unseen.

CHAPTER FOURTEEN

"He sure wasn't happy about something," Russell was the first to speak.

"How so?" Stacey asked.

They started to head back to Stacey's Colt, which was parked only a short distance away, "When he was standing there. You just had to look at him and you knew he would have shot you with that gun in his draw if you said even the nicest 'Good day to you, sir' to him."

"Do you think he knew?"

Pam answered that, "I don't think so. Otherwise he would have been more active in trying to find us. I'd say something else in his day didn't go too well."

"Maybe he isn't happy that his daughter is dating his worst enemy, if that's what it was," Russell laughed, though he wasn't entirely happy with the idea himself.

Stacey blanched, "What? Kristen?"

"Uh-huh. There was a family portrait on his desk."

"Holy-"

"That's what I thought."

"You just say it more colourfully," Pam jibed, "That certainly was an interesting phrase you used."

"Just something I made up."

They arrived at the Colt and got in. Russell took the back seat. He was glad to feel the presence of his wallet again in his pocket. Though that sounded kind of weird, so he didn't say it out loud.

"But what are we going to do about this bomb?"

"Bomb? What did you guys get up to in there?"

As always, Pam explained it all for Stacey. But she did it in a shortened version, "We found a file up there. All evidence points at Peerson having organised a bomb to go off at the Australia Day Concert. Unfortunately it didn't say where it was or when it was to go off."

"So you're saying it could go off with a full audience?"

Russell remembered hearing a couple of things. One that the Aus. Day Concert had been played to full houses the last five years and the tickets, which were free but ran on the policy of first in, best dressed, had all been grabbed in the first two days of them being available to the public. The second fact was that the Entertainment Centre had undergone three upgrades in the past twelve years to cope with the population growth. It now held over thirty thousand people, not that everyone could see, though they had large screens around to display whatever was occurring on stage or the deconstructable basketball court. The Centre doubled as a sporting arena also. It just required the moving of seating and the erection of support grounds and the laying of the court surface.

If it was at maximum capacity crowds, who knew how many people would be killed or injured in a bomb blast.

"That and that the effects would be variable, which I didn't understand myself."

"What do you mean?"

"There was mention of a Doctor Eryn. The designer of the bomb. He has somehow created a bomb that may not only kill, but have other side effects. There was something mentioning research, cause and effect."

"And my key ring."

Pam shook her head, turning in her seat to look at Russell, "No. Not that I'm aware of."

"No. But that's what he's talking about. My key ring. I told you how they believed my key ring was the cause of the change both his men and I went through?"

"So you think they've built a bomb based on his research of the effects on his own men, trying to reproduce the same effect on ordinary people?"

"Possibly. Alternatively, he just wants to blow up a lot of people."

"Do you actually think he'd go that far?"

"Well. Not really. But maybe it's something along those lines."

"We already know he's willing and able," Stacey was looking in his rear view mirror as he talked to Russell, still keeping half an eye on the road, "You're proof of that. That car park was hit for a reason."

"Good point," Russell said, "I hadn't really thought of that. So you think he was targeting someone in particular?"

"Quite probably."

"Or it could be a trap for us."

"I doubt it. He's simply grabbed Russell, he could have killed him then," Pam pointed out.

They sat and thought for a moment, and then Stacey spoke, "What about the other theory? The one of using the effects on the people at the event?"

"What would he gain?" Pam, ever the analytical journalist, "Unless he's worked out how to mind control everyone, how will giving super powers to thousands of people benefit him?"

Russell had been thinking about this since he'd suggested it. Maybe it had nothing to do with benefiting him, "Who says it will help him? What if it is intended to hamper others?"

Pam turned in her seat, "How so?"

"I was watching the news. The government are talking about finding out more about people with powers, stopping them. There is a lot of money potentially backing that, not to mention the government's investigative resources. What if he's trying to screw the government?"

Stacey cut in, "I saw that report. That idiot woman."

126

Listening to what he was saying, he'd actually changed his theory, "No! Wait, I'm an idiot. Of course it is for his benefit! He's got subjects to experiment on. He is currently the only person to have knowledge of how the powers were created in the first place. Could it be that he simply wants to profit from the government's proposal? Be the scientific brain behind it all. He'd stand to make a fortune!"

"Not to mention the fact that the resulting uproar would be devastating. If it were to succeed. Think of the panic. Thousands of people getting super powers. There could be any number of possibilities. With that many people, with that many abilities in a city this size, it could have massive repercussions. The panic could lead to riots or people may abuse their powers, causing even more tension. At worst, it could become a military issue and people aren't just going to lay down and die like good little puppies. You can bet they, along with me, will be using their powers to fight for our freedom, thus spurring on more conflict. It would be horrible."

Pam's eyes widened, "And Peerson already has military contracts. He'd gain funding on that side of things as well.

"Wow. I didn't think of it like that," Russell really hadn't, "So, either way, we have to stop that bomb. Am I right or am I right."

Pam smiled encouragingly, "Of course, it has to be the latter."

*   *   *

They didn't get much sleep that night. They had a lot of work to do.

The Concert was to start twelve o'clock the next day. The audience would be there and waiting to get to their seats by eleven. Russell had been to one of these concerts in the past and found he and his family had been stuck in a crowded corridor, nearly dying of over heating and suffocation from having so many hot and sweaty bodies around. It wouldn't be too surprising if people died just waiting to get in, even before the bomb went off. Russell wouldn't mind that. It wouldn't be his problem.

First things first. Russell had to talk to Kristen, find out all he could about her father and whether she knew anything at all. Meanwhile, Stacey would be trying to gain access to the Entertainment Centre in the hopes of finding the bomb itself, if it had already been planted. Pam would be trying to contact the police to inform them of the situation. These were going to be difficult hours. Just how difficult, Russell wasn't sure. When he arrived outside the staff entrance, which was the one leading to the bridge and the train station, at ten to nine the next morning, he found out life was going to be hell, not only for the next day, but for who knows how long. As he approached Greyson's he spotted her. Kristen. She was dressed for work. Not unusual. And she was walking with Louis, who also worked in computers. A decent looking chap who was not dressed for work on this particular day. Russell thought nothing of it. He was probably just there to check rosters or to buy something. Maybe he was working in logistics for the day. Regardless, Russell started to speed up to catch up with them when the two stopped. They spoke briefly and once more, Russell nearly choked on his heart. This woman was doing that to him a lot lately. If all this excitement didn't kill him, she would.

She leant over and kissed Louis. First it was a peck. Just a quick peck. Friends can peck, can't they?

But she went 'in' again. And this time it was more than just a peck. Russell froze, barely three metres behind them. He felt his eyes widen, as if trying to work out a confusing 3D puzzle, hoping what he was actually seeing was an optical illusion. He tried to tell his brain that what looked like Kristen and Louis getting it on was actually Kristen looking back and waving at him. When Russell managed to blink, he saw part of that was true. She was looking at him. Her own eyes wide with surprise. She was no longer 'into' the kiss and Louis realised something was wrong, pulling away.

Kristen quickly covered her shock from Louis, "I'll see you after work."

He nodded, "Okay. See ya." He turned toward Russell. Smiled, acknowledging his presence. But then his expression changed. Louis did know. He knew what was going on. But he simply said "hi" and walked on.

Russell couldn't move. Couldn't speak. His life force had been totally choked out of him. Even his heart seemed to have gotten stuck in his throat and stopped beating from lack of oxygen. The wound in his chest, as if Kristen herself had actually punched into it, taken hold of his heart and shoved it up there in the first place was throbbing with pain, but his brain just wouldn't register, still hoping to see that same optical illusion he'd been trying for earlier.

Kristen approached.

Russell tried to cover his shock. He knew he was over acting in the first place. It hadn't been a date. He thought not. It had just been a friendly thing. But she knew that wasn't what he had intended. She knew it.

And he asked, "Why didn't you just say 'No'?"

"I'm…"

"No. Why didn't you just say 'No'?

"I…"

Forget this. It was like a switch in Russell's brain. It clicked over and bang. It was gone from his head. He had work to do. He knew he'd come back to being hurt later on, but he couldn't afford to worry about it now.

He actually shocked himself the way he had switched over so suddenly. It wasn't like him at all. Normally he'd mope on it for hours. But that was all the time he had.

"Kristen. You're dad. Trent Peerson?"

"I- I'm sorry?"

That's what she had been trying to say before. It wasn't what he wanted to hear then, nor now.

He spoke slower, more directly, aware that his manner had changed toward her completely. No longer emotional. No longer as a friend would speak. More robotic, direct, "Your father's name is Trent Peerson. Correct?"

Her confusion was more than evident.

Russell found himself having that effect on a lot of people, even before he had his super powers.

"Yes. Why? What about-?"

"Later. Is he at work today?"

She hesitated before answering, unsure where this was going, "He's been there all night. Are you going to-?"

"Why all night?"

"Russell? What is this?"

"Please, just answer me?"

Her confusion was starting to turn to annoyance. He was starting to run out of her time, "We had an argument last night."

"About Australia Day? Rottnest?"

"No," she was obviously annoyed by the personal and invasive nature of his questioning. Deep down, he knew he was wrong, but it felt good. Mind you, how much longer she would answer his questions was getting debatable and he needed these answers, "We argued about you, actually."

That surprised him out of his robotic trance a little, "Me? Why?"

"Russell-?"

His human side started to rear its head again, "Kristen, please? Why?

"She must have realised the answer was important, perhaps from the transitions he was making in his moods, especially having ignored the present situation, "He told me a couple of days ago he didn't want me to have anything to do with you. That was sort of the reason I said yes to you. Normally I do what he says, but that got to me a little. I don't like being told what to do. Well, not like that anyway."

"Do you know what he's doing tomorrow?"

"Yes. He's going to be at the Australia Day Concert."

"I don't think so."

She was offended, "What?"

"No. You don't understand. I don't think he's going to be there. Look. It's a long story."

"I have ten minutes."

"It'll take longer than that."

"I have a lunch break."

"Fine. I'll meet you when?"

"Twelve, this afternoon. Out here."

"Great. I'll see you then."

He turned without saying a proper good bye and walked off. He knew she was still standing there, confused. But he didn't care. He had to get away. The pain was back and it was starting to reach his numb brain.

He didn't want to think about it. But he couldn't help it. She'd said yes only to spite her arsehole father. How typical! He was a tool. Being used.

He broke into a run and let the thoughts fall to the wind, which he noticed began to pick up, cooling his face which had begun to seethe with anger.

*   *   *

"It was no good. They didn't believe me."

"I don't see why not," Russell had had time to calm down. Having returned to the safe house, he had met Pam who was in the middle of a heated discussion on the phone.

"Why don't you just check it out? You may just find I'm right...Well screw you too!" She had hung up the phone the way she would hit a thug trying to assault her. Russell had let her cool a moment before speaking.

"Because of my background. They needed to know who I was and I was stupid enough to give my name."

"So?"

"Think about it. A tabloid journalist who makes her living off of mock stories like aliens landing and conspiracy theories. He just happened to read that crud I write. There's no way they're going to believe me."

"What if I try?"

"You'd be wasting your time. He's probably put the word out on me trying to raise hysterics, probably explaining it by blaming me for trying to incite a story. You call up, you already have ties to my stories and you'll be outed and possibly hunted for interfering with Police, time wasting and fraud."

"But it isn't fraud."

"And you won't be able to prevent the bomb from going off if you're in jail so you're damn right it wouldn't be. Our job, hopefully, is to make sure my call is fraudulent. Anyway. How'd you go?"

He decided to keep his personal story to himself, "She had to get to work. I found out what he was angry about last night. Probably why he went to work. It was exactly as I had guessed last night, though I was only joking. He'd found out about me going out with her and he was, well, let's just say, none to pleased. I've got to meet her for lunch to find out more details."

Pam smiled and winked, "So it's going well then, huh?"

"Yeah, Well..." Russell bluffed, "Hopefully Stacey got on better than we did."

As if on cue, in he walked.

"No good. Those tossers wouldn't have a bar of me. I tried eight different people. Eight different stories and none of them'd let me in. Not as a health and safety rep, not as a journalist, not as a member of the Australia Day Committee, not even as bomb squad. Paranoid little-"

"They're just doing their job."

"Yeah, so was I."

"So," Russell piped up, "We've gotten zip so far."

"We could try a frontal assault on Peerson?"

"Violence isn't going to solve this, Stacey. That's what we're actually trying to prevent in the first place."

"We don't have to kill anyone, Pam. Just maim and injure," he joked.

"Sounds good to me," Russell murmured under his breath.

Pam gave him a look of concern; "You alright?"

"A-one and raring to go," He lied, "If only we had a place to go."

"Well, you've got lunch in a couple of hours. I'm going to try direct with the committee and see if I can get in. Maybe I'll have a little more luck."

"And me?"

"You can come with. Try your same lines. We'll go with the journalist aspect first. Stiffs like that might not read our paper. We may have more credibility that way. Even if we ask for a tour. That way you can get shots, humour them by including some of them in it. I'll ask a few stupid questions and see if we can just have a little look around back stage."

CHAPTER FIFTEEN

Pam wasn't altogether surprised the committee chairman went for it. He seemed pretty egocentric and the notion that his picture 'may' be published in a newspaper tipped him over the edge. Egos were so malleable.

Stacey, fortunately, had kept his mouth shut. He had a habit of being rash sometimes, though he was a decent fellow.

Presently, they were both waiting for Mr Wallace to show for the 'interview'. If all went to plan, they could get inside, talk for a couple of minutes, take some snap shots while searching the set and the surface of the stage. Then, if they were lucky, they could check the dressing rooms and the front of house. That would cover some of the areas. There was still the lighting rig, the bio-box and a number of other tunnels and nooks and crannies to be searched. Hopefully the back stage crew would be helpful in revealing those spots. If they weren't too helpful to begin with, Pam could always use her 'feminine wiles' to get their assistance, as long as they weren't all gay; which she doubted. She knew enough theatre people to know the stereotype wasn't true. Not all dancers or actors or crew were gay. Just a larger portion than the general populous. Who knows? Maybe creativity is connected to that mythical 'gay gene'.

She smiled at that. Her own editor was proof of that.

A dark car pulled up on the street. The freshness of its paint and the perfection of its lines implied it was the man they were waiting for. A wealthy man who delves into politics while dancing on the stock market. The man really didn't have much to do with the performance aspect of the concert, thankfully. However, Pam knew those that were on the creative task still weren't the most creative or tasteful individuals the city had to offer.

Pam prepped herself as she would any interview. She brushed her hair back from her face, made sure her breasts were at full advantage position and her clothes were immaculate. She had dressed for the occasion in a dress-suit, a low cut blouse and a high cut mini. Already having checked her teeth for food remnants and her shoulder for lint, she was confident she'd make a great impression. Here was her chance to play at real journalism. Even if it was a mock up.

"Mr Wallace, I presume?"

The man beamed at her, his eyes alight with unconcealed lust, for lack of a better word. The fact he was wearing a wedding ring unsettled Pam slightly, but it took all sorts. She had read in a paper once that the smarter the men, the more likely they were to be adulterers. This man didn't have much going on upstairs, but he was still up there with the big leaguers.

He extended his hand for that first touch of her supple soft skin. Or that was how she read it the way he rubbed his thumb over the back of her wrist. She felt a shiver run down her spine of pure disgust. Men like this repulsed her, but she was playing a part for him, so she had to deliver her lines.

She wished she'd stuck to drama in high school. She had delved into some amateur theatre. A lot of directors took her, merely for her looks, but she did have the talent to back herself up. Or at least she hoped she did. But her new lifestyle wasn't the most idyllic one for actors.

"It's a real pleasure to finally meet you, sir," play up to his power.

"The feeling's mutual. I've read your work and it's fabulous," He lied. If, indeed, he had read her work, there was no way a man of this position would be agreeing to an interview. He was definitely getting more than he bargained for.

"I just hope I can do you justice, sir."

He smiled, nodded at the compliment. Arrogant prick, she thought, all the while maintaining the sickliest sweet smile she could manage.

"Oh, this is my photographer, Sta-"

"Shall we go inside, Miss Dauber. It is Miss isn't it?"

"Oh, yes. Miss it is."

He laughed, taking her by the arm, invading her space and making her skin crawl even more, "That rhymes."

Oh god! She almost tore her arm free and slammed him with a telekinetic blast. But there was too much at stake. She could almost imagine what Stacey must be thinking. Almost.

*   *   *

What a shit head!

Stacey followed behind, making sure he wasn't too far away as to belt the guy if Pam so wanted. He'd already been tempted. How could anyone treat such a wonderful woman with such disrespect?

The sleazy creep had all but felt her up. And if he even tried to cop a feel, He'd be looking at being treated for third degree burns.

They were led inside to the foyer that actually ran most of the way around the building with gates marked from A to W. Pam asked to look around a little, get a feel for the place to "Set her juices flowing" as she put it. That spurred the sleaze on, no end.

Stacey could hear what the man was about to say, even though it still hung onto the tip of his tongue.

"Mind if I snap some of the set up out here?"

"Go ahead."

Stacey knew the implication there. Mr Wallace, or Wally as Stacey was thinking of him, was going to hang back with the lovely Miss Dauber, while Stacey left him alone to work his magic.

'Well, I won't be going that far, I can tell you,' Stacey thought to himself. He moved away, prepping his camera for some shots, all the while keeping an eye out for both the bomb and Pam.

"You know, you're name's almost identical to that Mindy lady."

"I'm sorry, sir?"

"You know. Mork and Mindy. She was mighty pretty too. But you, well, there's no comparison there."

"Why, thank you," Pam actually blushed. Stacey did too, but it was out of anger. Was she actually falling for this? No. She was too smart for that. But she was sure playing her part well.

Toying with some of the flags in the pretence of trying to straighten them out, Stacey check behind each one. No bomb in sight or out of sight as far as he could see. There was still a long way to go in checking out the foyer, but from all appearances it was mostly empty, to cope with the number of people.

There was a first and second floor walkway that Stacey could see above.

When he could get Pam's attention, he shook his head and she smiled.

"Do you mind if we go inside, Mr Wallace? I've always been excited by the theatre. And this one is so big. It's amazing."

"Not a problem. If you'll do me the service of having a photo with me later on, hmm?"

"Oh, Mr Wallace, I'd love to."

She wasn't blonde, and Stacey knew most blondes didn't behave like this, but she was playing almost too well to the stereotype.

Inside the theatre, it was dark. Stage lights were lit, though alternating in intensity as the operator checked which frenell or profile was attached to which patch. It looked spectacular already, if not over crowded. Pam had described the photos she'd seen last night. What was on stage now was similar, but beefed up more. There was a huge zoo of stuffed animals from Koalas to Kangaroos, Quokkas to Platypuses, Emus to marsupial mice, though the latter was enlarged for cuteness factor.

The stage itself was massive. Brightly lit in numerous different colours. The surface was a patchwork of flags from around the world, representing the performers that would appear there tomorrow.

The idea of the Australia Day Concert was to showcase the different nationalities and cultures within Australia. From English to American, Russian to Cambodian. Everyone was represented here with either song or dance in a four-hour production. Then at the end, as they did every year, they would come together and sing three songs. First was the National song, which still hadn't been made the national Anthem, 'Advance Australia Fair', which Stacey thought sounded like a funeral dirge. Pam, though a proud Australian, had agreed with him. The other two songs, both of which would have made better Anthems or even National songs were 'Waltzing Matilda' and 'I still call Australia Home'. At the beginning was a massive dance piece involving the whole cast where they sang an excerpt from 'Advance Australia Fair' followed by

'We are Australian'. Another song that would be better representing the country.

In all, it was a load of sentimental hogwash as far as Stacey was concerned.

"It looks fabulous!"

"You think so?"

"Oh, yes. The colours. The animals. It's so Australian."

"Well, I gave the final approval."

"It couldn't be more obvious unless you added a few naked ladies and a tonne of whipped cream," Stacey grumbled.

"I'm sorry, did you say something?"

"Oh, I was just thinking I'm going to have one heck of a time trying to capture all this beauty."

"I'm sure if you're as talented as Pam, here. You don't mind if I call you Pam, do you?"

"No, of course not."

"Well, if you are as talented as Pam here, you shouldn't have a problem," He turned back to the lovely lady and continued aloud, "If he isn't, you should find yourself better help."

Pam laughed, flashing a warning look to Stacey who was about to take a swing at the prick's head.

He recovered and decided it was time to get to work.

He headed down through the large double doors that lead from the foyer into the auditorium and down the stairs, thumping heavily as he went, imagining he was stepping on Wally's face every time.

He kept his eye out along the rows of chairs, hoping to catch a glimpse of the device. No such luck.

The bomb would have to be huge. To do any serious damage or have any real effects, it would have to be the size of a car. Perhaps as small as a motorbike. Though, Stacey wasn't too sure of that. He wasn't a mechanical genius or bomb specialist so he was only guessing. But he figured it was better to start off big than worry about the small at present.

The problem was, how was one man supposed to get a good look at a stadium that seats thousands of people, not to mention backstage and everywhere else?

There was no sign of anything out of the ordinary as far as he could tell, apart from the massive gum trees made out of ply wood and the stuffed animals. Maybe one of them concealed the bomb? That would be very theatrical.

He hurried down onto the stage. A man dressed in black stepped up and stopped him, crossing his arms.

"It's alright. He's a journalist, with me," Wally called.

Okay, Stacey hated to admit it but that had been very useful. The man stepped aside and Stacey smiled his thank you before proceeding to the menagerie. Testing each one, he lifted them only slightly. Nope. Not a one over weight. They were simply stuffed. He then moved around the trees, hoping to spot something.

Nope. Of course, it wouldn't be hidden in plain sight for a techie to see.

So where was it? He looked up to the lighting rig. There were a few odd pieces up there, but it all belonged, such as the speakers, the seats for the follow spot operators to sit. Then there were the two massive screens on either side of the stage, one above it and several smaller ones dotted around the stadium. Anything could be hidden behind there. Maybe if he could get a closer look.

"Did you want to take some photos?"

"Sure," He had heard the slime approaching. His stomach had unceremoniously growled as he took the last step onto the stage, sending both he and Pam into fits of laughter. The way she was behaving, Stacey was actually starting to dislike her. Fortunately he knew what she was really like. He certainly didn't envy her position right now.

"I was wondering. Would it be possible for me to get up there to take a shot down toward the stage and the audience?"

He pointed up at the lighting rig.

"What for?"

"So I can have you, the main figure standing amongst such a massive backdrop. It would be fantastic, right Pam?"

"Totally. Think of it Mr Wallace," She stepped away from him, spreading her hands as if revealing a whole new landscape to him. It was as if she could actually see what she was describing, and as she talked, so could Mr Wallace, "You and only you amongst the tremendous array of sets and lights and seats. You'd be the central focus. All eyes would be on you wondering, 'Who is this charismatic man? Why is it the world is revolving around him? What makes him so wonderful?' Which is something I'd like to find out while Stacey here sets up."

"Well. If you put it like that, how can I disagree," He clicked his fingers, "Hey, Charlie," No one looked up, "You, in the black shirt," every one looked up, "You, messing with the wombat. Show this gentleman up to the rig. He wants to take some photos."

The man he was talking to; obviously not Charlie, nor a tour guide stood up to his full height. He was one tall bloke. Stacey was almost too afraid to go with him.

The man was about to say something when one of the women back stage spoke up, "Just do it, Troy. Humour him."

Troy grimaced, "This way."

Stacey hurried over to him, not wanting to upset him by keeping him waiting. When they were on their way he apologised, "Sorry about this. It was his idea. I just point and click."

"Whatever."

She was out exactly on twelve.

Russell had been waiting for fifteen minutes for lack of anything better to do. When he saw her this time, however, he felt the pang in his chest once more and he quickly looked away, his face turning a bright shade of red. Not out of anger or embarrassment. He just felt flushed. He didn't want her to see him looking at her. Nor for her to see him looking the way he did. The latter he had no choice on, but when she stepped out the door, he avoided making eye contact with her.

"Shall we go somewhere and sit?"

Russell simply nodded.

He turned around and started to walk back toward the inner city. She had to jog a little to catch up.

"Look, Russell. I'm sorry. I should have told you, but-"

"It was cruel, but I'm over it now. Let's just forget about it."

He slammed his hands into his pockets. He wanted to think about the bomb. But the only thing that came into his head was about Kristen. How much he liked her as a friend or whatever. But he couldn't look at her in that way any more. He couldn't look at her at all.

"Then you can tell me what the grilling was about this morning."

"I told you, it's a long story."

"I have an hour. You may as well start now."

"Okay," He paused for a moment, not too sure how to approach it. The simple truth would probably be the best, "You remember last Thursday. The explosion and all that?"

"Yeah. Hard to forget."

"Well, something happened. The bomb, it was, I don't know... Defective somehow. Well, I made it defective, by accident," He was starting to lose direction. Already. It was just talking to her that was distracting.

"You made it...?"

He quickly corrected himself, "No. I accidentally did something that set the thing off early. It also affected it somehow. I don't know what happened, but... Something happened. Anyway. I saw the van the bomb was in. A Mazda, white."

"Okay. So you saw a van. And?"

"I was later attacked by a similar van, obviously not the same one. A group of people tried to kidnap me or kill me, I wasn't sure."

"My God, did you call the police?"

"No. I had no real evidence," He covered. He knew the reasons were different, but still, "I was again chased later on, but managed to get away. Which brings us to Sunday."

"That fateful day," she said it so seriously. Maybe she was.

"You don't know how much so. It started that morning. The second explosion. It happened just up the road from my apartment."

"Coincidence?"

"Yes. Their target was an abandoned building. I'm still not sure of the motivation for those first two explosions. But at that second one, the same van that attacked me was there. So were the men. A friend of mine showed up. We followed them, got into an… altercation but we got away."

"This is getting a little complicated. But I still don't see how this all ties in with your questions."

"I'm getting to that. But I warn you, you're not going to like it. And no, I'm not saying it out of spite. This is too important to be kidding."

He sensed her mood change a little. He still couldn't look at her, but she slowed up a bit before regaining the lost ground, "I don't like the sound of this already. What is it?"

"That afternoon, as I was leaving work. I was attacked again. Aiden was hurt."

"That was over you?"

"No. Not just me. A lot more. Aiden just happened to be there and tried to help out. I feel bad about that. But it was the same men from that morning. They caught me. Kidnapped me. I was taken to this room where I was interrogated by two other men," He stopped again. He didn't want to say it. He knew even after his assurances, she was going to take it the wrong way. If what had happened this morning hadn't happened, maybe she'd be able to believe him more easily, but there were no guarantees now, "One of them was your dad. Trent Peerson."

She stopped, "Oh, yeah, right!" She turned around and started to walk back to Greyson's, "What a load of crap! Couldn't you think up something more pathetic?"

"Kristen, wait!"

She spun back, her face as red as his. She was furious, but more upset really, "I'm not going to listen to this kind of bull about my dad! How dare you! You have no right to say that!"

He finally worked up the courage to look at her, "Kristen! I'm telling you the truth. This has nothing to do with what happened this morning. I have proof. Well, I don't but… Look. Something is going to happen tomorrow and your Dad is going to be responsible."

"Shut up!" She started back to Greyson's, her arms flinging wildly.

He had to go after her. He couldn't just leave her like that. He hurried after her, catching up as she refused to run, an obvious sign of weakness, or at least that's what she thought.

"I'm sorry. Kristen, just talk to him. Ask him. If not, thousands of people could be hurt."

She stopped once more, looking directly into his eyes. He felt his own stinging. Her's were red, near tears, his own weren't far off. The number

138

of times they had shared a moment like this. Just looking into each others eyes from across the floor. From one department to the next. Then she'd always smile and give a little flick of her head, as if clearing a non-existent lock of hair from her eyes. It was a greeting and one he found most endearing. She gave no such flick this time. Instead she just stared, searching his soul, it seemed, trying to work out how honest he was. And she knew. She could see it in him that what he was saying was true. His eyes were always open windows to his soul. She could almost read who he was from simply looking into the deep blue eyes she had often admired. He was a good man. A good friend. And right now, she could tell he was an honest one.

"How?"

"What?"

"How will they be hurt?"

"A bomb. We think it's a bomb at the Australia Day Concert. That's why he wants you out of the way. Please, just ask him. This isn't about his vendetta against me, or mine against you, not that I have one, but this is far more important. Just ask him."

And that was it. He couldn't look any longer. He left. Simply turned and disappeared down the walkway. She didn't follow. She simply stood and watched as he vanished into the crowd.

"I'm still sorry," she whispered, hoping the wind may just carry it back to him.

*   *   *

Russell wasn't sure whether she'd do it or not. And even if she did, what would it accomplish. Maybe he'd reconsider it.

He stopped mid-thought.

The wind seemed to be whispering to him. A single word echoed in his ears, barely audible, but he knew its meaning. He closed his eyes for a moment and thought about nothing as he walked. Thankfully there were no people or poles in his way. When he re-opened his eyes, he was focussed again on the problem at hand.

Maybe he would change his mind if she asked. Maybe there was some good in Trent Peerson. Then again, after everything that has happened. Maybe not.

He hoped Stacey and Pam were having more luck than he was.

CHAPTER SIXTEEN

A small metal staircase, a long winding inclined tunnel and a small storeroom later, Stacey and Troy finally made it to the entry to the gangway that led to the lighting rig.

"Thanks. I'll be fine from here."

Troy grunted, still not happy with having been called away from his duties, "Touch nothing. Got it?"

Stacey tightened his lips into a thin smile and nodded as innocently as he could. Troy was more than happy to leave the cockney behind. He actually hoped the guy would get lost or killed by the ghost of the theatre. There was always a ghost in the theatre. Even the new ones. Someone was always killed on the land it was built on, or in the case of the older ones, inside the actual theatre. There were rumours about the ghost in the Entertainment Centre. A big fat opera singer. He had choked on a burrito only twelve years before. Ever since, he had haunted the dressing rooms of the female leads. Never letting up on his singing when they were applying their make up, or so the women say. The man, one Georgio Halberti, had been a reputable womaniser. Troy figured the reason he only sang when they were putting their make-up on, was because he had just seen them come out of the pre-show showers. He figured he'd be singing then too if he were a ghost.

Stacey could hear a small rumble from above. Machines at work, perhaps the air-conditioner. There was a small doorway that led back out to the backstage and a web of walkways in front.

Stacey made his way around, taking a few shots as he did so, for both cover as well as the view was quite spectacular. The spread of colours still dancing across the already bright stage and its menagerie of Australian plant life and animals, mixed with the patterns of the steeply inclining seating tiers enshrouded in darkness would make a well contrasted photograph. Instead of Wallace being the main feature, Wallace would actually be the main distraction. From this distance, however, you could hardly see the portly sleaze, though as Stacey zoomed in to check up on Pam, he could still see Wally with his arm around her waste, guiding her here and there to show her one unmiraculous marvel or another.

He knew he couldn't take too long. It wouldn't be fair on Pam. Not to mention he didn't like the idea of another man touching her, well, except her boyfriend, but even then...

He hurried along the gangway, running his eyes along the speakers and lights and then the auditorium, hoping to spot something. He even used the zoom to try and look at anything suspicious in the auditorium. But nothing out of the ordinary as far as he could see.

Once he had a few shots he could show Wally, he made his way around to a second exit from the gangway. He found himself in another storeroom. But where as the first one was empty, this one was full of signage pieces for advertising and boxes of set items and lights. Two doors led from here. The first to a third storeroom, packed full of boxes. A real possibility, excepting the fact none of it had been moved for what seemed like centuries. Besides, back here, it would have little effect on the crowd. The second door went out to another stairwell.

The grey concrete walls were lit only by intermittent fluorescent lights that revealed a range of multicoloured wiring, a steel length of piping as a banister and the stains that marked the walls and steps. Water or paint or whatever.

He took a couple of mood shots. Some of these images would be worth keeping later on.

He shortly came across a door part way down to the bottom. It was marked 'Authorised Personnel Only. Keep Out.'

Stacey never liked being told what to do. Besides, what sort of journalist would he be if he paid attention to those sort of signs?

He turned the handle and stepped into a large room with monitors lining the walls. This looked to be some sort of security room.

"So this is where it all happens."

Four people looked up. They all had close cropped hair, as if they shared the same barber, though he wasn't quite sure if they were all men either.

"What the hell do you think you're doing in here?"

"Wally… I mean Mr Wallace is doing an interview with my colleague. He asked me to come up and talk to you about how impressive the security set up is," He lied.

There was stillness and silence as the four people contemplated this. Then one of them shrugged, "Yeah, we run a tight ship."

Stacey smiled, as if impressed, but more at his own skilful escape. He walked across to a bank of monitors and examined the camera angles. Most were filled with techies adding finishing touches to lights, set or otherwise, however, one, labelled loading dock, seemed to be a hive of action.

"I can see. Mr Wallace was saying you lot were keeping things in order," He turned to regard them all. Were any of them working for Peerson? How could you tell? He kept talking, "I mean it's a pretty huge event. Thirty thousand people. Wouldn't want anything to go wrong."

Not one of their faces changed expression.

He spun back to the monitors, "So what's going on down there then?" He pointed at the loading dock, "It looks like it's busy as."

"They're just installing the boards down there," one, a woman it seemed, answered, "It's all going down there," she pointed at another monitor that showed a point just in front of the stage, "See. They're just bringing in the equipment now."

Stacey craned to have a look. Sure enough, several other people in black were carrying large lighting and soundboards, copious amounts of cables and computer equipment such as monitors toward the area she had indicated.

The bomb? Stacey thought. Could be.

"Great, thanks. Now, if you'll excuse me."

He made his way back out the same way as he'd entered and onto the stairs.

He poked his head back inside, "By the way. You sure have a great view from up here. How much would you charge for these seats?"

He vanished behind the door just as a large clipboard made contact with it.

"Charming," he laughed as he made his way down the stairs. Had to be fit to work here.

He watched the walls as he went. Solid concrete. There'd be no point putting a bomb here, especially like the one that went off in the car park. It caused damage to the cars, but the building itself wasn't massively damaged. With this much concrete, the effects wouldn't touch the audience. It had to be in the stadium itself.

Unless, maybe the building would collapse if the bomb was put somewhere strategic. Mass carnage, lots of death, but that didn't sound like what Peerson was aiming at.

When he reached the bottom, he was greeted by a crew in black t-shirts helping carry the equipment out the front.

He looked at his watch. It was already two o'clock. They had been here for just on fifty minutes. Most of that had been fumbling around back stage with Troy, trying to spot anything out of the ordinary. Much of it was, but nothing resembling a bomb. He had continued being awe inspired, or at least playing as such, by the workings of the back stage of the Centre up to the point Troy all but threatened to tie a fly rope around his neck and let it go.

Just to be on the safe side, he tried to get a look behind the screens as he walked from the backstage onto the stage proper. Nothing. He started to feel a little annoyed and frustrated. They hadn't gotten anywhere. Other than the equipment they were moving in, which he still had to check out, there had been no indication that a bomb was present. Had Pam been right in the way she read it? Or was Peerson just playing a practical joke? Maybe there wasn't a bomb at all and he was actually targeting something else. Or someone.

"Ah, here he is. Did you get your photos?"

"Just a couple more," He said as he hurried straight past them. He could see Pam was starting to tire of her charade. The look on her face when he appeared was one of gratitude and relief. When he walked straight by, he could see she was about to snap.

He stopped on the edge of the stage and lifted his camera. There had been a spot cleared for the equipment directly centre stage and a few rows back. He focussed his zoom, trying to spot any oddities about the lighting and sound boards, but came up with zip.

They seemed a-okay.

Still, a closer look would be better. So he jumped down and hurried to where the people were setting up.

"Do you mind?"

"Yes!" One man all but yelled.

"Fine, bite my head off. I just wanted to have a look."

"You shouldn't even be here," chimed someone else.

"But I am and I want to have a look," he declared almost childishly.

"You can sod off is what you can do."

He didn't respond. They were being snappy. That was their prerogative. But he couldn't see anything wrong with the equipment. Hurrying back to Pam and the sleaze he declared loudly, "Yup! Got the shots! They're gonna look fabulous!"

*   *   *

"You git! What took you so long? Another five minutes longer and he'd have had that slimy tongue down my throat."

"And don't say you didn't want it!"

Pam punched him hard on the arm.

"Hey what was that for?"

"The guy was horrible. He even tried to cop a feel."

If Stacey had seen the smirk on her face just after she'd said that he would have realised she was joking. But, as she predicted, he was a rash man who acted before he thought.

He was halfway to Wallace's car before Pam could grab him with her TK field.

He was literally seething. With his powers, the smoke had actually started to steam out of his hands.

"I was joking, Stace. If he had tried, I'd have flattened him."

"If I was there, you wouldn't have had a chance. He'd be charred cinders by the time you even thought about it."

She laughed. She knew how he felt about her. He was very protective. She even knew the way he wanted to see their relationship. And she wouldn't have minded. But he'd have to make the first move. Dealing with Pat would be a cinch. They'd been talking about it for a while now and with neither of them really ever home at the same time any more, who knows. But that was for another time.

"Did you find anything?"

"Nothing that flashed the words 'Bomb. Please disarm.'"

"You weren't expecting that, I hope," she joked.

143

He laughed, "It would have been nice. Civil also. You'd think those homicidal rich kids would at least have the courtesy to have something like that."

"Which world are you living in?"

"Uh- hu- Hmm."

He was lost for a come back. Never mind. They laughed anyway.

"Well, after I have a shower and wash the slime away, we can meet up with Russell, see how he went."

"Everything okay with him?"

"How do you mean?"

"He didn't seem all too chipper this morning."

"He's always a little moody. Perhaps finding out his girlfriend just happens to be the daughter of the tyrant trying to kill him has played with his mind a little. He'll get over it."

"I guess so."

"Why, Stacey Brownlin, are you getting concerned on me? This could be the beginning of something completely new and wonderful."

"Not on your life, sweet cheeks. So, how's about one of them tonguies," to emphasise the request he stuck out his enormous tongue and flapped it in the air. It was truly disgusting. She was sure he could touch the bridge of his nose with that thing, not to mention do whatever else with it.

"Eww. You're even worse than Wallace!"

"No one is worse than Wallace."

*   *   *

When the other two arrived at the safe house, Russell was already lying on the couch, a mug of tea sitting empty on the coffee table and a pillow over his face.

"Hello?"

He removed the pillow and sat up, surprised, "Hi, how'd it go?"

Stacey shook his head, "No luck. Not a thing. Not that we really had the time or resources."

"How about you. How did lunch go with Kristen?"

"I don't know if she'll talk to him, but I hope I got through to her."

Pam looked a little concerned, "How did she take it?"

"Better than I expected, I guess."

"Are you alright, lad?"

Russell smiled reassuringly at Stacey, not really fooling anyone, but letting them know he'd rather not talk about it, "Everything is peachy. Just peachy. So what do we do now?"

No one said a word. No one knew the answer.

"We were hoping to find the bomb so we wouldn't have to worry about that bit."

"That's what comes from being too optimistic," Russell explained.

Pam did some explaining of her own, "And if we were all so pessimistic, we'd have blown the bomb ourselves, right?"

"I guess," Russell hung his head slightly, a little ashamed. But he had a right to be a little angry.

"So, we sit around and wait?"

"Or we find Peerson, keep an eye on him and see what goes."

"Good idea, Pam, but how do we find him?"

"Russell?"

He shook his head, "Nope. Not me. I don't even know where she lives. They have a silent number so it isn't listed. All I know is she lives somewhere in the outer suburbs."

"Great. So I guess it's up to her now."

CHAPTER SEVENTEEN

He came home later than normal. Meeting, he said. Was it?

How could she look at him the same way? After everything Russell had told her. What if he was lying to get even for her being such a bitch?

No. His eyes would have told her. He was the only person she knew whose eyes told you everything. As long as you took the time to look, that was. He had such nice blue eyes. They always changed with his moods though, and boy was he moody.

But he may have been misled. Maybe it wasn't her dad.

She was waiting for him in the living room when he came in. Her mum was out at a Taibo class.

She heard the car, sat in silence as the doors closed and he trudged along the gravel path to the front door. The keys jangled as he found the right one. When he did so, he slid it noisily into the lock and turned the knob.

It was already unlocked.

The only light in the living room was the lamp beside the sofa. She sat, curled up against the opposing arm, away from the light, practically covered in shadows. She didn't want him to see her face. Not yet. But she wanted to see his. To see if he was lying, or if what Russell had said was true.

He locked the door behind him, not even bothering to look up and see if anyone was home.

"Daddy?"

He jumped, the keys falling to the floor.

"Kristen? Is that you?"

"Yes."

He bent down to pick up his keys, "What are you doing sitting in the dark, honey?"

Same old dad. He couldn't be doing what Russell said. Could he? No!

But she had to know. He had seemed so desperate. So honest. Even after what had happened.

"Dad, can you come in here, please?"

"In a minute. Let me just-"

"Please. Now?"

He stopped, a little unsure of himself. Yes, she was behaving strangely. She knew it. Now he did too.

"Is something wrong?"

"No. I just want you to sit down with me a while. So we can talk."

He smiled, thinking he understood. He placed his laptop and briefcase beside the door and stepped down into the living room.

"Where's your mother?"

"Taibo. She always has Taibo on Tuesdays.

"He nodded again, making his way to the other side of the couch, "That's right, I forgot. So. What did you want to talk about, and why all the darkness?""

The time was now. She had to ask. Not directly. If he could explain himself without her having to push too hard or too far, that would be better, "Dad. What's happening tomorrow?"

"You and your mother are going to Rottnest. I've arranged it all-"

"Why?"

"Don't you want to go?"

"Yes, but, why aren't you coming?"

"I've got work, honey."

She could almost hear the incorrect ba-boom from an old television game show, Family Feud.

"It's Australia Day. No one is working. Even the finance sector is shut for the day. Nothing is open on Australia Day."

"Delis are," He tried making light of the situation. She wasn't sure if he knew what he was getting at or not. She tried keeping her voice neutral. She didn't want to come on too strong. If Russell was wrong, she couldn't lose her father because of that. She wasn't even sure now if she was doing the right thing. But his eyes…

"So why are you working?"

He didn't say anything. Under the light, she could see he was fighting for an excuse. She knew already what he was about to say was a lie, "We have a big take over in the works. I have to oversee-"

"No one works on Australia Day, Dad," time to try a new approach, "What's happening at the Australia Day Concert?"

His head snapped up, trying to see her in the dark. Even silhouetted by the lamp, she could see the surprise in his eyes, "Why?"

"I'm thinking of going," she lied.

He moved closer to her, feeling for her hands, which she moved away. She didn't want him to touch her. Not until he explained himself. Why was he lying to her? What did he have to hide? She could already feel a lump forming in her throat. This was her own father she was questioning. Why was there a need for her to do that? What was he doing? Why wasn't he telling her?

"No. Honey. I arranged for you and your mother to go to Rottnest."

His own voice was starting to crackle. He wasn't so sure of himself.

"But I want to see the concert. I want Mum to see it, too."

"There aren't any seats," He snapped quickly.

She shook her head, "You've arranged seats for me before. For other concerts."

"Not this time, Kristen. I can't."

She tried to swallow, feeling it catch, "Dad."

"Yes, honey?"

"What is going to happen at the Australia Day Concert, tomorrow?"

147

He looked away, "I… Kristen… I don't like where this is going. Who…" He turned back, "Why are you having a go at me now?"

He was going to ask who she had been speaking to. She knew it. Russell was right. She didn't know what, whether it was a bomb or what, but he had something planned. Something bad and he couldn't tell her. He was lying to her.

"How could you?" She stood up, moving away from him.

He started to rise, "Kristen. Nothing is going to happen. Who have you been talking to? That Russell kid?"

"How could you?!" She screamed at him.

"Don't you raise your voice at me!"

"I asked you a question! How could you?"

"You don't understand. You couldn't understand!"

She lowered her voice, "Try me!"

"Honey, we stand a chance at being on top. I can't-"

"On top? We are on top? We were on top of the world until this."

"You weren't supposed to know."

"What? Wasn't supposed to know what? That you were planning to kill people? That you already had people kidnapped, beaten?"

"They're all lies," He reached out to her with his hand and with his voice. He was pleading for her to come back to him. But how could she? Not now. This wasn't the man she knew. This wasn't her father? How could he be?

Her father was a family man, a loving, caring, gentle man.

When she was younger she remembered looking up to him as if he was God himself, leaning down to protect her. Now she could only see him as the demon he really was.

"How could you!" She screamed; an accusation more than a question. She reached for the deadbolt, unlocked it and disappeared out into the night.

"Kristen! I-"

There was nothing more he could say.

CHAPTER EIGHTEEN

The next morning came with a beautiful sky. No dark clouds as an omen to what was to come. The sun was bright, the clouds white and fluffy. Russell had thought about the term, every cloud has a silver lining. From all his experience of late, he was starting to believe it. What with his new found abilities giving him the ability to see air currents as silver wisps, he just wished the figurative meaning was true as well.

But it was more or less behind him now. He really did have more important things to worry about.

As he walked into the room, he found himself walking into the tail end of a conversation between his housemates.

"Ha ha. Very funny," Pam saw him and quickly changed the subject, "We were just trying to see if we could spot anything."

Russell spotted an image of some technical looking junk, "How about that?"

"The lighting board? As far as I could tell, it was clean. It's possible all the different components housed different parts of the bomb. But it's very unlikely. All work the desks have to do to begin with, it would probably blow before the end of the first tech rehearsal, which they had last night. And there was nothing in the news this morning about it."

"So, still no idea?"

"Not a thing."

Russell fell back into an arm chair, "Well, I'd say we're royally screwed, not to mention a few thousand people as well."

"It's not over yet, Russell."

"Yet being the operative word there, Pam."

She ignored him, "Our best bet would be turning up. The least we could do is try and contain the blast when it happens and protect as many people as we can. Are we at least up for that?"

The two men nodded, determined not to fail at this.

"Well then, boys. Our sponsors and I have a little surprise for you then."

Russell leaned over to Stacey, "Who are these mysterious sponsors of ours?"

He shrugged, "Search me. She's the only one who has claimed to know them. I'm just hoping they're pretty reliable."

"Well they've done wonders for this place."

"You boys coming?"

Pam was at the door, waiting for them to follow.

"Where are we going?"

She raised a finger to her lips, "Sshh. It's a secret."

"Oh, don't be coy, woman."

"Stacey, humour me. We could all do with a little of that before we get into the grit this afternoon."

They did so without another word of complaint.

She led them both back toward the main entrance. Russell hadn't bothered checking the other rooms as yet, so he had no idea where he was going when Pam stopped at one of the doors on the right. She took hold of the handle and addressed her two companions.

"What you are about to see, you must promise not to laugh at," she was nearly laughing herself, which got the other two quite discombobulated. What exactly was she up to?

"What you are about to receive, you must promise to utilise to its full potential."

She paused once more.

"What you are about to do, you must tackle head on and do us proud."

"Come on, Pam, cut the crap and let us in already."

She laughed out loud now, "Fine. Gentlemen, I now introduce to you… Your new costumes!"

With that she flung the door inward to reveal a mid sized room, its walls a stark white. It was completely devoid of furnishings. But on the very far wall, three hooks protruded from the wall. And from those, three hangers. And on those, three not so garish, but very, very awkward looking heaps of material. They had no form, having been hung directly onto the hangers instead of display mannequins.

"You've got to be kidding me," Stacey beat Russell to it, "Costumes?"

She adopted a hero stance, hands on hips, legs wide apart, "We need to protect our identities," this was a new side to Pam Russell hadn't seen. He had heard tid bits from Stacey on her exploits with the chairman, but Russell thought he was joking.

"But won't protecting our identities by masking our faces actually create a little more tension. You know, masked vigilantes?"

"Oh come on, Russell. Just for today at least. Try it out. Who knows, looking at it from your perspective, we may never have another chance to wear them," she joked.

"Hey, I'm not always that negative!"

"I know, just toying with ya. The people in charge want to give them a test run, get public opinion polls or something. Now, grab your gear and get ready. We've only got a couple of hours before lift off."

It wasn't hard to see whose costume was whose.

Stacey's was on the right hook. A mixture of flame red and orange. There were hints of other colours there, but it appeared it was all done in 'flame' motif.

Pam's was in the middle. Crimson red with a lot of dark patches. She was bound to look hot in that one. Mind you, Russell thought, she looked good in anything.

The last costume, Russell's, was more sombre. Grey was a major colour, a deep almost wolfish grey, he supposed to represent storm clouds. The rest was made of black.

He slowly removed the hanger from the wall. Stacey followed suit.

"Come on guys, chop-chop. They should be the right size."

"But I was never measured," Russell argued.

"Just try them on. You'll see."

"But I'll look ridiculous."

"Russell, if you don't go and try it on now, you'll be hard pressed to convince me you aren't always a negative little git."

He exchanged glances with Stacey who looked as enthusiastic as he did. The Cockney shrugged and disappeared out the door.

*   *   *

To be honest, Russell's most embarrassing moment was the support. 'You just can't wear tights without a support', Pam had said. It sent shivers down his spine just to think she'd probably been the one to look after that little detail. Or anyone would have to look after it at all.

He put it on and found it also to be the most uncomfortable item he had ever worn, that was on top of the costume itself.

It's only just this once, he was thinking to himself. The way the damn thing was riding up, as it was supposed to, he could be sure to stay focused the whole blooming time.

When he put on the rest of the costume, after the initial difficulty of telling which was front and back, he was far more concerned about how his physique would look.

He wasn't exactly Arnold Schwarzenegger, was he? He was lucky to have pectorals at all, let alone biceps.

Thankfully, however, whoever designed the thing had taken that into account. There was some sort of padding built into the costume itself. He wasn't sure if it was some sort of armour or what, but when he looked in the mirror, he had a very decent, if fake, build. He smiled, "Not bad. Not bad at all."

There was a knock on the door, "You ready yet?"

"Give us a moment."

He had a cape. It was big, majority grey with a black patterning on the back. It could attach to the costume by the wrists and the collar and lower back. It looked pretty cool in theory, but how would it stand up in practice? Was it more aerodynamically in tune? Would it help him lift off better? Or would it just get in the way?

The last item he had to put on, other than adjusting the boots that made up the bottom end of his costume, was the mask. It was negligible when it came to protecting his identity as Pam had claimed.

It barely covered his eyebrows. But it sat snugly, adjusting easily to the contours of his face.

It was complete. Checking the mirror on the backside of the cupboard door, he made sure everything was on straight and sitting right.

The design on the body was pretty decent, as well. Again, mainly black, with black swirls down either leg. These extended from his upper thigh where the costume became completely black until it reached his waist line where, again it broke into cloud-like whiffs that ran up either side toward his arm pits. Matching patterns ran down from his collar to just above his wrist.

In all it was a pretty decent costume and it fit rather well, though he was still concerned as to where they got the measurements from.

As he stepped into the hall, he felt slightly self-conscious. At least, until Stacey stepped out of another room a moment later. He, too, looked pretty good. The flame motif actually made him look taller than he actually was. There was no cape on his, simply the base costume, but it actually stretched up his neck and the side of his face, stopping short of covering his hair. Russell wasn't sure how it stayed up like that, but it looked good. Stacey obviously had the same sort of padding in the costume because he looked like he was capable of lifting a truck.

"This padding is pretty cool, huh? Makes you look like Superman or something."

Stacey regarded him curiously, "What padding?"

Russell shut his mouth, more than a little embarrassed.

Pam was already dressed. She arrived from the stairwell. And to say she looked good in her suit was an understatement in Russell's point of view.

"How are we supposed to do anything with you looking like that?"

"Feelings mutual, Stacey."

He began to blush.

"Okay. We can't exactly go in like this," Pam continued, regardless, "We'll wear civvies over the top. If and when there's trouble, we may need to spruce ourselves up. But it is entirely up to you."

"Sounds cool to me."

"Ditto," Russell said.

He had already found the cape detaches at the wrist and can be wrapped around his body so it didn't look weird under his clothes. So he did as Pam suggested - wore his ordinary gear over the top, dressing up slightly for the occasion.

CHAPTER NINETEEN

They arrived at the Centre at Eleven o'clock. Television and radio journalists were already making their way in. But from the looks of it, through the glass that made up the foyer's external wall, the crowd was still kept outside and was gradually increasing in number. Soon their numbers would be spilling into the street.

"We don't have time to wait," Pam stated the obvious, "We'll flash our cards and get inside."

"What about me?"

"You stay out here. Keep an eye out. If anything suspicious happens-"

"Like someone choking on a hot dog or passing out from heat exhaustion?"

"Like the bomb going off out here instead. Just be at the ready."

He nodded, keeping his eye on the street, hoping to make out a familiar white Mazda van. No sign as yet. But there was a massive car park a few streets away for it to be stored.

Then a thought struck him, "Pam! Stacey! Wait."

They hurried back to him, "What?"

"The car park. What if they're attacking the car park again?"

She considered it for a moment. Then shook her head, "Too obvious for one. And no guarantees that someone will get caught. The weather could take it up and away from the crowd."

"Oh, come on. There will be thousands of people."

"Well, keep your ear out. We're spread too thin to be able to deal with that many options. It could be the train station for all we know. Hundreds of people will be taking public transport today. Just keep an eye and ear out."

He nodded, surveying the crowd as the two disappeared inside.

Great. All alone again. Then again, maybe this was better. If he could spot Dufus or Pipsqueak around, maybe he could distract the bad guys from setting the bomb off. Unless, of course, it's set on timer.

He looked at his watch. Brilliant. Ages to wait.

*   *   *

Inside, it was dark still. Some television cameras had been set up by the corners of the stage. Some men and women were carrying the portables, attached to hip braces to prevent drastic shaking and unsteadiness.

"There are so many places it could be," Stacey whispered to Pam.

There were too many people around to speak too loudly. They'd draw attention to themselves and any mention of a bomb would probably have them arrested.

"We just have to keep looking."

"I'll try back stage again. Maybe I'll be able to get around better with all the cast out there."

"Let's hope so. I'll stick out here. Maybe I'll spot someone or something."

They split up. They would have been wasting their time sticking together. Besides if the bomb went off underneath their feet, the best thing would be to have the only other help as far away as possible.

She watched as Stacey vanished out through one of the stage doors. It was now up to her to check the front. Sticking close to the journalists who were already present, she tried to listen out for any suspicious talk. All she heard, however, was the usual babble; some annoyed insults and received a few dirty looks.

These guys were no help.

Opting instead to do a once round the stage, hoping to spot something she, once again, failed to spot anything out of the ordinary. The only place left for her to go was into the seating.

Slowly, but casually, trying not to draw too much attention to herself, she moved up toward the make shift lighting and sound set up. There were two men working there already, going through preliminary tests, warm ups on the equipment and making thorough checks as to whether the boards were working correctly.

"Excuse me," she started.

"Yes," neither man looked up.

"I was just wondering. Last night, did you have any technical problems? Was everything running smoothly," she laid on a bit of the 'ditsy' air, hoping to fool them. What she had asked obviously caught their attention. They both looked up.

The man checking the lighting board answered, "Not particularly, why?"

"Just doing a comparison on the new Colonial Stadium in Melbourne. They had a few glitches, I believe for the Barbra Streisand concert a while back. Just wanted to make sure that we, a proud Western Australian establishment, are running perfectly."

The guys smiled. No evil here, she could tell, "You can count on us, miss, to keep things running right. We'll show them why we're the best city."

She smiled sweetly, "Thank you gentlemen. Much appreciated. Now if you'll excuse me, I want to check the state of your cleaning services."

They nodded in acknowledgement, sort of like a curt little bow and she moved off, up the stairs into the darkened auditorium.

Absolutely nothing. She could feel the frustration setting in. This was pathetic. How hard would it be to hide a bomb?

Stupid question, she knew.

Looking back and forth down either side of the isle, she watched for anything suspicious. Anything at all. And came up with zip.

With all the seating and all the aisles in this place, it would take hours to check them all.

She concentrated, pushing out lightly with her telekinesis, letting it fan out along the seats and around them, like covering then all with a tight fitting sheet.

It was hard work and took a lot of concentration, but she continued to push, feeling for anything out of the ordinary. Still coming up with zip.

"Oh, this is getting ridiculous."

"I'm sorry, ma'am?"

She spun around and found herself looking into a very broad chest.

"I'm trying to find my seat, she covered."

The massive behemoth looked down at her, quizzed, "It's first in best dressed, ma'am."

"As you can see by looking at me, sir, I know that," She played the prissy card this time.

He looked a little embarrassed and she hoped she didn't look too intimidated. A man this size should not be physically possible. He was gigantic.

"I meant, ma'am, that you can find a seat anywhere and take it."

She smiled, as if actually understanding what he meant, "Oh, so if I wanted to sit in that box over there, you'd let me?"

The man looked where she was pointing, finding it hard to turn around.

"Uh. No ma'am. That's for the Premier and his family."

"But you just said-"

"I know, Ma'am. I am awfully sorry. I was mistaken."

"What are you doing, you idiot?"

A smaller man, at least a quarter of the size of the first appeared. He spotted Pam and his eyes nearly leapt out of his head.

"Oh. I'm sorry to interrupt, ma'am. I didn't realise he was working. He has a tendency of wandering off."

"Oh, no. He was being most helpful. In fact, he has helped me chose my seat. Thank you very much gentlemen."

With that, she made her exit.

These two weren't kosher. In fact, she wouldn't mind betting they were the two both Russell and Stacey had encountered before. The size of the first man was unnatural and he did fit their description of him.

Well. At least she now knew they were in the right place. But why were they here if a bomb was going to be going off?

She paused for a moment, looking back at the two men who were watching her eagerly. She smiled and waved coyly before making her way down to the Premier's box. She had to play out the charade, at least for a little while.

"You idiot! You're going to get us into trouble!"

Good. They were still in earshot. Pam stopped, bending over to check her shoe, as if she had a stone lodged in it.

"We'll be in trouble anyway if we don't find her."

"No sign of her yet?"

"Nope. I was just checking the stairs when I started speaking to that one."

"Well keep your mouth shut and your eyes open."

She'd heard enough. Standing up again, she proceeded down to the box.

Who were they looking for? Was someone of importance supposed to be arriving? Maybe the bomb was designed to kill someone in particular. The Premier? But that was a man. So who was 'she'? Unless...

* * *

Stacey was lost. Once he had strayed from the actual back stage area into the change rooms, he knew he was out of his depth. He had already checked the sets, the people, and the loading docks. They had all come up empty.

He wasn't even aware of the changing rooms until he opened an out of the way stage door and stepped into a crowded corridor.

There were names listed on so many doors, he was surprised how many people this place was meant to hold back stage alone.

Still, each room was a potential hiding place for a bomb. He had checked several already. A lot were still empty. Being an hour from curtain up, he though that was a bit odd. Maybe the talent had gotten lost in the maze of corridors back here.

There was no sign of a bomb, or any sort of casing that could house a bomb at all. Most of the rooms were either filled with costumes, people or completely empty.

He approached the next door on his left and knocked gently. There was no reply so he opened the door.

There were several shrill screams as a number of scantily clad women hurried to cover up.

"Oops. Sorry. My apologies. I really am sorry."

He hurriedly shut the door and turned around to the one on the opposite side and nearly bumped into Trent Peerson himself.

"Holy..."

The tall man, whom he had only seen in the photograph, was stalking along the corridor, his eyes scanning the crowd.

Not having seen Stacey before, or at least he hoped, Stacey continued to move confidently across the corridor. Once Peerson had passed, he moved in behind him, trying to remain inconspicuous.

But what was this prick doing here? Shouldn't he be holed up somewhere away from the bomb?

Maybe he knew Russell knew.

Why were there always so many maybes in this business? There were never any straight answers. The same with journalism, really. No one could ever give a straight answer. Always the convoluted babble. Even if it's a question on the weather. Stacey knew he should be used to it, but found it hard to resign himself to the negatives of life. Though he had heard one politician amazingly give the following response to a simple question as to how he found the weather during his holiday in France:

'Well, according to the meteorology board in Venezuela, I have been informed that the effects of the continental weather patterns in Europe may adversely have a positive effect on the farming markets in China.'

A load of hog wash, no matter which country you come from.

But it paid reasonably well.

It still didn't answer his question, though. What was Peerson doing back stage when a bomb was set to go off in who knows how long?

Then he heard the man speak.

"Where the devil are you?"

This was his chance to get some answers, "Have you lost someone, Sir?"

Peerson turned on him, his anger and frustration very clear from the distance between them.

"What's it to you, you little piece of pommy shit?"

The corridor went silent. All the eyes turned to glare at the man who had spoken. And with his height, he stood out like a sore thumb.

Stacey smiled, "Not really a good idea, sir. Australia Day is the celebration of multi-culturalism in Australia. That sort of attitude doesn't go down too well."

Peerson bent down so only Stacey could hear what he had to say and there was no doubting what he said as he said it slowly and concisely, "Get out of my face or you'll regret ever coming to this God forsaken country."

Well, now he definitely wasn't going to get any straight answers. So Stacey continued to follow the prick at a safe distance as he continued on his way down the corridor, continually scanning the crowd around him.

*　　*　　*

It was nearing eleven thirty. The doors would be opening soon; thousands of people would pour into the auditorium, like sand through an hour glass. Except you'd be hard pressed to turn this flow back around. Russell could sense the excitement in the air. He could also feel the temperature in the foyer rising to about forty degrees centigrade, even with the air-conditioning.

Time for a little cool change, he thought.

With a slight nudge, he beckoned a few cold currents to sweep in through the glass doors to sweep over the crowd. He could hear a number of sighs as it caught up to some of the more elderly people. Everyone else simply kept talking, or yelling.

It was paradoxical. The louder one person talked to be heard over everyone else, the louder everyone else talked until it was a wrestling match to see who could out scream who. It was crowds like this that really got up Russell's nose. Being somewhat claustrophobic, he had problems with large crowds. Though, with his new abilities, especially the one he had just used, he found it easier to cope.

It was hard to see anyone in this crowd, or anything that looked suspicious. There were just too many people, a lot of whom were taller than him. He could see them clearly enough.

Sighing in resignation he looked back toward the entry into the foyer. And spotted one tall person in particular.

"Kristen!"

It was no good. She couldn't hear over the noise.

What was she doing here? He had told her about the bomb. Was she trying to get herself killed? He didn't even know when the damn thing was going to go off.

"Kristen," He knew it was useless. She was being sucked deeper into the crowd and further away toward another entrance.

As far as he could tell, she didn't look too happy. In fact she looked a little worse for wear as well. Still managing to look amazing, however.

Maybe she had talked to her dad. Maybe she had convinced him to stop the bomb. Maybe. Maybe. Maybe.

"Oh for goodness sake," He began to make his own way after her. He had to find out what was going on. Was the bomb going to go off? Had her father changed his mind? Had he lied to her and she was here simply to prove a point.

"Back off, loser!"

"I'm sorry," He tried pushing around another way.

"Hey, watch it! We're all going to get in, you know. Just be patient!"

It was no good. People were blocking his every move.

"Bugger me blue."

And then the doors opened.

He was nearly swept under foot as the crowd began to move along with the uprising of a choral sigh of relief and appreciation.

He managed to keep his footing and follow the crowd along. There was no fighting against it. He noticed they were checking tickets at the door. He didn't have one, but from the look of how many people pushing through without being checked, it appeared he wasn't the only one.

So he pushed harder. He had to get to Kristen and find out what was going on.

He watched her head bob its way through the other end of the crowd, getting pulled further away and toward another gate. Damn it, he was going to lose her.

Hopefully Pam would spot her. She'd seen her in the photo. Maybe she'd recognise her, pull her aside and work everything out. She had a knack of doing that it seemed.

He reached the door, receiving a couple of knocks, but finding the extra padding underneath was useful in more ways than one. He nearly laughed when he bounced around into people, like bumper cars. He barely felt a thing, though everyone else was giving him dirty looks.

Trying to keep his fun under control, he focussed on his support and the matter at hand. There was too much at stake to buggerise around.

He was swept inside, straight past the door ushers and finally found himself in relatively open air. Although it was enclosed, the auditorium was far more airy than the foyer. He could actually see the swirls of silver highlighted against the dark ceiling dancing to and fro with the motion of the air-conditioner. Good, he thought. I have plenty of firepower.

People stopped pushing him forward and started to fan out to the sides, trying to find a decent seat. Most of the lower seating had been nabbed already. Russell stood back from the door and tried to survey the crowd, hoping to spot anyone he knew.

It wasn't until he looked over at the Premier's box, traditionally kept aside and empty for the late coming delegates that he spotted Pam having a heated discussion with an usher.

He needed to get to her.

Pushing on with the crowd, he circled down the stairs and back up to the box until he reached Pam and the man she was talking to. She was remaining calm, almost laughing at the situation while he was turning a bright scarlet as he explained the seating was reserved.

"I'm awfully sorry for my sister," He took Pam by the elbow and leaned in closer to the usher, "Medical condition. Doctors say it's only temporary after the crash."

The man froze, his mouth open ready to respond. Thought better of it and apologised.

Russell merely smiled and led Pam away.

"I'm surprised he fell for that one," Pam muttered.

"Kristen's here."

"What?" She was incredulous.

"I saw her. She must be inside by now."

Scanning the crowd for herself, Pam muttered, "So that's who they're looking for."

"What do you mean?"

"Your two friends. The ones from the cathedral you were telling me about. They're here looking for some woman. I'd say it's her. She must have had a talk with daddy and threatened to come here to stop him setting off the bomb."

"Bomb?"

They both turned to see a young woman wide eyed and staring at them. She vanished into the crowd in moments but her concern was all too clear.

"We better keep our voices down. A panic would be worse than a-"

Russell nodded his agreement.

"Where's Stacey?"

"I haven't seen him for ages. I've been out here looking around, using my TK to do a fairly thorough sweep of the auditorium and can't find anything. He's out back somewhere, still looking around."

"We can't let the show start without finding out what is going on."

"Well, I don't think the thing will go off while your friends are here. And if she is here too, I have a feeling Daddy won't be far behind."

Looking at the hordes pushing through the doors and up the stairs toward the middle and back rows, Russell couldn't help thinking of them as ants or mice. And if they didn't do something soon, they'd all be going down with the ship.

"There she is!"

Russell pivoted to try and see where Pam was pointing.

By the stage. There was no missing her. Everyone else was seated while Kristen was making her way toward the central steps that lead directly onto the brightly coloured stage.

"She's going to show herself to her father. Let him know she's here."

"She could get arrested," Russell said, "If she's carted away then there would be nothing stopping Peerson from going ahead."

"Not if we can stop the authorities."

"How so?"

"Follow me," Pam started to stride down the stairs, taking them two at a time and Russell hurried closely behind, "We have to reach her before she gets up onto the stage. That way Peerson will see who she's with and we can give her a little defence from the police."

Taking the long way around due to some wheel chairs that had been set up in the isles, the two heroes hurried toward Kristen as fast as they could. They found they were actually able to manage a jog. There was no need to be inconspicuous now. Besides, there were plenty of techies running around doing last minute checks. They'd be like one of the crowd.

"Kristen!"

The girl faulted. So did Russell. That was Deep-Thr- Peerson.

He had appeared out one of the stage doors beside the stage. One, Russell assumed, was meant for the entrance of some of the performers. The doors swung open again, narrowly missing the first man and revealing a second. Stacey.

Russell had to get her attention, "Kristen!"

She turned at the sound of his voice.

She was only a few feet from the central stairs.

Pam continued her approach, slower now, keeping an eye on Peerson.

"Oh I see you've found her," Stacey said. Peerson, for the second time, turned on him. "Get your foreign little arse out of my face!"

"Gladly!"

He grabbed at Peerson, taking hold of his arm. He then proceeded to twist both it and the taller man around into an arm lock, so as his arm was lifted up against his back.

Peerson called out in pain as Stacey moved him forward.

"Leave him alone!" Kristen cried. Her voice full of emotion, but it didn't seem quite sure it knew which emotion to be.

She wasn't coping too well with the situation. That much was obvious. Russell didn't blame her.

Pam was nearly to her when the girl started to back away, eyeing the strange woman warily.

Things were going really weirdly, as far as Russell was concerned.

By now a couple of the audience members had started to take interest in what was going on.

Russell had to try again, "Kristen. She's a friend. You can trust her."

"No! I can't trust any of you! I can't even trust him. My own dad!"

Peerson, who had been manoeuvred around the side of the stage toward the other members of the drama that was unfolding by the stage, looked up at his daughter. Russell could see he was hurting, both physically and in other ways. Obviously he hadn't meant for her to find out. And from what Russell had learnt on the 'date', they had been close. There was no repairing this sort of tear in a family.

"You can trust me, can't you?" Russell tried.

She shook her head and jumped up onto the stage.

This got the authorities' attention. From the side-lines a couple started to move forward, unsure whether this was part of a pre-show display or not. One of the sponsors was Relationships Australia, of course. Maybe they were getting their two bits in.

"Back off!"

A new voice, followed by a bright green flare of light. Stacey was knocked backward as it connected with his chest.

'How would my padding hold up against that?' Russell thought.

Peerson broke free and rushed toward his daughter.

Not if I can help it, Russell nearly said. But it sounded too stupid so he merely ran and jumped up onto the stage, between father and daughter.

Both Dufus and Pipsqueak appeared from the crowd. Some of whom had stopped moving just to see what the light show was about.

"Where is it?" Russell yelled.

Peerson stopped, looked around at the crowd and then at the heroes before smiling nonchalantly, "I don't know what you're talking about."

"I'm talking about what had Kristen so upset."

"We had an argument, that's all."

"I'll bet."

"Dad! Stop it!"

"What? I haven't-"

"Stop all this bullshit!"

Her father was speechless, as was the crowd now. That kind of language was rarely used in a community based production like this. There were children and elderly present.

And then the earth began to quake. Russell could feel the suspension in the stage working to its peak efficiency, but the audience wasn't so lucky.

Russell turned to see the cause of the disturbance charging straight at him and nearly lost control of himself.

Dufus was not just a big man. He was like an elephant, and to see one of those heading your way, you knew you were in deep trouble.

"Uh-uh," Pam said ever so calmly.

And in an instant, Dufus went flying. He somehow tripped over mid air and somersaulted upward and forward, landing hard on his back toward the rear of the stage.

Boy did that woman have power.

She leapt up onto the stage herself and headed toward the giant brute.

"Don't even think about it," Stacey called to Pipsqueak who was raising his hands toward his female companion.

"Fine," and he shot a bolt of green energy at Stacey instead.

Stacey countered it with a small fireball that met it midway and exploded into a shower multi-coloured sparks and accompanied by a round of applause from the audience.

"Kristen. Come over here. We don't have time for this."

"How much time do we have then, Mister Peerson?"

Peerson ignored Russell as he tried to reach out to his daughter, "Kristen, please."

"Stop the bomb."

She said it so simply, but her delivery captivated the whole front seven rows.

"Since when did the Greens get a part in the Australia Day Concerts," one little old lady in the front row asked her neighbour.

"I can't. Eryn programmed it. I don't know how."

"Then I'd suggest you get him to do it," Russell informed the man. Peerson wasn't looking too good himself. He was looking almost green and very pale, as if he were about to throw up.

"Will you shut up! This is between me and my daughter!"

"Yeah, let him speak!" One audience member cried out, receiving a few laughs of his own.

At the back of the stage, Russell was aware Dufus was now back on his feet and looking none to happy. But Pam was there to head him off. It looked ridiculous. Such a small and very attractive woman against a bull of a man.

But that wasn't going to be a problem as Russell was about to see.

Dufus lashed out with both hands in an attempt to grab hold of her. But the air around her flashed a bright purple.

"Let's see how you last against someone your own size," and with that, a misshapen ball of purple light began to expand and reform until it was about Dufus' height and size. The man, not to mention the audience, watched in awe as Pam then corrected its shape, giving it arms and legs. In the end it was a veritable Sumo wrestler she was standing right in the middle of. Pam had adopted the stance of the Telekinetic man she had manufactured, linking her own movements to those of her creation.

Dufus took one moment to size up his new opponent before taking another swing.

She blocked it easily and made a lunge at him herself. The purple figure wrapped its arms around the man and began to literally wrestle him.

On the other side, Pipsqueak had taken the offensive again, sending a spray of energy balls at Stacey. The Cockney managed to lithely dodge a couple before careening backward in the air under the force of one of the emerald projectiles.

This was going to be one interesting confrontation.

"Kristen! This is your last chance. We don't have any more time."

"Dad, I can't. How could you?"

He could see Peerson was more than a little desperate. But he couldn't just accept defeat like this. So he couldn't stop the bomb. Maybe one of his friends could, or even himself.

"Where is it?"

Peerson looked at him for the first time, actually seeing him, "What?"

"Where is the bomb?" Russell called a little louder.

There was a horrible silence that spread through the audience at the mention of an explosive, this time the performer actually seemed to mean it.

From the looks of it, both Pam and Stacey had their hands full. It was up to Russell now. He had to find the bomb and put a stop to it.

"Mister Peerson, please. For the love of your daughter, where is the bomb."

"I…"

The audience was completely involved in the drama. Not entirely sure what to make of it, they watched in open mouthed awe as the four people traded supernatural blows while these three seemingly ordinary people debated between the trust and love of one's family and something they weren't quite sure of. And where did this bomb come into it?

Kristen and Russell called out together:

163

"Daddy, please!"

"Mister Peerson! Please!"

He answered. He finally answered. Defeated, he mumbled, "You're standing on it. It's under the stage. I'm sorry Kristen," and he bolted into the darkened auditorium.

Russell was speechless. Under the stage. Under the supports.

He had to act.

"Kristen, get out of here."

She was staring down at the floorboard beneath her feet, captivated by the idea she was standing on a bomb. Probably not registering it as being fact rather than fiction.

"Now!"

She looked up at him, finally realising what was going on. But she didn't move. She simply shook her head and said, "No."

"Fine. Then help me get this up."

The flooring had been laid in segments. Each segment was coloured with a flag of one country or another. They were only about two meters squared, but they weren't as light as they seemed.

Russell dug his fingers into the groove and heaved at the sides. He wasn't doing too well until Kristen came over to help. With her added effort, they managed to slide the cover aside to reveal exactly what they were looking for.

Hidden and supported amongst the suspension works for the stage - a large and very complicated piece of machinery. Its dark metal reflecting the bright lights from above, creating so many new curves and shapes to its already convoluted surface. The only thing Russell was able to identify was a bright red timer that was slowly ticking away the final few seconds on the count down.

"Run," He said it so simply. So quietly, he wasn't sure if she had heard.

She looked up at him. This item represented all the lies her father had been telling. The final truth to all the mess that had made its way into their lives.

"For god's sake! Will you just get the hell out of here?"

He stood up, addressing the whole crowd.

"All of you! Get out! Get out of here now!"

There was silence. Even the fighting had stopped. Everyone's attention was on Russell, his small figure commanding a huge presence on the massive stage. Even those sitting at the back had stopped. But no one was sure what to do.

"This is no show! This is for real! Get your arses out of here."

He looked down at the counter. There was no time. He watched in silent horror, though his own voice was still echoing through the auditorium, as the counter reached the final count down.

And he focussed as hard as he could. There was no margin for error. He snatched out with his mind, forcing all the air currents in the building

164

to bend to his will, his control and to do his bidding. He reached out...
Out through the entrances. Out past the foyer and into the open air
outside and yanked, for all he could, the currents that were dancing out
there.

Before the bomb exploded, the glass wall that made up the foyer's
external wall shattered inwards under the force of the air under his
control as he commanded it to come to him.

The wind was doing as he bid and it was doing it with such force even
he wasn't sure what to expect.

It started as a quiet whistle through the entrances as the first of the
silver strands answered his call, but it built up in intensity so quickly, the
change in air pressure in the room made everyone's ears pop.

The howling as it belted through the door became nigh unbearable, but
still Russell pushed on. Or rather, pulled. He drew it all to him, gathering
all the air he could, feeling the strain in every fibre of his body as his
mind scooped it all up. He could feel the veins in his neck and temple
flaring as he squeezed even more juice from his very body.

The air raced at him like an invisible tidal wave, food items, papers,
tickets, hats all came with it, swept up in the torrential gusts. And when
they reached him they continued to race around, knocking Kristen away,
sending her sprawling across the stage. He didn't have time to be
concerned about her now.

When that timer hit zero, he had to be ready.

Screams were coming from the audience as the realization that this
wasn't part of the show set in. People began scrambling over chairs and
other people in an effort to make their way to the exits. It was fruitless.
With his own power, he had all but prevented anyone escaping through
the sheer tunnels of wind that continued to blow through every exit,
every orifice from outside.

And when the final red digit flickered out, Russell was ready.

With all his remaining strength, he enveloped the device in his own
private silver cocoon. Only Russell himself saw the near blinding flash of
light as the bomb went off. A split second later and he felt searing heat.
Ignoring it, he sent the force of the explosion, driven by the very winds
he commanded straight up into the sky. Bracing himself against the sheer
power of both bomb and air, he watched as it punched its way up and
through the ceiling of the theatre. The lighting rig, support beams,
construction pieces didn't stand a chance against the brunt of this
directed assault.

Bright orange flames, along with its poisonous orange smoke was
sucked upward and out of the building, debris from above going with it,
rather than falling down, protecting the stunned crowd.

In seconds, his outer clothing had been scorched away and he did his
best to redirect the gusts he controlled. His cape unfurled and began to

billow out behind him. It had to be an impressive sight, but he wasn't in the frame of mind to think about it.

It felt like an eternity as, along with the raging storm of flame and smoke went the last remaining ounce of strength in Russell's body.

And in only a few seconds more, it was over. No longer was the theatre lit by the bright orange aura of the bomb. All there was was darkness as the Centre's lights faltered under the onslaught of Russell's powers.

And he finally let go.

His legs gave way and he felt himself sink to the floor.

All the pent up energy he had left, encircling himself and the bomb, was released, sending a shock wave of fresh air out over the audience, who were finally free to breathe. And darkness claimed him once more.

CHAPTER TWENTY

People were evacuated faster than was expected. All they wanted to do was get outside and away from whatever it was that had happened.

Russell awoke to Pam's smiling face. His head cradled in her lap. Looking to her side, Stacey was squatting; his own costume was showing a little beneath tattered and scorched clothing.

"Did we make it?"

"Damn right we did, lad. You were brilliant!"

"And Kristen?"

Pam shook her head, "Gone after her father, along with the police. We won't have to worry about him anymore. He's their problem."

Stacey put his hand on her shoulder and she looked at him. Russell couldn't read it from this angle, but there was something in her expression.

He didn't want to think about it now. They had won. Instead, he smiled, enjoying the moment, unable to do much else, "So I can go home now?"

"Sure can. Here, let's get you up," Pam provided support as Stacey reached underneath his arms and hauled him to his feet. Russell winced in pain as every bone in his body seemed to crumble to dust.

"A few days hard rest and you'll be good as new," Stacey joked. Russell could only chuckle. Anything harder made his chest hurt.

"And Dufus?"

Pam shook her head.

"They got away, just after your spectacular light show. They're still our problem. I think they always will be."

"We can handle it," Russell offered.

"Damn right we can!" Stacey yelled as he helped Russell out of the now empty theatre. Leaving behind only several policemen who had already gathered statements and the debris that had fallen after Russell had ceased his assault on the roof. 'Maybe it's time for an open air theatre,' he thought to himself.

Stacey wrapped his coat around Russell trying to conceal the costume and prevent any further attention.

Outside there was just the hint of a breeze – the air itself seemed to be tired, worn out.

CHAPTER TWENTY ONE

Friday night.

The safe house had become a party house. Surprising Russell and Stacey both, Pam had organised a party in one of the lower ground rooms. It had somewhat spread out from there, however, into some of the other rooms, though Pam had locked those doors she wanted kept shut.

The front rooms on the ground floor were actually rather spectacular. They were styled as Victorian ballrooms complete with bar, some tables and chair and a separate dance floor on a lower level. A crystal chandelier hung from the ceiling and the rooms seemed to take up both the ground and first floor space.

Russell wasn't even sure who half the people were, but both Pam and Stacey knew them. He figured most of them were journalists. Maybe some were the 'others' they had mentioned when the couple had first approached Russell outside his apartment.

All the same, they were here for a good time. And he was going to have one, aching or not.

Even after a couple of days rest, he was totally vamoosed. But the music was good, there was plenty of coca cola, because he didn't drink alcohol, not that he minded anyone else drinking it; he just didn't like it, not that he felt he had to justify that to anyone. Pam gave him a little smirk when they had had that conversation.

"So. You still up for it?"

He looked sideways at her. She had nonchalantly turned to admire the view, which consisted of a number of people bobbing up and down to the music.

"Up for what?"

"Oh, come on. The whole costume deal. The heroing?"

He shrugged, "Maybe. Maybe not."

"You've been hanging out with Stacey too long," Then she turned to look directly at him, "But seriously. Are you?"

He considered the small amount of coke left in his glass, swirled it around a little and actually considered it all over again.

"You know," he started, "You couldn't hold me back, even with all the telekinetics in the world. Though I think we can forgo the costumes."

She whooped for joy and punched him on the arm, sending a fresh bout of pain running through him, "Oh. Sorry. I forgot."

"That's cool. I guess I better get used to all these little knocks."

They had talked for a while longer about the party, the events of the last week and about the prospects for the future. He found it hard to believe only a week before that he had been a normal person moping all the way up the stairs in a lowly car park.

168

Now, he was a freak of nature, who still did his moping, but had opted to keep his new orange Telstar at home before forgetting about public transport. Surprisingly, in some ways it was safer.

Right now, he bobbed to the beat, watching as everyone had a good time. It was great. The music set up, the lights. They had gone all out for this party.

And then Stacey appeared from among the dancing couples and wrapped his arm around Pam. Russell had noted that Pam had not invited her boyfriend. Was that a sign, or had something finally clicked between these two? He wasn't going to pry.

Stacey beamed, "Hey, whatcha up to?"

"Just finishing my drink," as if to emphasise this, Russell took the last swig of his coke.

"Well, I know someone who wants to talk with you," Stacey pulled Russell in close and pointed through the crowd. In all the flashing lights, it was still easy to spot who he was talking about.

Kristen was standing tall and proud, looking like a million dollars. She already had a drink in hand, probably shoved there by Stacey.

What was he supposed to say? He had practically ruined her life. If he'd kept his big mouth shut, maybe she would still think her father was a good bloke. But would that be solving the problem?

She spotted the two men and made her way over to them.

"I'll leave ya to it," Stacey's voice stank of alcohol. Thankfully it didn't linger as he too was swallowed by the crowd along with a smiling Pam.

She started, "Hi."

"Hi."

She started again, "Nice place."

"It's Pam's, I figure. Have you met Pam?"

"She's the one who invited me."

"Oh."

There was an awkward silence. He didn't know what to say. He half expected them to speak at once, like in those movies. But he couldn't work up the courage to say anything. So she spoke again.

"Look, Russell. I'm sorry."

"No. I am. I'm sorry it all worked out this way."

"It wasn't your fault."

He wasn't sure whether she was referring to the bomb incident and her father or the date. He tried his luck, "I got the wrong idea."

"No. You didn't."

What did that mean? Where was he standing now?

"Look. Russell. I do like you. I like you a lot."

He nodded, knowing what was coming next. There had to be a 'but'. So he said it first, "But only as a friend."

"Exactly. I'm sorry."

"That's cool. I deserve it after all the crud I put you through."

169

She laughed, "Ditto. But that's what friends are for, right?"

He laughed, "I guess so."

The music changed; a song by the band Aqua began to play and Russell smiled at the idea. Then he thought about it for a moment. Then finally asked, no longer with his heart beating in his throat, "Want to dance?"

"Sure. But-"

"Yeah, I know. Friends."

"Just that."

The two moved further onto the dance floor and into the music.

He could be happy with that. Friends. He'd made some good ones this past week. Not to mention enemies, but you take the good with the bad.

He chuckled to himself and she pulled away.

He smiled, "Just friends remember."